ROYAL EL

TWISTED KINGDOM

ROYAL ELITE
SCHOOL

RINA KENT

To the survivors.

AUTHOR NOTE

Hello reader friend,

If you haven't read my books before, you might not know this, but I write darker stories that can be upsetting and disturbing. My books and main characters aren't for the faint of heart.

Twisted Kingdom is a dark high school bully romance, mature new adult, and contains dubious situations that some readers might find offensive.
If you're looking for a hero, Aiden is NOT it. If you, however, have been itching for a villain, then by all means, welcome to Aiden King's world

To remain true to the characters, the vocabulary, grammar, and spelling of Twisted Kingdom is written in British English.

This book is part of a trilogy and is NOT standalone.

Royal Elite Series:
#0 Cruel King
#1 Deviant King
#2 Steel Princess
#3 Twisted Kingdom
#4 Black Knight
#5 Vicious Prince
#6 Ruthless Empire
#7 Royal Elite Epilogue

Don't forget to Sign up to Rina Kent's Newsletter for news about future releases and an exclusive gift.

The kingdom isn't supposed to fall.

The truth screws you over before it sets you free.

Masks drop.

Secrets unravel.

Elsa's race after the past blinds her from the present.

I'll fight for her.

I'll bring her back.

I'll protect her even if it's the last thing I do.

We made a promise.

She's mine.

Are you ready for one final game, sweetheart?

PLAYLIST

I Fell In Love With The Devil—Avril Lavigne

Paradise—Coldplay

Church—Coldplay

Daddy—Coldplay

In My Place—Coldplay

Things We Lost In The Fire—Bastille

Another Place—Bastille & Alessia Cara

Torn Apart—Bastille Vs GRADES

Every Second—From Ashes to New & Eva Under Fire

Natural—Imagine Dragons.

Death of Me—PVRIS

Blood // Water—grandson

Of These Chains—Red

Night Of The Hunter—Thirty Seconds To Mars

Fallout—UNSECRET & Neoni

Numb—8 Graves

The Fighter—In This Moment

Mother Tongue—Bring Me The Horizon

Grave—Wage War

How It Feels to Be Lost—Sleeping With Sirens

You can find the playlist on Spotify.

ROYAL ELITE BOOK THREE

TWISTED KINGDOM

ONE

Aiden

Past

W*e will always be together. You're the reason I'm alive, Aiden.*

My mother's voice drifts in my head like warmth in the middle of the cold.

The shackle rattles and protests as I pull my legs to my chest. The freezing floor sends icy bursts through my entire body, but I don't have the energy to stand up.

My toes are numb. The welts on my back burn. The red marks left by my ankle cuff have deepened to purple.

I think that's bad.

What seems like hours pass, and I still don't have the energy to stand up, let alone take a closer look at my wound. My upper body slumps to the cold floor. The ground smells like the stables at my father's friend's house.

My teeth chatter and I bite my lip several times, trying to stop it.

"Mum…" I whisper in the pitch-black room.

She said we have a special mother-son bond, and she can feel my pain. My mother knows the day I'll fall sick before I even wake up. She must be feeling my pain now. She must be crying.

I don't like it when Mum cries, but I want her to find me.

This place isn't like any I've been in before. This place hurts.

My stomach growls like an animal.

I press my hand to it, but that doesn't quiet the sound. If anything, it turns louder and higher as if taunting me.

I lick my dry, cracked lips and stare at the empty bottle of water at my feet. It's the only thing I've had since being separated from Xander and Cole.

Are they hungry as well? Were they also hurt by the red woman?

I don't know how much time I've spent in this dark, dirty place, but it's been long enough that my stomach has been growling non-stop for what feels like hours.

If I don't eat soon, I won't have the strength to open my eyes, let alone stand up and search for a way out.

Mum is waiting for me.

She becomes sad when I'm not with her, and I hate it when Mum is sad.

The door squeaks as it cracks open. I jerk up and flinch when the hard stone wall cuts into my bruised back, but that's the least of my worries.

The red woman is back.

The chain lies all around me. I grasp the cuff and pull with the little energy I have left. I know it won't come off. I know I'm just scraping my skin, but it's all I can do.

If I don't get out of this, the red woman will hurt me again.

She'll beat me.

She'll make my skin burn.

Soft light appears in the otherwise dark room, blinding me. I squint as the echo of footsteps comes closer.

There's no clicking of the red woman's high heels.

My breathing slows down a notch and my grip loosens from around the cuff.

With the light between us, a peaceful face comes into view. A white halo surrounds her, complete with her white cotton dress and bunny shoes.

An angel.

She's like the angel statue Mum has in our garden.

She's the same girl from the other time. I think it was yesterday.

Since she's wearing sleeping clothes, it must be night time again.

She drops the light on the floor and crouches in front of me. Her little hands are dragging a heavy bag behind her, but I don't focus on the sound or her bag.

I focus on her.

The girl who looks exactly like one of Silver and Kimberly's dolls. The girl with golden blonde hair and sparkly blue eyes watching me with a frown.

The girl with milky white skin and flushed red cheeks.

Do they make Silver and Kimberly's dolls into real people who can move and drag things?

She waves a hand in front of my face, the two lines between her brows deepening. "Can you hear me?"

"Are you real?" My voice sounds far away as if I'm speaking from another room.

I touched her yesterday. I grabbed her hand and asked her to help me, but maybe I'm seeing ghosts.

Maybe I'm becoming like my mother when she can't sleep at night.

Maybe the red woman is trying to torture me again.

"Of course I'm real, silly." She grins, showcasing a missing tooth.

Okay, Silver and Kimberly's dolls don't have missing teeth.

She retrieves a smaller bag and unveils a napkin. The scent of bread and Marmite hits me straight in the stomach. The growling sound can be heard from another continent.

"I brought you —"

I snatch the piece of bread from between her fingers before she has the chance to finish the sentence.

If my father saw me eating right now, he'd yell at me for my lacking manners. I don't even chew, I don't wait for the first bite to go down before snatching the next one.

"I'm sorry. These were the only things I could find in the kitchen this late."

The girl approaches me carefully. I turn away from her like a starving dog protecting his food.

She rises and wraps something fluffy and warm around my shoulders. "It's freezing in here."

I stare at her while munching on a piece of bread. I cough and choke on the bite.

She reaches into her wonder bag and brings out a bottle of water. I grab it from her and drink half of it in one go.

The cold liquid soothes my scratchy throat like honey. I miss the honey sandwiches Margo used to make for me.

I go back to devouring my bread. I start to taste the Marmite near the end.

Something warm connects with my skin and I pause chewing to stare at the girl again.

She's wiping my face with a wet cotton cloth, but the more she wipes the more her expression falls.

Her fingers comb through my tangled hair then she glides the cloth over my arm, forcing me to eat with one hand.

A fat tear slides down her cheek. I swallow the last bite of bread and remain completely still.

Why is she crying? Did I do something wrong? Is it because I told her that she's not real?

"I know you're real." My voice is less scratchy than before. "Don't cry."

"I'm sorry them monsters did this to you. They took Eli, but don't worry." Her palm flattens on my cheek, determination shining in her sparkling blue eyes. "I won't allow them to take you, too."

TWO

Aiden

Present

This is the worst fucking scenario that could've happened. The disaster part is, I didn't see it coming—and I always see things coming.

The most catastrophic mistake any general can make is to feel comfortable and ignore the outside world.

Today I was blinded by Elsa and her closeness, I was over my head with irrational feelings and thoughts and I didn't try to control them.

Elsa has that effect on me; she has the power to fuck up the best-laid plans ever set.

After last night, I wanted her to have a peaceful birthday without allowing the outside world to ruin it.

Result: I've been caught off guard.

Ethan Steel is alive and he's standing in the middle of the Meet Up's lounge area—a place my mother considered a sanctuary.

Elsa hasn't taken her gaze off him since the moment he walked in. Her blue eyes have widened and her jaw has nearly hit the floor. I don't think she even notices it, but her limbs slightly tremble as if she can't control her reaction.

Jonathan isn't holding up better. His menacing gaze studies

Ethan like he's watching a demon rise from the ashes. Judging by the tightening of his jaw, he wasn't expecting to see Ethan alive.

Ever.

Elsa's father just shuffled all the chess pieces by showing up from the dead like a fucking ghost.

Queens stands at the entrance, shrinking against the wall. She holds onto her phone with a death grip and watches the scene unfold like it's a freak show.

I'll deal with her later for not letting me know about Jonathan's arrival and for having Elsa find out about the engagement this way.

Jonathan must've shown up at her doorstep unannounced and made it impossible for her to refuse, but she could've sent a fucking text.

Life as she knows it will crush to pieces. I'll make sure of it.

My attention slides to Van Doren who stands beside Ethan with a proud smirk on his bruised lips.

The fucker.

I knew there was something up with him since the first time he walked into RES, integrating himself into Elsa's life like a parasite.

I just didn't know he was part of Ethan Steel's plan.

Well played, old man. Well fucking played.

"It's you... Dad." Elsa's haunted whisper echoes in the walls, surrounding us like a prayer.

There's an innocent sparkle in her eyes reminiscent of her childhood. Seeing her father again has pushed her ten years back in time.

She's again the seven years old girl who always brought up her father in every conversation.

She called him her superhero.

Her invincible hero.

Now he's back and he'll take her away from me after I've finally found her.

Who the fuck does he think he is to waltz in after ten years of playing dead and take away what's mine?

It's time for us to go home?

Fuck no.

Fucking never.

"Yes, princess. It's me." He smiles with so much warmth, I want to poke his eyes out and shove him back to the grave he crawled out of.

It is him, I recognised him as the man rather than Elsa's father.

Ethan Steel—Jonathan's former friend and most worthy rival.

He's aged since the last time I saw him, but he still has the same black tailored suits style as Jonathan. He still sports his chestnut hair slicked back with purpose and power; he still wears Prada shoes and diamond cuffs and a watch that costs a third world country's yearly budget.

He's Steel Empire's emperor back for his heir.

Elsa's bottom lip trembles as if she's about to cry, but there are no tears. When I look closer, I can almost see Ethan's reflection in her electric blue eyes.

She takes a shaky step forward. Her damp blond strands stick to her face and wet clothes, but I'd bet one of my limbs she's not trembling because of the cold.

I grab her arm, stopping her from taking another step. She doesn't acknowledge me and continues to try getting to her father.

"Get your hands off of my daughter. *Now.*" Ethan orders in an authoritative tone that would've scared any other person.

Ethan isn't a man to be taken lightly. He's as ruthless as Jonathan, if not more. If he puts someone in his sight, he won't stop until that person is eradicated. The fact that he rose from the dead is one more proof of his ruthless personality.

But he doesn't scare me.

The only person I care about is this beautiful girl who won't even acknowledge my existence.

"Let her go, Aiden," Jonathan finally speaks.

I tune him out. "Elsa, look at me."

She doesn't.

I stroke my thumb along her arm, caressing softly. "Sweetheart, look at me."

"Are you engaged to Silver?" Elsa continues staring at her father, but her words are directed at me.

The sudden question stops me in my tracks. How do I answer this without triggering her ugly side?

"It's not what you—"

"Yes or no?" She cuts me off, still not sparing me a glance.

I grind my molars at the apathetic way she's addressing me. I can't blame her, but my brain crowds with only one thought: throw her over my shoulder and get her the fuck out of here.

I'm restraining myself only because she's reuniting with her father and will never forgive me for taking her away. And while I don't give a fuck about him or anyone else in this room, I give lots of fucks about her.

"Elsa, there's so much you need to know," I speak in my calmest tone.

"It's a simple question, Aiden. Yes or no?"

"Yes." My left eye twitches as I say the word.

Elsa goes completely still; she doesn't even blink.

I expect her to turn around and hit me. I would let her. If it'll help her blow off steam, I'll let her hit me all she likes. As long as she finally fucking faces me, I'm ready to do just about anything.

She jerks her arm out of my grip. My hand curls into a fist by my side, but I don't grab her again.

It guts me to have her close and not touch her, but if I reach out for her, I'm really kidnapping her the fuck out of here.

All the shaking from earlier disappears. Her spine jerks upright, and her chin lifts high as she takes purposeful strides in her father's direction. Away from me.

"Elsa." Her name leaves my lips like a pained growl.

"Let's go home," she tells her father with such determination, it echoes around the room.

Ethan wraps an arm around his daughter's shoulders. She snuggles to his side like a kitten.

He nods in our direction. "Looking forward to crushing you, Jonathan."

Then he's out of the door, Elsa and Van Doren walking on either side of him.

Go after her.

Bring her back.

Kidnap her if you have to.

It takes everything in me not to follow my beast's demands. If I use any type of force with her it'll only backfire and burn me. If some distance will help cool her down, then so fucking be it.

For now.

I face Jonathan, expecting him to be seething about Ethan's sudden appearance.

My father likes to use the element of surprise, but he sure as fuck doesn't like to be its victim. Ethan's rise from the dead has shuffled all of his cards and ruined the plan he's been concocting for ten years.

A sadistic smirk sits on his lips. He flops on the sofa and forms a church steeple at his chin with his fingers. I can only imagine the number of fucked up scenarios running rampant in his mind.

Queens approaches me with careful steps as if she's walking through a minefield. "I didn't want to come here, but —"

I hold up a hand, shutting her the fuck up. "Leave."

Her voice and face are the last things I need in my immediate vicinity right now.

"You deserve it, by the way," she whispers so I'm the only one who hears. "This is what happens when you fuck people over. You get fucked over in return."

I give her my best 'do you have a death wish' glare in response.

She lifts a shoulder and huffs as she announces, "I'm leaving."

Jonathan barely acknowledges her, still lost in his own head.

We're the same that way: when there's a target to eliminate, we tune out the outside world and get lost in our internal chaos.

He's probably counting his options and coming up with a plan to destroy Ethan. Quick wit and the ability to make snap decisions under stress are the reasons why Jonathan is what he is today.

When other people freak, Jonathan is focused on finding efficient solutions. If he falls, he doesn't dwell on the smash, he dwells on how to never fall again.

"You really didn't know he's alive?" I ask.

The smirk still tilts his lips. "If I did, I wouldn't have gone after his daughter. Interesting. Maybe he kept in hiding to see how I would've handled the existence of his only heir."

I wouldn't be surprised.

But unlike Jonathan, Ethan is affectionate towards Elsa. He wouldn't erase himself from her life and make her believe he's dead just for a game with Jonathan.

Besides, Ethan is a businessman. He wouldn't have willingly left his empire for ten years without a reason.

I shove a hand in my pocket. "Ethan won't waste time and will attack straightaway."

"Then we attack first." He stands and buttons his jacket. "Call Levi. We have a war to plot."

THREE

Elsa

They say one second is all it takes for everything to be flipped upside down.

I had many seconds like those in my life.

When I erased my memories.

When I met Aiden for the first time in RES.

When I almost drowned in the pool.

When I recalled some of my dark, bloody past.

However, the second I set eyes on my supposedly dead father is, without a doubt, the highlight of all.

Since he walked through the door, all I could do was stare at him. I even stopped myself from blinking, too afraid he'll disappear into thin air the moment I close my eyes.

Dad, Knox, and I ride in the back of a car. I haven't paid attention to what type of car it is, but it must be luxurious considering the high-quality caramel leather seats. There's even a driver who's separated from us by a window.

Knox's headphones rest around his neck as he sits beside my dad without a care in the world. He smiles like an idiot while scrolling through his phone.

Please tell me he's not going through memes right now.

I'm over here, opposite them, my frozen hands tucked between my legs. Strands of my wet hair and clothes stick to my skin and a shiver shoots from my scalp to my toes despite the heat in the car.

None of it matters.

All my attention zeroes on the man in front of me.

Dad.

My dad is alive.

In the nightmare I had this morning, he was drowning in a pool of his own blood, shouting at me to run.

How can he be here now?

He's watching me with warmth glinting in his eyes especially tailored for me.

Hazy memories filter back in.

Back then, Dad used to be stern and a control freak. The staff and Daddy's friends who wore black—whom I now recognise as bodyguards—trembled at the sight of him. He was the type of man who commanded any room he stood in.

Ethan Steel—the emperor of Steel's fortune. A ruthless businessman and an unforgiving enemy.

My father.

When I was younger, I saw him from a different perspective than everyone else. To me, he wasn't the merciless, heartless man everyone feared and cowered away from. He was Daddy.

Just Daddy.

He was the type of father who wouldn't just read me bedtime stories, but he'd also perform them for me. He tickled me until I broke into giggles.

He took me on long runs in the rain.

He saved me from the monsters in the lake.

Daddy never frowned when he looked at me. When he was having a bad day, it'd take a glance at me and a smile would break on his face.

"Are you comfortable, princess?" he asks with a low, yet warm voice.

Princess.

Back then, I was his princess. His favourite. His legacy. His masterpiece.

A lump lodges deep in my throat. I can't speak even if I want to, so I nod.

For long minutes, silence is the only language in the car.

I watch the lines on Dad's face. He has a sharp jaw and high cheekbones that give him an untraditional type of masculine beauty. From afar, we look nothing alike, but up close, I share the thickness of his lashes and the shape of his eyes—mine are just a bit bigger.

He places his elbow on the edge of the car seat and leans on it as he watches me. We're like two injured animals that don't know how to accept offered help.

Or maybe I'm the only one who feels that way. After all, Dad knew exactly where to find me.

"I understand this can seem too much." Dad's posh accent fills the car.

Can seem too much?

Is he kidding? He just returned from the dead. Surely, there are some other words he could use.

"I told you she's not ready." Knox doesn't avert his attention from his phone.

"That's up to me to decide," Ethan tells him.

Knox lifts a shoulder. "Just saying, Dad."

Dad?

My gaze snaps to Knox. Did he just call my dad *his* dad?

He's about my age, when the hell did Dad have him? Is he from another woman?

"Are you…" I clear my throat. "Are you my brother?"

Knox lifts his gaze from his phone and winks. "Foster brother, babe."

Oh. Okay.

He does bear some resemblance to Eli. Is that why Dad took him in?

Although I doubt Dad would take in anyone just for that;

he doesn't like anyone to get into his familial bubble. Now that I think about it, Dad's concern for privacy came before all else. That's why he kept us away from civilisation.

However, all of this is only a speculation based on what I remember about Dad. It's been ten years, he could've changed into an entirely different person.

"I'm hurt you don't remember me." Knox pouts like a child who's been deprived of his favourite toy.

"Remember you?" I ask.

"Yeah. You ought to remember me after —"

"Knox." The warning in Dad's tone is loud and clear.

Knox shrugs and goes back to scrolling through his phone.

Okay. That's weird.

Super weird.

I meet Dad's brown eyes. They're so wise and deep, you could get lost in there and never find a way out. He must use his penetrating gaze as an intimidation method during business meetings.

"You've been raising Knox all this time?" I try not to sound bitter, but I'm not sure I succeeded.

Dad left me for ten years. All this time, I thought he was dead and buried somewhere I would never find while he was actually alive and well. Hell, he's been raising another child while his only daughter lived with relatives.

"Nah, not really. We raised ourselves," Knox says.

"We?"

He smirks. "There's another one."

"Another one?" I meant to shout, but my vocal cords constrict so the only thing that comes out is a choked murmur.

"Shut up for a second, Knox." Dad sounds both exasperated and resigned.

"Whatever."

Dad focuses back on me. He removes his jacket, and before I can react, he wraps it around my shoulders.

My fingers dig into the expensive material as he settles back into his seat.

It smells like cloves and cinnamon. It smells like Dad.

"You're shaking." He taps the wall between us and the driver. "Turn on the heat, Joseph."

"Yes, Sir."

I'm not shaking because of the cold, but I don't say that.

My mind crowds with so many questions and theories, but I struggle to form words. My head keeps flashing back to the vision of blood while Dad lay in it. This is how it feels like to be shackled by the past. It's always there, wrapping wires around your neck, threatening to chop it off.

"How much do you remember?" Dad asks.

"Not everything." My voice is barely above a whisper.

"Told you," Knox says.

Dad shoots him a glare before he focuses back on me. "Do you remember the night of the fire?"

I shake my head once.

A mixture of disappointment and relief covers his features. "I see."

"I dreamt about blood, though. You… You were shot and covered in blood, Dad. How… How did you… H-how…"

"Hey." He slides to the edge of his seat and takes my hand in his bigger, warmer one. "Breathe, princess."

"You died!" I scream at the top of my lungs. "I thought you were dead for the past ten years. Why did you show up now? Why not before? Why, Daddy? Why?"

"Do you think I would've left my princess alone if I had a choice?"

I stare at him through wet lashes. "W-What happened?"

"I was shot, and I've been in a coma since. I only regained consciousness a year ago. If it were up to me, I would've found you the moment I woke, but I didn't want you to see me in that state."

"True that." Knox counts on his fingers. "He had to go through physical therapy and mental therapy and a whole bunch of other therapies that drove me bonkers."

I watch Dad closely. Even though he appears fine now, that doesn't mean he has been fine all along.

Dad was in a coma for nine years.

I read once that coma patients suffer immensely through re-habilitation and struggle to get back to normal.

Is there a rock I can hide under?

I was a little brat about the fact that he disappeared when I didn't know the entire story.

"I kept an eye on you," Dad says. "I just didn't show myself."

I gasp. "The black Mercedes."

He nods. "And Knox."

The latter waves two fingers my way. "Always at your service, my lady."

Pieces start falling into place. Since Knox showed up in my life, he has always been near even when I didn't need him to.

"You owe me, remember?" Knox winks.

I nod.

He taps the bruise at the side of his mouth. "And your green-haired friend owes me for this."

"Kim?"

"That Xander bloke did this." He leans in to whisper. "Your Aiden watched, by the way, then he drove off into the sunset as if he saw nothing."

My lips part.

Truth is, I'm not surprised Aiden was involved. I suspected he had something to do with it. However, I *am* surprised Xander indulged in violence. He has never shown violent behaviour.

Except for that time at the cafeteria.

"He's not her Aiden," Dad deadpans. "He's Aiden King, son of Jonathan King, who ruined our lives."

I swallow, and it's not only because of the reminder of a feud between our families.

Dad is right.

He's not my Aiden.

Here's the thing, Steel, you have no future with Aiden because he's already engaged to Silver.

Jonathan's dispassionate words scratch at my defective heart, ripping it open.

Silver was right all along—he never belonged to me.

He reduced me to playing the most loathsome, despicable role: the other woman.

Chaotic feelings claw at my chest, but I choose to tune them out.

I refuse to be dragged into that hell. Not now.

I focus on my dad. "Are you okay now?"

"I am."

"Will there be side effects of the coma?"

"According to my physician, I'm stable."

"But he needs to do regular checkups," Knox chimes in. "Sort of like you."

Tears well in my eyes at the reminder. Just like me, Dad was shot that day.

We were both victims.

Or were we really victims?

Everything is blurry and without any solution in sight.

There's one thing I'm sure about—Dad is here. He's not dead. He kept his promise to not leave me as Eli did.

He came back for me.

"Dad?"

"Yes, princess?"

"C-can I hug you?"

The corners of his eyes soften, and without hesitation, he opens his arms.

I dive straight in and bury my face in his chest. Dad's arms wrap around me in a warm, soothing hug. The tears I fought since I saw him today stream down my cheeks. "You're... Y-you're back."

"I promised you I would never leave you. I'm sorry I'm late, princess."

I shake my head frantically. "You're back."

For what seems like forever, I continue to cry against his chest. My fingers dig into his shirt as if I'm back to being that little girl.

Daddy's little girl.

"I'll never leave you again. I promise."

I hiccough into his chest, my breaths coming in and out in a frenzy.

"We're here!" Knox shouts and then murmurs. "Thank God."

"Are you ready to go inside our house?" Dad strokes the hair away from my face.

I pull my head from Dad's chest and nod, but even then, a riot starts at the bottom of my stomach.

Am I ready to go into the house where I lost my childhood?

Only one way to find out.

FOUR

Elsa

Home.

Such a strange word.

Here I am again. In Birmingham. At home.

Knox has already hopped out of the car as if his arse was on fire.

The distance from the front gate to the mansion is long. A stylish garden extends as far as the sight goes, and it's filled with trees cut into different geometrical shapes.

A tremor shoots through my limbs as Dad and I stand in front of the mansion's grand gate.

Two lion statues decorate the entrance, just like in my fragmented memories.

I don't think I ever realised just how big our mansion was when I was younger. I remember the wires, the private lake, and the long runs Dad and I took within the perimeters of our property.

Our house is larger than the King's mansion. Perhaps it's because they're in London while we're far away from the city, in Birmingham.

The cloudy sky casts a gloomy shroud over the two towers standing tall on the eastern side.

A shudder runs through me at the sight, clawing at my

ribcage like a prisoner needing release. There's something about those towers, but what?

"Welcome home, princess."

I rip my gaze from the architectural masterpiece to stare at my father. He watches me with pride and accomplishment like he wanted to bring me back here all along.

"I… I thought the whole house was burned down in the fire."

"It was." Nostalgia covers his gaze before it soon disappears. "It wasn't easy, but we renovated it to make it look like before."

"I see."

It's all too… surreal.

If it becomes red and foggy right now, I would know for sure it's a dream. Maybe I'm still in Dr Khan's office, reliving the memory of my first meeting with Aiden.

Maybe this morning never happened. Maybe Aiden isn't engaged to Silver.

I inwardly shake my head. I won't think about him. I won't think about him…

Dad takes my hand and interlaces it with his arm. "Let's go inside. You must be tired."

My feet move of their own volition as we step into the foyer. Marble.

That's the first thought that jumps to mind. Marble flooring, marble stairs, and even a marble lion statue.

Wait. Is that a thing?

A middle-aged man—who resembles Robert De Niro—and two women dressed in maids outfits bow upon our entry.

I nod back awkwardly. It's so weird to have people bow like we're royalty. Though, from what I've learnt about Steel Corporation, Dad might as well be considered nobility in Birmingham.

He doesn't seem the least bit fazed by the staff. He acknowledges them and moves along.

I'm like a lost orphan walking by his side. With my semi-wet clothes and dishevelled hair, I also look the part.

Dad and I stride into the enormous lounge area with its vaulted, golden ceilings and dazzling light. Two large lion statues decorate the sweeping marble stairs. Two tall Chinese warriors paintings stand on either side of the stairs in perfect symmetry.

Now I know where my love for old Chinese war books and philosophers comes from.

Several French windows are strategically lined throughout the lounge area, allowing a peek into the garden.

It's exactly like in my vision.

Maybe this is a vision, too. Maybe I'm hallucinating, and my father isn't alive.

That thought brings a bitter, sticky taste to the back of my throat. I squeeze his hand in mine to make sure this isn't a mind trick.

No. Dad is here.

He came back for me.

"There you are."

My attention snaps to my right. A middle-aged man comes down the stairs with a polite smile on his face.

He's dressed in a three-piece, striped suit, appearing fit and well-built for a man his age. His pale blue eyes resemble a snow tiger and, although he doesn't appear old, his hair is peppered with white strands.

Wait.

There's something familiar about him.

I take a closer look at the man and my eyes widen. "You."

"Told you she'd recognise you." Knox crashes into the man from behind, wrapping an arm around his shoulder, grinning with mischief. "Pay up the hundred, Agnus."

"Do you recognise me?" The man—Agnus—asks without paying attention to Knox.

I nod slowly. "You were always at that coffee shop."

"Bingo!" Knox smirks, extending his palm. "My one hundred. Any day now."

"For the record, you made the bet. I never agreed." Agnus

reaches into his pocket and retrieves his wallet. Knox snatches the bills and grins while counting the money.

"Can someone tell me what's going on?" My gaze bounces between the three of them.

"This is Agnus," Dad says. "He's my right-hand, adviser, and best friend. He's been taking care of the company and the estate while I was unable to."

"You don't remember me, Elsa, but I was your favourite uncle when you were younger."

"Uncle Reg was my favourite." The words fall from my lips in a haunted whisper.

Agnus's face turns blank. Knox tenses so visibly, he nearly rips the money with his fingers.

Dad's expression remains unreadable. "Reginald is no more, princess."

"He was my twin brother." Agnus smiles with ease considering the situation. "You could never tell us apart."

I do a double-take on Agnus' face. He does have slightly bulging eyes, but they're not as prominent as the ones I had in my nightmare about Uncle Reginald. Besides, Agnus is handsome in a silver fox kind of way. I don't remember Uncle Reg ever being handsome.

"How did he die?" I ask.

"The Great Birmingham fire." Knox shoves the money in his pocket. "Like a roasted pig."

"Knox," Dad scolds. "Go to your room."

"Nah." Knox throws his weight on the sofa, flings one of his legs over the other and wraps his hand around the sofa's back. "Hey, T. You owe me a fifty. Elsa isn't a bitch as you predicted she would be."

A tiny girl saunters inside with earbuds shoved in her ears. She has such petite features, they're adorable. Her midnight-black hair falls straight to her shoulders; her eyes are huge and black— or are they dark-brown? Her lips remind me of a rosebud, and her nose is tiny like the rest of her face.

Despite the cuteness of her overall appearance, like a Snow White of sorts, everything else screams she doesn't like it. For one, she's wearing dark purple lipstick and black eyeshadow that give her doe eyes a witchy appearance. She also has skull earrings.

Even her stockings have skulls on them. Other than that, she's wearing denim shorts, a black leather jacket, and a crop top that reveals her pale belly.

I pause to read the red writing on her white top.

Sometimes the king is a woman.

Interesting. This girl must be a lot more than her appearance suggests.

Plucking out her earbuds, she stares at me intently with empty, desolate eyes. It's like she's thinking about ways to cut my head open and look inside.

"Elsa, this is Teal." Dad squeezes my hand, bringing me out of the staring competition with the new girl. "Teal, Elsa."

"The spoilt princess." Teal plays with the earbuds. "Who doesn't know about her?"

"Pay up, T." Knox snaps his fingers. "You owe me."

"Not yet. I have to make sure for myself."

"Knox, Teal," Dad speaks slowly but with an authoritative edge. "I expect you to get along with Elsa. Am I making myself clear?"

"We already get along." Knox winks at me. "I even beat her in math."

"No promises, Dad." Teal flips her hair back and heads outside without a glance.

The first droplets of rain start beating down on the glass, but she doesn't seem to care. Maybe she also likes the rain and its ability to cleanse.

"Give Teal some time." Dad smiles at me. "She's not good with changes or outsiders, but she'll get used to it."

"Is she also…" I trail off.

"Foster sister." Knox snaps his fingers. "Bingo."

"How many more do I have?"

"Just two." It's Agnus who speaks. "Welcome back, Elsa."

Okay.

This home isn't like I remember it. A lot of things have changed, including the addition of two foster siblings, an uncle I don't remember, and the maids.

It'll take me some time to understand the new dynamics, but being here is progress on its own.

I have returned to where it all started—and ended. This is the place that can answer all my questions and lead me onto the right path.

I take a deep breath, the scent of jasmine and spices filling my nostrils.

No matter how much has changed, this remains home.

My home.

Maybe, just maybe, this is where I'm supposed to be.

FIVE

Aiden

"I'm here. And by the way, I don't want to be here."

Levi flops on a seat at the dinner table and thanks Margo for preparing his favourite steak.

She throws one last glance at us with worry etching deep between her brows. Levi, being a proclaimed gentleman, gives her a reassuring nod as if saying 'No, we won't eat each other for dinner.'

Margo tells us to call her if we need anything and retreats with brisk steps. The dining room's double door closes behind her with finality.

It's just the King men and their screwed up heads.

Good times.

I can't remember the last time the three of us sat down for a meal. Since Levi started his relationship with Astrid and moved out, he barely shows up anymore, and when he does it's only with her by his side.

Jonathan and I both know Astrid coaxes him to keep in touch with his family. That's the reason my father accepted her over time despite the fact that she's a Clifford.

Newsflash about the Cliffords; Jonathan doesn't like them.

Her mother killed Uncle James in an accident—in which both of them died. Jonathan being Jonathan still holds a grudge against Astrid and her lord father as if they're the ones who shoved drugs down Uncle James' throat that night.

That's Jonathan in a nutshell. He's vengeful, and he's ruthless about it.

He occupies the head of the table while Levi and I sit on each side of him. The chandelier above us casts a white light on the food as if we're in a cooking show.

I drag the knife over my steak, but I'm neither cutting nor eating.

My thoughts keep spiralling back to how Elsa left yesterday. The numbness on her face still lurks inside me, tying a noose around my heart.

How the fuck could I let her go like that? She doesn't even have her damn phone. Not that she would've answered my calls or texts.

It's only been a day, but it feels like we've been apart for an eternity—and I don't even believe in eternity and all that shit.

I sit here, wondering when exactly it was she became such an integral part of my life and the fucking air I breathe.

Was it when I claimed her as mine? When I first touched her? When I reunited with her two years ago? Or maybe it all started in the damn basement.

"You're here today because we have an enemy."

"You mean *you* have an enemy." Levi scoffs, taking a generous bite of his beef and chewing without a care in the world.

"The King household has an enemy, you little punk."

Levi rolls his eyes but says nothing. I've already briefed him about Ethan Steel's return. Whether he likes it or not, Levi is a King and Jonathan's precious legacy. He was already a part of the game before he was born.

Like me.

Like Elsa.

"Knowing Ethan, he'll try to disrupt our formation before attacking." Jonathan cuts his meat with ease like he's not talking about attacks and wars.

"You *knew* Ethan. Past tense," I say.

"Ethan doesn't change his attack methods." Jonathan pauses eating. "Besides, my resources tell me he was in a coma for nearly nine years. The past is all he remembers."

"Your resources couldn't tell you that before he made a surprise visit?" Levi mocks.

Jonathan glares at him.

"Stating facts, Uncle. He who only knows himself and not the enemy suffers a loss for every battle won, remember?" He recites the old strategies Jonathan used to shove down our throats.

Levi isn't even trying to feign interest in the whole thing. He has already built his life as a professional football player. He has his girl and his future ahead. For him, this entire ordeal is a waste of time and he won't stop reminding Jonathan of that fact.

"I know my enemy." Jonathan smirks as he takes a bite of his food. "A lot more than I know myself."

"What's the plan?" I ask.

"Now we're talking." Jonathan points his fork in my direction. "First of all, you'll stop your idiotic escapades with Steel's daughter and commit to Silver. Her father and I are friends and go way back. I won't have you ruin that."

Yeah, no.

Queens and I didn't get together because of what our fathers expect. We got together for a different reason, which will soon be eradicated.

"You go way back with Sebastian Queens, as in, you share business interests with him," Levi speaks without lifting his head. "You know, with how he uses his minister power to let your ships go unnoticed. Oh, and you promised to fund his campaign for Prime Minister. Very friendly of you, Uncle."

I hide a snicker.

"Am I making myself clear?" Jonathan ignores Levi, focusing on me.

I nod absentmindedly. He doesn't need to know my move

until I make it. After all, he's not the only one who's fond of the element of surprise.

He's not the only one who likes to destroy.

"Perfect." He points his fork between me and Levi. "We're invited to a fundraiser hosted by the Rhodes family this Friday. Both of you will be attending."

"Pass." Levi feigns a yawn.

"Not interested," I say at the same time.

Jonathan knows better than to drag us to his friends' parties and fundraising bullshit. We do attend one gathering once a year, and that's already happened.

"Listen, you two." Jonathan slams his fork and knife on the table. "This isn't just any fundraiser. The Rhodes are aristocrats who have recently returned to business. They're looking for a long-term partner, and that's going to be King Enterprises. I've been preparing for months for this project, and I won't accept a loss on such a huge opportunity."

"What do we have to do with this?" Levi asks.

"You will bring Clifford's daughter. Those with titles like people who resemble them. If they see a member of the King family in a relationship with a lord's daughter, they'll soften."

According to Jonathan, Cliffords are bad until there's a use for them.

"And me?" I chew on the food, but I don't taste much.

"You're my heir. It'll put their minds at ease to see the future of the company as diligent as his father."

Levi rolls his eyes, and I sigh.

I'll find an excuse to skip the whole thing. If it were under different circumstances, I would've put on the show of a lifetime for Jonathan's friends and persuaded them to sign with him on the spot. If I score my father a huge deal, he'll leave me alone afterwards.

However, I'm not in the mood to kiss Jonathan's friends' arses.

There's a ton of things I need to do and they all lead back to Elsa, not my family name.

She didn't show up for school today. I shouldn't have been surprised, but a part of me hoped she would. A part of me thought she'd confront me and drive me crazy with her stubbornness like before.

Even Reed hasn't heard anything from her since yesterday and was having a mini panic attack about walking in the halls alone.

If I were a better person, I would've offered her my company. Unfortunately for Reed, I'm not. Astor spent the entire day with her, though. Knight killed him in a thousand different ways in his mind, then nearly broke his leg in practice.

Good times.

Back to Elsa. If she isn't talking to her best friend, how the hell am I supposed to contact her?

I tell myself that she needs time, and that after a while, she'll be open enough to listen to me.

The problem is, I'm not a fucking patient person.

Being away from her for an entire day is messing with my senses. I'm on a fucking withdrawal and it's irritating and pissing me off. I can only return to normal when Elsa's beside me where she belongs.

She promised.

She fucking *promised*.

If she thinks I'll let her get away she must not know me after all.

I'm happy to have her relearn me all over again.

"Ethan will make his move during this fundraiser."

Jonathan's words bring me back to the present.

"How can you be so sure?" I raise one eyebrow.

"He must know I've been after this deal for months. It's not mere coincidence he returned when the contract is near completion. He likes disrupting his enemies' patterns."

"Will he rival you?" Levi asks.

"Probably. I'm still not sure about his tactics, but I'll be there to ruin every last one of them."

"It's been ten years, Uncle and you both lost your wives. Isn't it time for bygones to be bygones? You can even ride into the sunset and shit."

Jonathan cuts him a glare so harsh, Levi shakes his head.

"Just saying. Jesus."

"You'll both be there." Jonathan wipes his mouth with a napkin. "That's final."

If Ethan goes, then Elsa most likely will, too. Not because she likes this sort of thing, but because Ethan will seize the chance to show off his daughter and Steel Empire's heir to the world.

She'll be there.

I can almost smell her coconut scent all the way to Friday.

"Fine," I tell Jonathan.

He nods with approval. "See you both on Friday."

"Wait a minute. I didn't agree," Levi protests.

But Jonathan is already out of the room. He'll probably spend the night in his office making the world a bit more horrible.

"Little fucker." Levi throws an apple at my head.

I catch it and take a bite.

"This is about Elsa, isn't it?" he asks.

I lift a shoulder.

Everything is about Elsa, but neither he nor Jonathan need to know that.

Showing weakness is the easiest way to be beaten at your own battle with your own soldiers.

I throw the apple back at Levi and stand up, another plan forming in my head.

He catches the fruit and crunches a bite. "You don't deserve her."

"Just like you don't deserve Astrid?"

"At least I changed for her. What did you do for Elsa?"

"I found her again."

And no one will take her away from me.

I leave the dining room and retrieve my phone. A number called me 1001 times today. It's an exaggeration, but yeah, he called me non-stop. I'm surprised he didn't raid the school.

"Elsa, is this you?" Jaxon Quinn's concerned voice filters through the phone. "You said you'll come back today, but you weren't at school. Your aunt is filing a missing person report."

So they did raid the school.

"This is Aiden King."

"Aiden." He sounds taken aback, but he quickly adds. "Is Elsa with you?"

"No."

"No?" he shouts, and I have to hold the phone away from my ear to not go deaf. "Where is she? What happened to her? Why didn't you call and inform us?" He launches on a series of clipped questions.

"Ethan Steel took her to Birmingham."

After telling him the details about Ethan's reappearance, I hang up with a smile on my face.

I might not be able to bring her back, but her aunt and uncle will.

SIX

Elsa

For the past two days, Dad has been taking me on long tours of the property.

I remember bits and pieces from the past, but they're barely thirty per cent of my childhood. It's like my memories have been frozen and there's no way to 'unfreeze' them.

Dad has been patient, talking about how both of us used to come to the garden after he returned from work. I was home-schooled at the time and he often helped me with my homework.

The topic of my mother has been on the tip of my tongue, but I stopped myself from mentioning her. One, I didn't have enough courage. Two, Knox always joined us on our walks, challenging me about beating him in becoming Dad's favourite. They're jokes on the outside, but I can feel the rivalry deep inside him. While he appears lighthearted, Knox is in fact lethal when it comes to what he wants.

Being with him is fun, though. It reminds me of the friendships I left behind.

My chest aches at the thought. It pains me how much I miss Kim and Ronan and even Xander and Cole.

I miss the easy friendship we share, the laughs, and even the secrets lurking under the surface. The horsemen might be royalty in RES, but each of them carries a mystery so tangible, it's enticing.

As for Aiden…

Nope.

I've been blocking him from my mind since I arrived here. He doesn't deserve my thoughts or my tears. Not now, not ever.

Maybe if I keep numbing myself to him and his enigmatic existence, I'll eventually erase him.

Delusional much, Elsa?

I squash that voice as soon as it rises.

"Do you remember that tree?" Dad motions to an old plum tree at the eastern side of the garden. "You used to climb it all the time and then you had trouble getting down, like a kitten."

I smile, stopping in my tracks next to Dad.

Agnus needed Knox to help him with the house's inventory. My foster brother—it's still weird to think of him that way—only agreed when Agnus promised him the new expensive headphones he's been eyeing.

For some reason, I think Agnus pulled Knox aside because he knows Dad and I need alone time.

I wrap the coat across my chest. It's not raining, but the chilly weather hits me to the bones. The dark-grey clouds hang above us with a sinister promise of a starless night in the near future. Like Aiden's eyes.

Nope. Not going there.

Why the hell does he have eyes the colour of the clouds before the rain? Now he'll barge into my mind whenever it rains. In a country like England, that's pure torture.

It's like being caught in the eye of a hurricane, smashed and wrecked to pieces, and having no way out.

I push him out of my mind and focus on Dad.

He's wearing a black, tailored suit but no coat. It's like he doesn't get cold.

Like Eli.

When we were little, my hands were ice cold, but Eli's felt like cosy winters and hot chocolate.

We drank it a lot together. Hot chocolate, I mean.

A wave of sadness hits me at the memory of him—or the lack thereof. His face is still a blur, even now.

This is the first time Dad and I have spent time alone; it's my chance to ask questions. Who knows when Knox will decide to join us again?

I motion at the empty space near the tree. "There was a swing there. Ma used to hold me in it and sing to me."

Dad freezes as if I've just spilt a bucket of ice water over his head.

I tense like a rigid cord. What have I done? Did I say something wrong?

"You remember." It's not a question, more like an observation—and not a very happy one at that.

"A little." A long sigh heaves out of me as if I haven't released a breath in ten years. "I know Ma wasn't mentally stable and she became worse after Eli drowned. I know all about your bet with Jonathan King, the Great Birmingham fire, and Aiden's kidnapping."

A gush of wind blows my hair and my coat back. I grit my teeth against the cold and… something else.

I didn't mean to blurt it out in one go, but I guess my thirst for the truth got the better of me.

Dad remains motionless, but I'm not sure if it's due to shock or contemplation.

"Your mum never wanted to hurt you, princess. She was mentally unwell. People do things they don't mean when they suffer from mental illnesses."

"But she did hurt me, Dad." My voice trembles like the tree branches. "She hit me on the back with a horsewhip."

"She… did?"

The tick in his jaw almost makes me want to stop talking,

but I don't. I've been silent for ten years, and now that I started speaking, it's impossible to go back. I owe myself this much.

Tears fill my eyes as I probe my useless head for answers. "I think it was when she found me near the basement. I didn't tell you because I didn't want you two to fight."

"Princess…"

"She tortured Aiden," I blurt. "He was a child, Dad. He was as old as Eli at that time, and he had red marks all over his skin and was chained to the wall. Did you know that he still has those scars? His back and ankle are a witness to Ma's abuse."

The need to cry for Aiden hits me out of nowhere. True, he's a monster now, and I won't ever forgive him, but that doesn't deny what happened to him as a child.

Ma ruined his innocence.

She smashed and crushed it to the ground, leaving a broken boy in her wake.

No wonder he's chosen to be a monster. In his warped logic, being a monster is better than being a weak mess.

I can't even blame him.

Deep down, I want to cry for the little boy he used to be. The boy with tousled, black hair and metal eyes.

That boy was my friend, my light in the darkness.

Eli sent him to me.

A sigh rips from Dad. "That was my fault."

"Your fault?"

"Kidnapping Aiden was only supposed to be a scare. He should've returned like the other two boys if I made sure of it personally."

"You mean Ma kept him without telling you?"

"With Reginald's help."

"U-Uncle Reg?"

Dad takes my hand in his and leads me to a bench nearby. I follow him like a lost puppy, my head wrapped in knots so complicated, it's hard to think straight.

Uncle Reg helped Ma kidnap Aiden.

The thought bounces in my head like a wrecking ball. I understand the words, but I can't wrap my mind around them.

Both of us sit on the wooden bench that smells of fresh paint. Dad angles me towards him so we're facing each other. "I wanted you to get used to home before any talk about the past, but I don't have a choice now. You might never see your mother the same after I tell you this."

"You can't make me hate Ma more than I already do, Dad."

He winces but doesn't comment. Perhaps, like me, Dad recognises just how much she ruined our lives.

"You have to understand that Eli's death hit your mother hard. Before we got married, Abigail suffered from manic episodes, depression, and anxiety. She didn't like doctors and often hid her medicines. Sometimes, she stopped using them altogether. When she got pregnant with Eli and gave birth to him, she didn't need her pills anymore. It was like she had found purpose in life. So when he died, her purpose died with him. It's safe to say we all lost a part of ourselves that day."

I inch closer to him and wrap my hand around his, silently communicating my support.

"Your mother's only way of survival was to imagine Eli was still alive. Two months after his death, she brought a boy home and told me she had found Eli in the market. I gave him back to his parents and apologised. Then, she started doing it behind my back with Reginald's help. That scoundrel did anything for money. He was smart, too, and only brought her homeless, orphaned, or runaway boys because no one misses them. Abigail's only condition was that they needed to look like Eli."

My frown deepens. "I vaguely remember that."

The pieces slowly come together.

I used to call Uncle Reginald a superhero because the monsters disappeared when he came along.

In my small mind, I used to categorise Ma's manic episodes as monsters. She wore white, hugged me to death, and took me to the lake. When she was white Ma, she never smiled and always seemed out of this world.

She was a monster.

However, when Uncle Reg came along, she wore her red dresses and put on red lipstick and makeup. She was stunning. She smiled more and had so much energy it baffled me sometimes.

She took me outside and played with me. She read me stories, laughed, and joked.

She was my ma.

My eyes widen and my heart nearly hits the grass.

Does that mean Ma only became cheerful when Uncle Reg brought her a boy from the streets?

"What did she do to them?" My voice is so haunting, it scares the shit out of me.

"Hug them and tell them she's glad her Eli was home." He sighs. "She never hurt them, so I allowed her to keep that habit."

"You *allowed* her?" I squeak.

"They came for lunch and stayed with her for a few hours. When the day was over, they took money and clothes and left. It was a win-win. The boys had a meal and shelter for the day and your mother was happy."

"Wouldn't it have been better if you took her to a shrink?"

"I did. I even left her in a psychiatric hospital under their recommendations, but she got worse and started cutting herself. I had to bring her back. At the time, I was still grieving Eli. I couldn't lose Abby, too."

Abby.

He still calls her that even after all this time.

I mull his words over, but I can't form clear thoughts. For a moment, Dad and I watch the distance, the freezing wind and the darkening clouds.

Those grey, *grey* clouds.

Screw you, clouds. Why do you have to add to my misery?

"Ma hurt them at some point, didn't she?" My voice is barely audible. "Aiden was tortured, Dad."

"At first, she only had lunches with them and talked to them about their day. Those street urchins loved her. Abby was kind and patient and had a knack in dealing with children."

"What changed?"

He runs a hand over his face and wipes his forefingers over his brows. "I don't know. She escalated, I think."

"Escalated?"

"One day, I came home and found her sitting in the bedroom. She was singing and brushing her hair with blood all over her hands. I ran straight to your room, scared she did something to you. Thankfully, you were sleeping safely."

"W-What happened?"

His jaw clenches and I recognise the gesture as anger. Dad doesn't show his emotions often, and I probably got my blank façade from him. "I found two children in the basement. They were on the verge of famine and their knees were scraped and cut horizontally. It was horrific."

"Two of them?"

He throws a fleeting glance in my direction. "You saw them back then, but you don't remember."

"Were they… Alive?"

"Yes. The wound wasn't fatal, but they were starving and on the verge of dying. Abigail usually fed the children and never laid a hand on them. When I asked her why she did that, she said they didn't have Eli's injury from when he fell off his bike so she fixed it."

I gasp and cover my mouth with my free hand "And you still allowed her near children?"

"No." He shakes his head. "Not after that incident."

"Thank God."

"She took it out on you, princess." He squeezes my hand in his. "I tried to protect you as best as I could, but I failed."

"Dad, don't say that."

"I admit failing you. If I could go back in time, I would've locked her in the psychiatric ward."

I shake my head. "I know you couldn't. It was right after Eli's death. If you and I lost both of them so close together, it would have ruined us."

"It would've been worth it. At least, I wouldn't have been separated from you for ten years." He pauses. "And she wouldn't have done what she did to Aiden."

I perk up, blinking away the tears. "Why did she do that to him?"

"After the incident with the two children, Abby remained without a 'fake Eli' for three months. It messed her up badly so when she finally had Aiden, she took it out on him." He runs a palm over his face. "I was busy with the aftermath of the Great Birmingham fire, HR, and police procedures so I didn't come home for a while. If I did, none of this would've happened. Doesn't matter anyway. What-ifs are…"

"Useless," I say with him.

We smile with an edge of sadness at one another.

Dad taught me it's useless to run after what-ifs when everything is said and done.

"We have each other now, princess. Nothing will keep us apart."

The first droplet of rain hits my nose.

"Come on, let's get you inside."

We hurry in the direction of the house, and for a moment, I imagine myself as the little girl who hung onto Dad's hand with all her might, giggling and screaming with delight as we ran in the rain.

The memory sends bolts of happiness through me.

Dad might be ruthless to the rest of the world, but to me, he's just Daddy

However, I'm not that seven-year-old child anymore. I'm not blind to the facts in front of me.

For one, although Ma tortured Aiden, Dad was the one who

kidnapped him. He was the one who started the vicious circle of ill fate between the Steel and King families.

Or maybe Jonathan is the one who started it by setting a fire that, while unintentional, killed dozens of people.

Jonathan and Ethan's ambitions and hunger for power are the reasons behind this entire feud.

However, Ma was the one who tortured Aiden and took the fucked up situation a notch higher. She was the reason Alicia drove in the middle of a storm and crashed into the cliff.

Ma is the reason Aiden became a cruel monster.

My head hurts from the entire situation.

Dad's phone rings as soon as we're at the entrance. He takes a look at it then smiles at me. "Go in first. I have to take this."

On my way inside, his no-nonsense voice drifts after me. "Yes. I want no mistakes… Perfect… Friday night…"

Agnus nods at me on his way to the kitchen. I smile back, but it's awkward at best.

Not only was he watching me the entire time on Dad's behalf, but he's also Uncle Reg's twin.

One was Ma's supplier of orphan boys and the other is Dad's right hand.

Weird dynamics.

I take the stairs and stop at the sound of music coming from Knox's room across from mine.

He must've finished the job for Agnus.

Now that I think about it, we haven't talked about returning to RES. Dad said he'll move us back to a private school here in Birmingham; Teal and Knox's school.

I haven't made up my mind yet, but that's probably due to the load of information my brain is trying to process.

If I talk to Knox, we might come to an agreement.

The sound of metal music blasts from the room. I knock, but there's no response. He probably hasn't heard me because of the music.

I push the door with my fingertips and then stop.

Knox is splayed on his back on the bed, wearing a short-sleeved T-shirt and shorts. He's laughing out loud while looking at his phone.

I'd bet a hundred he's going through memes.

Teal rolls her eyes from her position at his desk. She's going through some programming software and huffs as Knox laughs.

She has denim shorts without any stockings this time. I strain to read the quote on her blacktop.

A scar means I survived.

Just like mine and Aiden's scars.

The words hit me harder than I like to admit.

We have those scars because we survived. We're survivors.

Why the hell do I keep finding things to share with that bastard?

Teal hasn't been exactly warm to me since I arrived, but she hasn't been hostile either. She's basically been ignoring me.

Both Knox and Dad told me to give her time, so that's what I'm doing.

I'm curious about how they ended up with my father. They call him Dad, but neither of them is his biological child—per his confirmation the other day.

I'm about to knock again and go inside when something in my peripheral vision catches my eye.

A teddy bear sits on the shelves. It appears out of proportion for Knox's room. The walls are all black and filled with metal graffitis about Metallica, Slipknot, and Megadeth. There shouldn't be any teddy bears.

Oh, my God.

No, no, no…

This scene is familiar.

Way too familiar.

A shiver goes through my entire body as my mind jerks to the past.

"Daddy? Who are they?"

"Elsa? What are you doing here?" Dad stares down at me.

I grab his leg and lean to the side to stare at the door.

Two pairs of eyes look at me. One is light, the other is pitch black like the night outside. Their faces are all dirty like they haven't showered for days. Their dark hair flies all over the place as if they don't brush it.

I hug my teddy to my chest so tight, I'm sure I suffocate him.

"They just need help, princess." Dad crouches in front of me. "Now go back to your room."

"They don't have a teddy," I say.

"No, they don't," Daddy says with sadness.

I frown, tears filling my eyes.

Everyone should have a teddy bear. Mine is my favourite toy. Daddy gave it to me when I was three and I never leave without him. He's my sleeping buddy and my friend. We have tea parties together.

But Daddy says they need help, so they need Ted more than me.

"Here," I offer them Ted. "He'll help you. Take care of him, okay? He doesn't like to be cold and he doesn't like swimming."

The one with lighter eyes takes it from my hand with a sheepish smile.

My gaze falls to their knees. They're all red and bloody.

"Daddy! They're hurt!"

I'm thrown back to the present with a gasp. I stare at the scene in front of me with bugged eyes.

My gaze bounces between Ted, Knox, and Teal.

My heart nearly stops beating when I squint. Both Knox and Teal have faded horizontal scars on their right knees. Just like the scar Eli had after falling from his bike.

It's them.

Knox and Teal are the first ones Ma hurt.

Aiden and I aren't the only survivors.

SEVEN

Elsa

During breakfast the following day I keep to myself and barely touch my food.

Usually, I would participate in Knox's conversations, but today, I can't even look him in the eye.

Not after what I remembered yesterday.

Dad and Agnus are talking about stocks and the FTSE 100. Knox gave up on anyone hearing him out, so he just plays around with Teal's food. She kicks him under the table, the sound echoing in the dining room. He howls as if he's being murdered.

I wonder if he screamed when Ma cut his knee back then.

Don't.

If I allow those dark thoughts to sweep over me, I won't be able to function. I would stay up all night, hugging my knees to my chest, like I did last night.

I continue lowering my head so neither Teal nor Knox can see my heated cheeks or the pricking of my skin.

Can the earth open up and swallow me?

What would it be like if Aiden was sitting beside me right now? For one, he wouldn't feel ashamed. For two, he would know how to deal with this situation.

Damn you, mind. Aren't we supposed to block him out?

It's only been three days since I last saw him. Meaning, he and his fucking engagement are fresh in my mind.

Nope, brain. That's not how it works. Block him out. Block him the fuck out.

"We'll be in my office if you need anything, princess." Dad and Agnus stand.

I was too caught up in a conversation with my brain to notice they stopped talking.

Dad smiles down at me. "Let's go for horse riding afterwards."

"I don't know how to ride a horse."

"You do." He smiles. "We'll just have to refresh your memories."

It's only after he and Agnus disappear at the top of the stairs that I recall I'm at the table with Knox and Teal.

Alone.

Oh, God. What the hell am I supposed to do now?

Run? No, that would be rude.

Hide under the table? That'd be crazy.

I slap a generous amount of jam on my toast and take my time shaping it like I'm an artist or something. At this point, I would do anything to escape their company, but I don't trust my legs enough to carry me out of here.

"Are you okay?" Knox bites into a scone. "You've been silent since last night's dinner."

Teal stares at me from underneath her long, thick lashes but says nothing.

You're an adult. Own up to it, dammit.

Taking a deep, shaky breath, I finally lift my head, still clutching the toast.

Two pairs of eyes watch me closely. Hazel eyes and midnight eyes.

That's why both Knox and Teal looked so familiar when I first met them—or met them again.

"I remember meeting you years ago." My voice is heavy with

clogged emotions. I can barely breathe, let alone talk. "I'm sorry for what Ma did. I-I'm so sorry."

"Finally." Knox taps his chest. "I was hurt when you didn't remember me. It hit me right in the tiny white space in my heart."

"Your apology means shit to me," Teal speaks casually as she sips her coffee. "It doesn't give me back what I lost."

I wince.

"You sound like a bitch, T," Knox says with nonchalance like it's a normal occurrence. "There's something you need to know about Teal, Ellie. She has a weird way of expressing herself. Okay, now, T. Repeat that after thinking about the words."

"Right. Okay." She lifts her head, a crease etching between her brows. "I meant you don't need to apologise for something you didn't do."

"See?" Knox grins. "That wasn't too hard, was it?"

Teal isn't focused on him, though. Her entire attention falls on me and I feel like a mouse stalked by a cat.

That's… weird.

"Although you do look so much like that woman, I keep thinking about stabbing you to death with a fork while you sleep." She takes her coffee and disappears around the corner.

"Haha, very funny." Knox offers me a lopsided smile. "She's kidding… mostly."

My shoulders slouch. "She's right, I'm a carbon copy of my mother. How can you be so easy going about that, Knox?"

"Because you're not her. I'm going to be honest, the day of the pool's incident, I was the one who lifted you when you fell to your knees in the car park. I think you were so out of it, you didn't notice me. I was also so confused, thinking that woman had returned. Imagine my bloody shock! So anyway, I followed you and I found you floating in that pool." He runs a hand at the back of his head. "For a second, I did contemplate leaving you there, but I didn't because I knew you weren't her. The more time I spent with you, the more I was positive you weren't her. Give T some time, and she'll come to the same conclusion."

"Thank you, Knox." I fight the tears in my voice.

"No. Thank *you*. Ted was the first toy Teal and I received. Dad says it was your favourite. Children don't give their favourite toys to anyone. Hell, I don't give away my things now either."

I swallow. "It was nothing."

"It was something for both of us. T and I were the kind of children who weren't allowed hope, but you gave it to us in the form of Ted." He smirks. "We took great care of it, by the way."

"Are you and Teal siblings?"

He nods. "Twins."

"Twins?"

"Fraternal." He winks. "I got all the looks."

I'll have to disagree with that. Although Knox is handsome, Teal has a unique beauty that's rare to find; both innocent and hard. Adorable and dangerous.

"We were street kids," Knox continues. "We ran away from a druggie mother who was about to whore us out for money and all that jazz."

I gulp at the image and drop the toast. Not that I ever thought about eating it in the first place. "How about your father?"

"Never knew him. Dad is the only father we had."

My heart warms as if I were thrust from a dark icy winter night straight into a summer day. Dad took two lost children and gave them a home.

"Did he take you in since the basement incident?"

He nods. "We used to live in a separate home with Agnus, but Dad came by all the time. After the fire, we moved in with him."

"But he was in a coma."

"He was still Dad even while he was sleeping."

Everything that Knox told me about his father before makes sense now. He never stopped considering Dad his father even after he was in a coma with a slim chance of ever waking up again.

"Thank you for being there for him when he needed you."

"Hey, don't go all sappy on me. He's my dad, too." Challenge sparks in his eyes. "And I'm his favourite."

I smile and take my first real bite of food this morning. Knox and I talk about the times he stopped himself from finding me. Apparently, Agnus didn't like for us to get in touch without Dad in the picture.

We chat for a bit when a commotion sounds from the front door. I stand and Knox comes to my side. We both frown in confusion as we follow the source.

The butler talks to someone at the door. I barely manage to take a step forward when I'm hugged out of nowhere.

Nina Ricci's perfume clogs my nostrils as slim arms hold me so close, it's nearly suffocating.

"Elsie," she cries in my neck. "Oh my God, you're all right. You're going to be all right, hon."

"Aunt?"

"I'm here. Aunt is here." She pulls back to search my face with frantic eyes. "Are you okay? Are you hurt? Have you been eating well?"

"I'm fine, Aunt."

"Calm down, Blair." Uncle's voice is as soothing as I remember. He holds my backpack and stands with stone calm by the entrance.

I smile faintly at him.

I'm such a horrible person. It's been two days since I told them I'd come home, but I disappeared without a word.

"I'm sorry," I whisper to him.

Even though I'm still mad about how they hid the truth for a decade and actively forbade me from searching for it, Aunt and Uncle are still my parents. One way or another.

"Let's go home, hon." Aunt digs her nails into my arm. "Let's leave this place behind."

"Absolutely not." Dad's voice echoes from behind me like thunder, strong and non-negotiable. He stands beside me and addresses Aunt, "You're welcome to stay here all you like, but Elsa isn't going anywhere."

Both Aunt and Uncle freeze, watching him as if he's a ghost—which he is in some way.

I can't say I blame them. My reaction was the same when I first saw him.

"You are alive," Uncle whispers.

"I don't care whether you're alive or not," Aunt snarls. "Elsa is my adoptive daughter."

"Those papers can be annulled any time now that her real father is alive."

Aunt's lips tremble, but she visibly straightens and guards her cool. "I won't leave Elsa with you so you'll destroy her like you destroyed Abigail."

"You of all people know Abigail was unwell way before I married her." He takes a menacing step forward. "I was there for her until the end, but where were you, Blair?"

Aunt flinches as if he slapped her.

This is the side of Dad I never get to see; ruthless and merciless.

She touches the side of her neck. "Elsa, let's go, hon."

Somewhere deep inside, I miss Aunt and Uncle, and I do feel sorry for her—for her past, and her abusive father.

It must've cost her a lot to come to Birmingham when she associates this place with trauma. She's been slightly shaking since she hugged me, and I'm sure it has to do with this place as much as with me.

A few months ago, I would've taken her hand and followed her without question.

However, that was the Elsa of the past.

I gently pull my hand from her. "I'm staying."

Uncle briefly closes his eyes with a pained expression.

Aunt's mouth opens and closes like a fish. "W-what?"

"I'll stay with Dad." I swallow. "I'll call and visit. I promise."

"Is that your final decision, pumpkin?" Uncle asks with a note of sadness.

I nod once.

He passes me my backpack. "Your phone and necessities are in here."

"Thank you."

"No. No, Elsie. Don't do this." Aunt grabs me by both my arms like a dying woman holding onto her last breath. "You *can't* leave us."

"I'm not leaving you, Aunt. I'll visit."

A sob catches in her throat as Uncle pulls her back.

I watch them as Uncle drags a numb Aunt towards his car. A tear threatens to fall free, but I seal it in. I won't cry.

I will *not* cry.

Dad holds me to him by the shoulder and Knox—who has been watching the entire scene silently—smiles.

I smile back with so much internal peace.

Aunt and Uncle aren't my only family.

EIGHT

Elsa

On Friday night, Dad takes us to a fundraiser held by one of his friends.

Oh, and it's in London.

I'm not panicking or anything.

Scratch that, I'm totally panicking.

He told me that I could stay back in Birmingham if I wanted to, but it would make him happy if I stood by his side in his first official appearance.

I couldn't refuse him. Truth is, I want to appear on my father's side. I want the world to know I'm his daughter.

We have been separated for too long.

Knox is the most excited amongst us. He's game for any party—his words, not mine. He's wearing a stylish dark blue suit with rolled-up sleeves and a white T-shirt with Metallica's logo on it.

When Dad told him he can't attend a fundraiser at a duke's house with that shirt, Knox rolled his eyes and buttoned his jacket.

I laughed so hard when he said, "You just insulted the die-hard metal fans. Happy, Dad?"

I swear Knox and Dad have the strangest, most entertaining interactions ever. They're so different and yet, they're in tune.

Knox's competitive streak about being Dad's favourite is so entertaining, but can also be threatening sometimes.

If Eli didn't die so young, I wonder if his relationship with Dad would've been the same as Knox's.

Teal joined us, too, but she has a bored expression like this is the last place she'd want to be.

When she came down the stairs wearing a denim skirt and a T-shirt with 'Annoyed' written across her breasts, Dad and Agnus motioned for her to go back upstairs, put on a dress, and remove the gothic makeup.

She changed into a dark blue dress with a wide tulle skirt that stops a bit above her knees. Her inky hair shines in blue under the light and falls on either side of her face. She still has dark eyeshadow and eyeliner, but she's put on light pink lipstick for a change.

Cute is an understatement. She really has pinchable cheeks.

Me, on the other hand, I opted for a black dress I'll have to lift it so I don't fall on my face. I pulled my hair up and put on mascara and barely-there lipstick.

Oh, and Dad is the one who chose our clothes—except for Knox's Metallica T-shirt.

Teal and I interlace our arms with Dad's as we take the large stairs leading to the Rhodes' mansion.

Actually, it's an estate.

Expensive cars fill the driveway. Women wear stylish gowns and men rock tuxedos. Hell, even the stairs are covered in a red carpet as if we're at the Oscars.

The four of us head to the entrance.

Agnus hasn't joined us yet, saying he'll come by later. He and Dad have been locked up in their office the past few days conspiring. I'm not curious enough to ask, and I'd rather stay away from Dad's business world. After all, he and Agnus seem to have everything under control.

A butler bows to us after checking our invitation.

"Welcome to the Rhodes Estate, Mr Steel & Mr Van Doren."

Knox points at himself. "That would be me."

Teal shoots him a glare before she focuses back on the steps. Like me, she doesn't seem comfortable in heels.

I'm glad Dad chose our clothes or we would've been a joke at a place like this.

One step after the other. You can do this, Elsa.

One step. Just because I'm in London again doesn't mean I'll meet Aiden.

One step. I have to survive this night in peace and then go back to Birmingham.

Besides, I missed Kim, Ronan, and the others. I talk to them via text, but it's not the same as seeing them in person.

I haven't told Kim I'm coming tonight, in case she tells Aiden. However, I'm sure one of the horsemen will be here. Probably Ronan or Xander, since their parents are active in the political and public scheme.

"Are we ready or are we ready?" Knox interlaces his arm with my free one, cutting off my focus on my feet.

Like in the films, two butlers bow as the door opens.

Bursts of colours, sounds, and smells explode ahead of us.

The hall is the largest I've seen in my life. Golden chandeliers hang from the vaulted ceilings. In the middle sits a black jaguar statue, as well as a statue of a white knight riding a black horse.

The contrast is so riveting, I can't help but stop and stare. Dad has mentioned the Rhodes have real jaguars on their estates and it was the reason they earned their title hundreds of years ago.

That's impressive. Although I would rather not meet any jaguars in real life.

The strong mixture of designer perfumes and appetising food float in the air. Rows of self-service tables extend until the end of the hall.

An orchestra sits at the far end of the ballroom playing classical music. The piece is familiar so it must be Beethoven or Mozart—the only ones I know.

Whoa. This is what it feels like to have old money.

We all head towards a man wearing a tailored black tuxedo. With his black hair and eyes, it's like he's cut from the darkness. He appears to be in his early thirties.

"Mr Steel. It's an honour." He offers his hand.

Dad shakes it. "It's an honour to be here, Your Grace."

"Tristan is fine." He smiles.

Wait. He's *the* Tristan Rhodes? I don't know why I expected someone in his sixties with a bald head and a fat belly.

"These are my children, Elsa, Knox, and Teal."

We shake hands with Tristan. How does one greet a duke, anyway? It's the first time I've met one.

"This is my cousin Aaron Rhodes…" Tristan drifts off when he searches on either side of him but finds no one. "Or *was*. He's probably playing the invisibility game."

I like this Aaron Rhodes. Can I play the invisibility game with him?

"It's fine." Dad chuckles. "We can meet him later."

"No, please. We have a lot to talk about." Tristan smiles at us. It's both welcoming and formulaic.

He communicates so much with a mere smile. It's like he's saying, 'Yes, welcome to my house, but I'll rip your heart out if you break anything.'

"Do you mind if I steal your father for a while?" he asks us.

The three of us shake our heads in sync.

"Make yourselves at home." And with that, he disappears with Dad in the crowd.

"Okay, time to raid the food." Knox rubs his hands together. "Be right back." He takes two steps then stops. "Scratch that. I won't be right back."

He strides in the direction of the reception area as fast as he can without running.

Teal and I are left alone together.

Awkward.

I was never one for small talk, so I stay silent. If I say anything it'll sound awkward and ruin the mood. My relationship with Teal is already like walking on thin ice. I don't want to ruin it furthermore.

"This is so stupid." She sighs and retrieves her phone from her bra. "They had a show on the Cold War on National Geographic tonight."

"You're interested in the Cold War?" I ask carefully.

"Sure." She scrolls through her phone. "Wars are fun."

"Fun?"

"Uh…" she trails off. "I mean they're interesting. There's so much knowledge and human stupidity."

"How about ancient wars?"

"Like Napoleon? Roman?"

"I was thinking Asian? Chinese? I'm a fan of *The Art of War* by Sun Tzu."

"Oh, that. It's cool."

"You read it?" I gasp.

"Sure."

Whoa. It's so rare for someone my age to know about *The Art of War*, let alone having read it.

Teal's appearance is not what meets the eye, that's for sure. There's so much depth in there, it's kind of exciting to get to know her.

"I thought that was you, Ellie!"

I'm attacked by a hug from behind. Before I know it, I'm lifted off the ground and spun around.

I laugh as Ronan finally puts me back onto my feet.

"Hey, Ronan."

"Don't give me that, *petit traitre*." He glares down at me jokingly. "How can you disappear on me like that? I'm having withdrawals. I demand payback."

"I told you over text, a lot of things happened."

Xander and Cole join us. The three of them are rocking stylish suits; Ronan is in dark-blue, Cole is in black, and Xander is in dark-brown. With their hair styled, it's like they're out for a fashion show.

This is the side of them I don't know—or more like I haven't met yet. I'm sure they attend parties like these all the time.

Before I can rejoice about seeing them again, dread tightens in my stomach. The three of them wouldn't be here without Aiden. He must be hiding somewhere biding his time to come out and attack.

Like a fucking predator.

"And who is this?" Ronan drawls in Teal's direction.

"Teal." I motion at her. "This is Ronan, Cole, and Xander from school."

She nods, barely sparing them any attention before she returns to her phone.

"*Bonsoir, ma belle.*" Ronan devours her with his eyes, openly, with no shame. "This means we'll be seeing a lot of you."

"Not really," she says, still not looking at them.

"Yeah. We live in Birmingham," I say.

"No," Ronan clutches his heart dramatically, closing in on her. "I might die if I don't see you again."

"Then die." Teal turns around and heads in Knox's direction without a glance back.

"Hashtag, burn." Xander clutches Ronan by the shoulder.

"Someone actually turned you down." Cole raises an eyebrow. "I'm impressed."

"Fuck off, both of you." Ronan's face is unreadable for a second before he grins at me again. "Where were we? Right. When are you coming back, Ellie? I need my dose of you like I need weed."

"Did you just compare me to weed?"

"Hey! Weed is cool. It relaxes you and makes you happy."

"Well," Xander laughs. "Ronan and weed share an endless love story, so comparing you to it is kind of a compliment."

"*Exactement!*" Ronan clasps Xander's shoulder in a bro hug. "So Ellie, when are you coming back to be my happy place?"

I'm about to tell him I don't know if I'll ever come back when the hairs on the back of my neck stand on end.

A flush covers my skin from my cheeks all the way down my chest underneath my clothes. Something familiar races down my spine no matter how much I try to suffocate it.

No, no.

Please, please.

It's useless to beg when the disaster hits you straight in the face. It doesn't delay the inevitable and surely doesn't erase it.

He's here.

I feel it over my skin, and straight into my insides. As I slowly turn around, I hold on to my delusional bubble, my safe space.

I should've known better. There's no safe place from monsters.

The darkness is their playground, and the world is their theatre. If they choose to, they'll drag you into the shadows and it'll be all over.

I thought the worst monsters were the ones from my childhood. Turns out, my worst monster had the most hypnotic metallic eyes and the inkiest black hair. He has a penetrating gaze that dissects me and sees straight into the darkest depths of my soul.

My monster is all tall, powerful, and beautiful.

My monster is Aiden King.

NINE

Elsa

Considering all the tiny bursts of panic I experienced tonight, I should've been ready for Aiden's appearance.

I'm not.

Not really.

Not at all.

I fist both sides of my dress just to have something to twist.

Jonathan saunters inside with his infuriating confidence on display as if he owns the place and everyone in it. He looks down his arrogant nose at everyone in his vicinity.

Aiden and Levi stride on either side of him like generals waltzing into a war zone. Astrid hangs onto Levi's arm seeming more uncomfortable than I am currently feeling.

The three King men are wearing sharp black tuxedos that flatter their developed physiques. My attention bounces back to Aiden. I try to fight it, you know.

I try to look at Astrid's beautiful dress, at Levi's easy grin, or even at Jonathan treating everyone as peasants.

I can't.

Something pulls at my strings and leads me straight back to Aiden.

I hate that something. I loathe it from the bottom of my defective heart.

Said defective heart flutters, and I squash it while I focus on Aiden. On the way he strides with confident ease. On his slicked, stylish hair. On the cloth that tightens around his biceps and his muscular, tall thighs.

He put on an effort tonight. He wants to be as presentable as possible—and lethally attractive. He's using his appearance to help his manipulations.

The moment his eyes meet mine, I freeze. It's like those grey clouds have entered the hall and will now transform into a storm, wreaking havoc in its wake.

Or perhaps, that storm is only meant for me.

I keep sucking air, but I'm not breathing properly. I'm not breathing at all.

Silver is the queen to the King's name.

That reminder hits me like a jab to the ribs. My temper flares and all the blocking I've managed thus far threatens to smash to pieces.

I break eye contact with effort and face the guys. "I have to find Teal."

Ronan protests, but I lift my dress and walk in the opposite direction.

No idea where Teal went, but if I can find her and Knox, I won't have to face Aiden and his bitchy fiancée who must've come with him.

A whirlwind of bitterness grips me out of nowhere. My hands itch, and I curse myself for not bringing hand sanitiser.

The breathing shortage from earlier swings back with a vengeance. I nearly topple over from the force of it.

Air.

I need air.

Stumbling, I find a patio door open and I slip outside.

The music from the banquet dies down a little as the fresh air hits my face. Goosebumps cover my bare arms, but I don't wrap my arms around myself. That's for weak people.

Running away is also for the weak.

My teeth sink into my bottom lip. The wound is still fresh. I'm sure with time, I won't run away. There will be a day when I'll see Aiden and walk right past him without sparing him a glance.

I hope so.

I really hope so.

Pain is temporary. Pain dulls over time.

However, I doubt there'll be a day when I think about him and don't feel ache, but I'm sure it won't be this sharp or damning.

You're strong, Elsa. You're a Steel.

As Dad used to say, 'no one fucks with a Steel and lives to talk about it.'

Taking a deep breath, I whirl around. I'll go back inside and pretend he doesn't exist.

I falter, my heels catching on the floor. Aiden stands in front of me like a grim reaper.

No, not a grim reaper. A monster.

My monster.

He doesn't make a noise as he steps outside, purposefully invading my space and my air.

But that's what Aiden does, isn't it? He pushes you into a corner, and soon enough, you'll realise there's no way out.

He's more intimidating and handsome than anyone should be. He has his father's arrogant nose and the aura of a God amongst humans. Or rather, a king amongst peasants.

"Did you think you could run away from me, sweetheart?"

His voice is still the same, rough, deep, and sinister. No idea why I thought his voice would change in the span of a week.

My repressed anger catches on fire and boils through my veins. Profanities fight and claw to be set free like a hurricane brewing in the distance.

However, I remain silent.

Aiden is the type of deviant who feeds on hysterics. The best way to win against him is to reverse his own tactics, disrupt his thought process, and keep him in the dark.

Due to his lack of empathy, he has a knack for reading people.

He relies so much on intuition and logic; they're his greatest assets. It's almost impossible to shuffle his formation or make a move he didn't already anticipate.

However, I have one advantage.

I know him so well that I'm able to look him in the eye and seal all my emotions inside.

If he's searching for a fit of anger, he won't be getting any.

"You disappeared on me," he continues after a moment of silence. "I understand you're angry, but you didn't hear my side of the story, Elsa."

Angry? How about waking up in the middle of the night to find myself crying and my chest squeezing painfully? How about the sense of betrayal I've been blocking out so I don't break into pieces?

His side of the story? Fuck that.

Fuck *him*.

He has no side of the story. He kept a fucking engagement a secret while I was going berserker on the girl who had more right to him than I ever would.

The bastard reduced me to being the other woman.

It's such a dirty, humiliating place to be, and I'll never forgive him for that.

I lift my dress and start to pass him.

Aiden grips me by the arm. His touch would've set me on fire before, now it's just… so cold.

So freezing.

So wrong.

"I said," he enunciates as if I didn't hear him the first time. "You didn't hear my side of the story."

I wiggle my arm free and surprisingly he releases me.

That's a first.

I take two steps when his lethal, hard voice stops me in my tracks. "You made a promise, Elsa. Fucking keep it."

"If you don't keep your promises, why should I keep mine?" My voice is so calm, it's kind of haunting.

I don't turn around or face him.

He chose this. He chose to have us in a place where my back is the only thing he sees.

"I don't give promises I don't keep. You're the one who does that over and over again. I told you loving me is a one-way road. I told you not to say the fucking words if you didn't mean them."

I throw a glance at him over my shoulder. "I meant those words. I love you, Aiden, but I also love myself enough to walk away from you."

And then I head back inside.

The urge to cry hits me like a sudden natural disaster; hard and destructive. Still, I don't cry. I won't shed tears for him. I won't be reduced to the victim he wants me to become.

Pain grips the centre of my chest. It's deep and affects every layer of my heart.

I thought if I admitted I still love him, the pain would lessen.

I thought wrong.

Will it always be like this? Chaotic and painful? Will I have to walk counting my steps?

One day, I'll attend one of these parties and watch Aiden waltz inside with Silver hanging off his arm as his wife.

His fucking *wife*.

Acute nausea coats my throat and sticks my tongue to the roof of my mouth.

I won't survive that. I can't.

My thoughts rob my air again. I stop near one of the food tables to catch my breath. There's another patio to my right. Will anyone notice if I hide out there for the rest of the evening?

Movement catches in my peripheral vision.

In the corner of the patio, a man and woman are shrouded in darkness as they talk in a hushed tone. I can't hear them due to the music and the general chatter.

There goes my plan to hide out there.

I'm about to turn around when something else catches my attention.

The man speaks so low, it's almost threatening. The girl shrinks back against the stone railing. The dim light catches in her... green hair?

I barge outside. "Kim?"

The man—Xander—slowly pushes back but not before giving her a harsh glare. "I mean it. Don't fucking test me."

And then he's back inside.

Kim's chest rises and falls so fast, I'm afraid she'll have some sort of a heart attack. Her pupils are dilated as if she's coming down from a high.

I rush to her and take her hands—shaking and sweating—in mine. "What happened? Are you okay? What did he do?"

"I'm fine." Kim fakes a smile.

She needs to stop faking smiles when she's this horrible at them.

"Kim!" I scold. "What the hell? You look on the verge of a breakdown."

"It's just Xander being Xander." She waves her hand in dismissal and fixes the hem of her dark green dress. "I missed you."

Her arms wrap around me. Even though I don't want her to change the subject, I don't pull away.

Kim takes shaky breaths and I realise how much she needs this hug. She's a loner and I'm practically the only friend she has. Except for Kir, her family aren't the affectionate type. I always feel like she needs human touch more than anything. She's just not so good at expressing her needs.

"I'm here for you, Kim. You know that, right?"

She nods into my neck without saying anything.

When she finally steps back, a reluctant smile is plastered on her face. "How about you? Are you okay?"

I FaceTimed with Kim and told her all about Aiden's engagement with Silver, my father, Knox, and Teal.

Every time she tried to ask me about my feelings considering Aiden's engagement, I shut down and ended the conversation.

I knew she'd bring it up again when we met face-to-face.

"What are you doing here?" I try to deflect.

"Dad brought me. He's all over fundraisers." She pauses, narrowing her eyes. "You don't get to change the subject."

Brilliant. Here we go.

"King doesn't see Silver as a woman. Cross my heart and hope to die." Kim places a hand over her breast. "I would bet Kir's life on it and you know I'd never do that unless I was sure."

"They're fucking engaged, Kim. They're getting married."

Every day, I wake up hoping last week's revelation is a nasty nightmare, but I'm brought back to reality all too soon. The fall hurts, you know. It's like crashing and burning at the same time with no way out.

"It could be something arranged by their parents." Kim taps her chin like a detective. "Jonathan King and Sebastian Queens are childhood friends and have been allies for as long as I can remember."

"Aiden isn't the type who could be forced into doing anything."

"This must've happened way before you came along, Ellie. King is the logical type, and if he thought marrying Silver would ensure his future and his relationship with his father, he would have agreed to it."

"Then why did he keep me in the dark about it?"

"I don't know. He's the only one who can answer that." She rubs my arm. "All I know is that King isn't interested in Silver, and honestly, I think it's the same for her."

I raise an eyebrow. "So now you're an expert on how Silver feels?"

"We were all raised together, remember? Silver and I were friends once upon a time."

"Wait. What?"

"It was before my fall from grace." She throws up a hand dismissively. "Anyway, she's a bitch, but I don't think Aiden is her endgame. Silver is the type of person who hides her real favourites so no one snatches them away. When we used to play together, she'd take out all her dolls except for her favourite, *Anastasia*. She hid it in a place I couldn't find. I hate her, but thinking logically, if she really loves Aiden, she wouldn't be all territorial about him in public. She would've made her moves in the background."

Kim's words bring back what Tara told me some time ago. She said Silver isn't interested in Aiden but does her best so everyone knows he's hers.

Tara also mentioned rumours has it that Silver has a secret boyfriend and is camouflaging him by using Aiden as a front.

If that's the case, then Silver runs a lot deeper than I thought. What's her endgame exactly?

Not that I care.

It's not Silver who matters. It's the fact that Aiden hid his engagement to her knowing full well how much his history with her bothered the living bejesus out of me.

"I really don't want to do this, but I can talk to her if you like?" Kim asks with a careful tone.

"Thanks, but you don't have to." I drag her with me by the arm. "Come on, let's find Knox."

"And Teal!" she squeals. "I'm super excited to meet Knox's twin sister. I'm sure she's as fun as him."

Since I told Kim about Knox having a twin, she's been dying to get to know her.

"She's special, yes, but she's nothing like him," I say.

We spend a few minutes parading between the tables.

The classical music stops. Tristan Rhodes clinks a fork against his glass of champagne, commanding the entire room's attention.

The residual chatter comes to a screeching halt.

Kim and I freeze in place. Knox joins us, stuffing his face with scones.

He offers us one, then grins when neither of us accepts. "More for me."

"Where's Dad?" I ask.

Knox motions ahead. Sure enough, Dad stands in the front row, but he's not alone.

Jonathan and Aiden King are beside him.

What...?

The urge to go and stand by his side overwhelms me. I should be beside my father just like Aiden is beside his.

A sense of calm falls over me when Teal inches closer to Dad. I can feel her determination all the way from over here.

Go, Teal.

"Ladies and Gentleman." Tristan's voice commands the entire hall. "We are honoured to have you here. Your donations for the orphans' association are bound to save lives and offer hope for people without any."

He goes on to talk about the association and the number of children they're helping. I steal a glance at Aiden, but he appears completely engrossed in the speech. His poker face is strapped in place; his demeanour screams calm.

I can do that, too. I can act as if nothing happened.

Tristan raises a toast to the money raised tonight then continues, "I would like to take this chance to thank everyone who participated in the growth of the Rhodes Conglomerate. We have enormous plans for the future. For that, we have recruited two of the best companies as potential partners."

Tristan tips his glass in Dad and Jonathan's direction. "Mr King, Mr Steel. May the best one win."

Everyone raises their glasses, Dad and Jonathan included.

The look in their eyes can only mean 'Game on'.

Aiden spins around and his cloudy eyes meet mine. He doesn't have to search for me as if he knew exactly where I stood. Even though his expression is unreadable, I'm almost sure that his thoughts match mine.

The real war has started.

TEN

Aiden

Past

I pace the length of the basement as far as the chains would let me.

They rattle behind me, their heavy clink is the only sound surrounding me in the looming darkness.

No idea if it's night or day. Back home, I associated the dark with nighttime, but there doesn't seem to be a sense of time in this place.

The red woman didn't show up.

I'm never sure if she'll hug me or hit me across the face, telling me to bring back her son.

There's also the girl who looks like a doll—Elsa. It's been a long time since she came by.

Time here is so messed up. It feels as if I've been trapped for two months.

Maybe it's less. Maybe it's more.

Mum used to say that when you're free, time flies by, but it becomes long when you're trapped. I didn't understand her back then, but now I do. Time is weird that way. Time is endless and short all at once.

The door slowly creaks open. I come to a halt, the chains slowly hissing to a stop, too.

It's the girl.

The red woman wouldn't open the door slowly, she'd barge in, sometimes startling me from sleep.

Elsa's small footsteps echo in the empty basement. She brings light with her—and it's not only because of her torch.

It's her entire presence. Her little bunny shoes and her tiny sleeping dress.

She smells of marshmallow, honey, and the beginning of spring. If light has a smell then Elsa is it. Just like Mum smells like warmth.

Sometimes, I wonder if I'm talking to imaginary people like Mum. I thought of Silver and Kimberly's dolls and then brought them to life so I can stay calm.

Dad says to always stay calm. Emotions can be my downfall. Just like my mum. He says she feels too much, and that's why she cries a lot.

I think she cries a lot because he doesn't feel enough.

Elsa tiptoes close to wrap the blanket around my shoulders. Since I'm taller, she strains and huffs in frustration, blowing on her golden strands.

My lips twitch as I lower myself so she can properly do it. She grins with triumph and drops her bag on the floor. There are a sandwich and a bottle of juice today.

"I did them behind Uncle Agnus' back." She puts a finger on her mouth. "Don't tell him."

I sit on the cold floor and take a bite of the sandwich. It's filled with bacon, ham, and all sorts of cheese.

Elsa likes putting cheese everywhere. I don't really care for it, but I eat anyway.

The red woman only gives me water, if it weren't for Elsa, I would've starved.

"Thank you." I swallow my first mouthful.

"If you want to thank me, tell me your name."

She crouches in front of me, crossing her arms over her knees and leaning her head on her arm.

It's become a habit of her to watch me like that.

Like I'm an alien.

I chew on my next bite slowly, thinking about her words.

Dad always says to never give my name to someone with bad vibes. Elsa doesn't give bad vibes, but she lives in a place that does.

The red woman looks so much like her, too. Maybe one day, she'll be the same.

Elsa frowns. "Why don't you tell me your name? I told you mine."

I remain silent.

"I'll just call you Grey Eyes then." She grins as if she came up with the most unique nickname.

"I had a teddy bear named Ted, but I had to give it to two children like you. If I still had it, I'd give it to you."

I continue chewing silently.

"If I can't find the keys that open your cuff, I'll tell Daddy when he comes back. He'll save you like he saved them."

Still, I say nothing. One, I'm hungry. Two, I like it better when she talks. Her voice is like a classical melody, soft, elegant, and… peaceful.

"How old are you?" she asks.

"Eight."

"I'll also be eight soon." Her missing tooth shows when she smiles big. "We can be friends."

"I have friends."

"Oh." Her expression falls.

I want to kick myself for making her feel bad. Cole keeps saying I should make my words less direct.

No idea what that means.

However, I don't want Elsa to feel bad. What if she never returns and I'll stay in the dark all alone?

She peeks at me through her eyelashes with puppy eyes. "Can't you add one more friend?"

I open my mouth to agree.

"Wait!" She reaches into her pocket and retrieves a small

pack of chocolate balls. "I'll give you two of my Maltesers. They're my favourites."

The sound of the bag fills the basement as she opens it and brings out two small balls. She bites her lower lip, eyes squinting hard, then retrieves another one. "Okay, I'll give you three."

She reaches out her hand then drops the three pieces back into the bag and offers it to me with a resigned sigh. "You can have them all if you become my friend."

When I don't take it, she shoves it into my lap. "I gave you my Maltesers, you have to be my friend."

I smile at her funny expression. She looks on the verge of taking back her chocolate and running away to eat them in the corner.

"Okay," I say.

"Okay?"

"Okay, I'll be your friend."

She claps, giggling. "Yes!"

I take one chocolate ball and offer her the rest. "We can share."

Her teeth sink in her bottom lip. "Are you sure? I gave them to you. I don't want to be rude and take them back."

"Friends share everything."

"Really?"

"Really."

She snatches the bag of Maltesers and stuffs her mouth with two balls of chocolate. "Hey, Grey Eyes."

"Hmm?" I watch her twinkling eyes as she chews. Some of the chocolate sticks to her upper lip.

"When I grow up, I'm gonna buy you a bucket of Maltesers."

"Why?"

"Because Dad says you have to buy gifts for the one you marry."

"Marry?" I whisper.

"Yup!" She grins. "When I grow up, I'm going to marry you."

"You can't marry me."

Her face contorts. "Why not?"

"Mum says you have to love someone to marry them."

"Then you can just love me." She throws her hand in the air. "What's so hard about that?"

I remain silent. This girl is crazy.

"Hey, Grey Eyes." She scoots closer. "When I give you the bucket of Maltesers, are you going to share it with me?"

I laugh and she laughs with me. Her laughter is like the sunshine after a rainy day. It's the sun peeking through the cloudy sky.

As I watch her, I realise I want to see her laugh all the time.

Maybe she's right. Maybe after we grow up, she needs to stay close so I can see her laugh this way every day.

She has the most beautiful laughter I've ever seen.

"Promise you'll marry me." She holds out her pinkie.

I curl mine around hers. "I promise."

ELEVEN

Aiden

Present

School is the last place I want to be.

However, every day I wake up, get ready, and hope against hope she'll show up.

I don't even do the hope thing. I'm a doer.

It's been more than thirteen days since she left to Birmingham and didn't return.

Five days since the Rhodes' fundraiser.

Five whole fucking days of sleepless nights.

Five days of angry handjobs while thinking about her.

Five days of contemplating how to barge into her world without making her hate me even more.

How the fuck am I supposed to get her back if she's on the other side of the country? How am I supposed to reach her if she won't hear me out?

The numb, apathetic expression on her face at the party still guts me every time I think about it.

As a result, all my handjobs end with a pathetic, non-satisfying release.

Elsa is slowly pulling away from me. I can feel it down to my soul and damn bones.

I can't even push back when she's volatile.

Elsa is so closed off about my involvement with Queens, she won't hear anything contrary to what she already believes in.

Stubborn fucking girl.

I slam my car's door shut and walk the small distance to Nash's black Jeep.

He appears completely at ease as he retrieves his books from the passenger seat.

I know better.

If I spent last night running hills and swimming, he spent it blowing off steam in the only way he knows how.

I prop my elbow against the side of his car. "Are you going to stop being a little bitch?"

"Are you going to stop being a fucking whore?" He doesn't miss a beat.

"You know that's not what happened, Nash. Stop thinking with your dick."

"Is that so?" He slams the passenger door shut and faces me, holding his books with one hand. "Why don't you tell me what happened, then? I'm listening."

"You don't trust me?"

"I'll pretend I didn't hear that."

Smart.

Nash's intelligence is the reason I got myself into this whole fucking mess in the first place.

The challenge and the games are what we lived for. I never thought there would be a day when I would regret them. Partly because I don't do regrets. And also because I didn't see Elsa coming back into my life with such power.

"Talk to Elsa," I say.

"Why would I do that?"

I want to smash his face into the car and pick his neurons apart.

I don't do that.

Nash is one of my rare tickets to get Elsa back.

"She likes and trusts you more than ever after you ran your fucking mouth about the kidnapping."

"She does, doesn't she?" His lips curl into a smirk.

Fucker knows his strengths all too well. He didn't only tell Elsa about the kidnapping to get back at me, he also did it so she'd trust him.

"Too bad I'm not in the mood to help a fucking whore." He slams his shoulder into mine.

I clench my jaw and grab him by the shoulder. "I'll owe you one."

He stops and slowly turns around.

Nash, of all people, knows I don't like owing anyone shit. This is a drastic measure. I'm giving him the chance to make the first move and strike.

"You'll end it." He squares his shoulders so we're standing toe-to-toe. "*All* of it."

"Soon."

"And you'll tell me what the fuck is your deal with her."

"Deal."

Sorry not sorry, Queens. I warned you. Now, you're on your own.

If I were a better person, I would've sent her a warning text, but I'm not. Besides, this is payback for when she didn't notify me about Jonathan.

It might take days, but I always pay my dues.

"When are you going to talk to her?" I ask.

"After you do."

"If I could talk to her myself, I wouldn't ask you to do it for me."

"Elsa isn't like us. She needs to hear it straight from you and Silver or she won't believe it."

"She wouldn't fucking talk to me."

"You deserve it."

"Nash," I warn low.

"Just saying. Ask for forgiveness and show her your true

feelings—as fucked up as they are. Knight, Astor, and I can talk to her all day, but if she shuts down from you, there's no bringing her back."

"When did you become an expert on relationships?"

"Since you keep fucking up." He starts towards the building. "Show up for practice and make an actual effort or I'll have to ask Coach to bench you."

Little—

"Oh." He smiles. "We have an interesting addition to the team."

Fuck if I care.

We walk through the school's hallway. Girls from the gymnastics and track teams bat their eyelashes at me.

They think because Elsa is out of the picture, they have a chance.

I'd pity them if I could.

There's no one before Elsa and no one after her. She's a constant, and soon everyone will know that.

Elsa fucking included.

Astor joins us and chats about his latest bang and the upcoming game, but I filter him out.

My head hurts from lack of sleep. It's been three days since I last slept, and I still couldn't collapse. I'm this close from seeing people as caricatures.

Wait. That's their everyday appearance.

"So, King." Astor wraps an arm around my shoulder and the other around Nash's.

I don't even have the energy to remove his arm or threaten to break it.

"When are you going to apologise to Ellie and bring her back? Hmm? Hmm?"

I glare at him.

"Knight and I can prepare a carriage filled with flowers and chocolate and shit."

Elsa doesn't like chocolate. Well, except for Maltesers. I

wonder if she'll remember anything if I give her those little chocolate balls.

"I can even sing." He snaps his fingers. "Wait! Cake bunny hookers! Ellie would fucking love them. Am I right or am I right?"

"You're never right, Astor," I tell him.

"And stop inserting cake bunny hookers in every idea," Nash chimes in.

"*Fais chier, connards.* Someone needs to acknowledge my fantasies or I'm cutting a bitch."

My feet come to a halt of their own volition.

Blonde hair bounces down slender shoulders with blinding elegance. Like a light in the darkness, Elsa walks down the hall with Van Doren and a tiny girl.

I'm pushed back to that basement when she brought light with her.

Literally.

Figuratively.

This thing inside me that beats for her is boundless.

I can't stop looking at her. At her electric blue eyes, her radiant face, and those fucking kissable lips that are mine.

She's all mine with a capital M.

And now, she's back.

This time, only death would do us part.

TWELVE

Elsa

Dad agreed to let us go back to RES.

Shocking, I know.

With what happened at the Rhodes' estate, I thought he'd be opposed to RES now more than ever. However, when we sat down and I told him I want to finish the year at my school, he didn't object.

And I'm glad. It was rushed to even think about leaving the school in the first place.

I'm done running and hiding.

I'm done disappearing when I should be walking the halls with my head held high.

I did nothing wrong.

Dad's agreement might have to do with the fact that he needs to be in London to prepare for the Rhodes' project.

Knox is all for going back to RES. His previous school in Birmingham is boring as fuck—again his words, not mine.

Teal isn't as ecstatic about the move. She only came along because no one stayed in Birmingham except for the staff.

Dad's house in London is close to Ronan's neighbourhood. It's a bit far from Aunt and Uncle's house, but I promised to visit them today.

Teal, Knox, and I walk down the hall towards our class. I

try not to focus on Aiden standing by the entrance, all powerful and polished. Both his hands are shoved into his pockets, which means he's stopping himself from doing something—what, I don't know.

He watches me as if I'm the only one in the busy hallway. The interest in his eyes is paralysing, suffocating even. His gaze studies me close, so *close*, as if he's relearning my features, the curve of my shoulder, and the line of my collarbone.

Almost like... he's making sure I'm real.

He gave me that look once upon a time.

Was it in our childhood?

I shake myself internally. Just because I came back to RES doesn't mean I'll get entangled up with Aiden all over again. My return has nothing to do with him and everything to do with my self-worth.

RES has my grades and my track practice and my friends.

It also has Aiden and my bullies.

Oh well, all places have advantages and inconveniences.

I breeze straight past him, ignoring his stupid broad shoulders and ridiculous tall frame.

One day, I'll stop seeing him as an attractive bastard.

Attractive or not, I'm not falling back into his orbit.

This is more than my attraction or feelings. This is about my worth.

I deserve better than being the other woman.

I deserve better than being a mere pawn.

I deserve better than *him*.

Knox, Teal, and I sit close together, and I listen to Knox talking about how Agnus tricked him into helping for free.

Aiden strolls inside but doesn't take a seat, instead he remains near the entrance. I can feel him watching me closely even without lifting my head.

A part of me wants to watch him back. I want to engage in that glare for glare battle. I want to see him see *me*.

The betrayal, anger, and bitterness.

But he'll only use those emotions to hurt me all over again. I'm done being hurt by Aiden and his fucking games.

"Ellie!" Ronan hops on my desk, nearly knocking my pens on the ground. "I was just telling King about how to bring you back. I even offered to sing."

Teal snorts from my side.

Ronan grins at her, but it's fake. It's rare to see Ronan fake anything, he's about the most honest out of the horsemen. "You have a problem, *ma belle?*"

She searches around me. "Did you hear someone talk, Elsa?"

Ronan leans in to whisper, "I'm happy you're back and all, but why did you bring this freak?"

"I heard that," Teal deadpans.

He feigns innocence. "Did you hear someone talk, Ellie?"

I smile, shaking my head.

This is the first time I see Ronan go out of his way to show passive-aggression towards anyone. He usually avoids confrontation—except with his friends. But I guess, just like in football, Ronan gives twice as hard when he's attacked.

He's Death after all.

Mrs Stone comes inside. All residual chatter dies down and everyone takes their seat.

During the entire class, the hairs on the back of my neck stand on end. I'm supposed to concentrate, but my attention keeps bouncing back to a certain someone who's watching me like a hawk.

Without turning around, I can feel his cloudy gaze darkening and fixating on me. I can almost see the twitching in his left eye and the tightness of his sharp jaw.

When the day is finally over, Kim invites us for coffee. Knox is all for it and forces Teal to come along.

I agreed to stay with them until I have to visit Aunt and Uncle.

Before we head out of RES, I excuse myself to go to the toilet.

As I wash my hands, a violent sound of heaving comes from one of the stalls. I stay behind after drying my hands.

Does she need help?

"It's okay. It's going to be okay." The familiar voice chants as she steps out of the stall.

Both of us freeze.

Silver stands there, her hair in disarray and her uniform dishevelled as if she was thrown out of bed.

Acting as if she didn't see me, she wipes the side of her mouth and heads to one of the taps.

She splashes water on her face. "Pretend you didn't see anything."

"Your life doesn't matter to me, Silver."

"No problem, then. Good talk." She starts to breeze past me.

"Wait." I clutch her by the arm.

She swings around, her hand wrapping around her midsection. "What are you doing?"

The fear in her eyes hits me straight in the chest. I drop her arm and step back. "I'm not going to hurt you."

She studies me suspiciously but doesn't move.

"Do you…" I clear my throat. "Do you need help?"

Silver's huge blue eyes widen, appearing as stunned as I feel.

I never thought there would be a day when I'd offer Silver help. I guess I'm not so monstrous after all.

"N-no." She takes a step back, then stops. "I didn't want to be in the Meet Up. I'm sorry."

And then she breezes out of the bathroom.

I stand there for a second, gathering my wits around me.

Did Silver just apologise to me?

Also, what does she mean about not wanting to be at the Meet Up? Being there or not doesn't change the fact that she's engaged to Aiden or that Aiden hid it from me.

It doesn't matter anyway.

Not when it's over. Only, it didn't start in the first place. She was right all along. From the beginning, Aiden was never mine.

He was hers.

The itch starts under my skin and spreads all over my body. I wash my hands again and dry them.

The moment I open the door, someone shoves me back inside.

I shriek, but a hand swallows all the sound. The bathroom door closes with a bang.

He spins me around. My back hits it as my gaze meets Aiden's metallic eyes.

I scream.

THIRTEEN

Elsa

I remain still.

Completely.

Like a board.

Despite the war zone in my heart. All the wars start in my stupid, defective heart.

My scream dies out.

Screaming is useless when Aiden's hand covers my mouth. His strength is like a unified battalion; dangerous and wrecking.

The hardness of his chest crushes my breasts as his entire body imprisons me against the door. I can feel his heartbeat, loud and raging. I'm tempted to reach out a hand and feel the pulse under my fingertips. His normal, healthy pulse.

The only thing that makes him human.

The temptation is taken away from me when he grabs both my wrists with his free hand and slams them against the door above my head.

The sound pulls me out of my induced stupor.

This scene is familiar.

Whenever Aiden doesn't get his way, he resorts to establishing his dominance. It's part of the push and pull game he plays so well. A game in which all I'll ever be is a pawn.

A game I always lose.

"Welcome back, sweetheart," he murmurs in his raspy, chill-inducing voice.

Is there a way to throw acid on his voice and stop it from being this good on the ears?

His lips hover inches away from my mouth covered by his hand. Whether it's a threat or a promise, I don't know.

"Are you done running away?" His thumb caresses my cheek in a sensual rhythm. Up and down, like a lullaby with skin against skin.

For a second, I'm lost in his touch. In his closeness. In his scent.

Damn his scent.

He smells like pain and pleasure. Sweet and bitter at the same time.

I would be lying to myself if I say I didn't miss him, and I promised to never lie to myself again.

I missed his maddening touch and that heated look.

I missed his kisses and the baths he ran for me.

I missed his scent and his crude words.

But most of all, I missed *him*.

The man, the monster.

It's all in vain though. No matter how much I miss him, it doesn't erase what he did. It doesn't change the fact that I've been a pawn on his board all along.

So I hold on to the boiling anger, hate, and bitterness. I hold on to how empty it felt to be told I was merely a game.

The itch to fight him and spout profanities at him awakens in me like a phoenix from the ashes. My muscles tighten ready for a fight, for a duel.

However, I bite my tongue. Confrontation will only give him leverage over me.

Instead of giving him what he wants, I go slack in his hold and lower my gaze, cutting off eye contact.

I erase him and his metal gaze, sinister features, and tousled hair.

"Look at me."

I don't.

He watches me in the quiet of the bathroom. I feel it like needles at the top of my skull about to cut it open.

The silent war goes on for minutes or hours. I just stand there, watching my black shoes and filling my head with Sun Tzu philosophical tactics.

The supreme art of war is to subdue the enemy without fighting.

Silence is my only weapon and I'll use it until the very end. No matter how suffocating that silence is.

In the quiet, Aiden releases my mouth. I don't scream. I keep the sacred silence as if my life depends on it.

He grips my jaw with two rough fingers and forces my head up. "Fucking look at me."

I stare at the ceiling with its white lights.

"Elsa," he growls, the sound echoing around us like a dark promise. "Don't push me."

"Show me your worst," I say with a levelled tone.

His lips crush to mine. I keep my mouth clamped shut. He'll have to bite my lips off if he wants to kiss me.

He grunts against my mouth and nibbles on the tender skin.

I don't open up.

I don't give him a way in.

I hold on to the anger and pain. Anger and pain allow me to ignore my body's reaction to him.

Anger and pain turn me numb to his touch.

Aiden pulls back but doesn't release my wrists. "Are you sure you want to play that game with me?"

I say nothing.

I'm safely tucked in a numb halo right now. If I say anything, I'll lose the shelter this place offers.

Aiden yanks my skirt up. Air hits my bare thighs and goose-bumps cover my skin. His strong palm grips my pussy over my boy shorts.

My breathing hitches, chest rising and falling like I just

finished a hundred-metre run. My toes curl in my shoes. I stare at an imaginary dot on the wall beyond Aiden's head.

He lied to you.

He has a fiancé.

You are the other woman.

He slips two lean fingers under my boy shorts and rubs them over my folds.

"Hmm, you're not wet." His dark voice reaches my ears through my chanting. "Is this a challenge, Frozen? Do you want to bet how long it'll take for me to make you wet?"

I continue staring at the invisible dot, silently repeating the mantra.

He doesn't deserve my words. He doesn't deserve anything.

Aiden circles my clit, slowly teasing the swollen nub. If I don't focus on it, I'll feel nothing.

Nothing at all.

"You'll be wet," he rumbles near my ear, the sound shooting straight to my core. "You'll be soaking my dick when I fuck the defiance out of you."

"Or you can rape me and use the blood as a lubricant."

Aiden stops, his fingers freezing over my folds.

He leans back and watches me closely. Intently. Like a stone.

This time, I meet his gaze. I meet those cloudy, sinister eyes that sometimes seem like an endless void. A place where you go and never return.

I want him to see my expression. No idea what it looks like right now, but I hope it's filled with anger and hate. I hope he sees he did this to us.

He *broke* us.

Broke me.

He told me he chose me, but he never did.

Not really.

His choice has always been a barbie doll with 'Queens' as her last name.

"You think I'd do that to you?" He enunciates his question, almost as if he's angry.

"You've done worse. Being mentally and emotionally raped is worse than being physically raped."

I mean it. If he shows me his worst, I'll be able to hate him once and for all. I'll stop dreaming about him and his touch and his damn freaking scent.

As if reading my mind, and deciding to go against it—as usual—Aiden releases my sex and my wrists. My arms drop on either side of me like lifeless body parts.

I don't move from the door. Not even when he steps back further.

His face remains impassive, but when he speaks, his voice hits me like thunder in a winter night. "Well played, Elsa. Well fucking played."

"Are you done?"

He smiles, but it's neither mocking nor in triumph. It's a challenge at its purest form. "I just got started."

"You can use my body all you like, but I'll never forgive you, Aiden."

"Then I won't touch you."

My eyes widen.

Perhaps my ears are damaged because I could swear I just heard Aiden say he won't touch me.

His strongest weapon has always been physical intimidation. Hell, except for today, I've always become a wanton mess in his hands.

I narrow my eyes. "Is that a promise? Not touching me, I mean."

"Until you forgive me, I won't fuck you."

"Which means never."

"Believe me, sweetheart. When you know the truth, you'll beg for it."

Dinner with Aunt and Uncle never felt so awkward.

Aunt is walking on eggshells around me and Uncle seems as if he doesn't know what to say to dissipate the tension.

"Are you taking your meds?" Aunt asks while cutting shrimp and putting it on my plate. "You have an appointment with Dr Albert soon, so you have to watch your calorie intake and —"

"Blair," Uncle cuts her off.

"Right." She touches her temple. "You're with Ethan now. It's none of my business. Old habits die hard, I guess. Did he at least book your appointment? I emailed him all the dates colour-coded. There are tests and consultations and —"

"Blair." Uncle touches her arm.

"Fine, fine. Let's just eat."

But she doesn't just eat. Aunt basically empties the entire table on my plate.

"I forgot the soup." She stands up. "I knew I forgot something."

"Is she okay?" I ask Uncle after she disappears into the kitchen.

"She just needs time to get used to the new change. It's not easy on her."

I nod.

Uncle clears his throat. "Blair has always felt guilty about Abigail, she just didn't show it. I'm not asking you to forgive her, but can you at least try to understand? She was shaking the entire way to Birmingham the other day. She loathes that place with a passion."

My hands pause on the knife and fork.

I can relate to her. It's not easy to go back to a place that traumatised you. During my entire stay at our house in Birmingham, I never had a full night's sleep.

Not to mention the basement.

It's still there at the far end of the tower, taunting me to come close and relieve bloodied memories.

Dr Khan said revisiting the place where a trauma started can trigger my subconscious. Dad also said that the basement now has a fingerprint-lock that I can open any time I like.

Truth is, I'm scared of that basement.

I'm scared to know what happened in there. If I step over that line, I would never be able to return.

I have the scar to prove it.

Maybe, just maybe, I don't want to learn more monstrous things about Ma.

"Eat, pumpkin." Uncle offers me his warmest smile. "She spent the entire day preparing this dinner."

I swallow past the clog in my throat and take a bite of the shrimp. It's hard to taste over the stickiness at the roof of my mouth.

Aunt returns with the soup, her eyes wet as if she's been crying. It's like having an arrow shoot straight to my heart.

"Aunt —"

"It's your favourite." She cuts me off, her voice shaking at the end. "I might not be a good parent, but I can at least cook what you like."

"It's okay, Aunt. I understand what trauma feels like." I stare at my lap before facing her again. "I shouldn't have blamed it all on you. Mum was sick. Even if you were there, I don't think much would have changed."

Her mouth hangs open. "Elsa…"

"I'm sorry."

"No. I'm sorry, hon." She leans over and wraps me in a motherly hug. It's warm and smells like cotton candy and summer. "I'm sorry I wasn't around from the beginning. I'm so sorry."

Me, too.

What would it feel like if I were born to a normal mother?

I guess I'll never know. Whether I admit it or not, my mother was a monster.

I'm the daughter of that monster.

Now, I just have to decide whether to fight or embrace it.

I have to decide if I'm the type of person who locks children up to torture them like Ma or the type who sets them free like Dad.

Death or life.

Darkness or hope.

As I wrap my arms around Aunt, I know exactly who I want to be.

FOURTEEN

Elsa

For the following week, Aiden doesn't leave me alone.

He's there during lunch, dropping off my special food. I don't eat any of it, opting to have lunch boxes, but he keeps bringing it anyway.

He's also there during practice, passing me water and his sports drink.

I stopped counting the number of times he wanted to talk to me and I refused.

He offers to drive me home after school. I refuse to and choose to ride with Knox instead.

His jaw clenches and his left eye twitches whenever I do that. He clearly doesn't like it, and I expect him to drag me by force more than once.

He doesn't.

Every time we cross paths in the hall, he watches me with a disarming intensity. He confiscates my air and tucks it somewhere beyond reach. I often stiffen, expecting him to drag me into a corner, announcing the game is over, and teach me whom I belong to in his sadistic dominating ways.

None of that happened.

It's weird.

No. It's disarming.

His nice, grovelling side is starting to freak me out.

Aiden doesn't do grovelling. Aiden takes without permission, leaving disaster in his wake.

I toss and turn at night thinking he might be genuine, maybe he really changed. Then I recall who he is, *what* he is, and quickly squash those thoughts.

People like Aiden don't change. They're too comfortable on their high and mighty pedestals to stoop low.

All this must be another ploy to make me trust him just so he can fuck me over again.

I'm done being that fool.

I'm done being played.

To his credit, I barely saw him with Silver in the school's hallways. But who knows what's going on behind closed doors.

Not that I care.

"Are you coming?"

I'm brought back to the present by Teal's voice. She's wearing her usual bored expression as she studies her black-polished nails.

"Yes!" Kim grabs my arm. "Let's go."

I can't believe I agreed to this, but then again, Knox tricked me.

Apparently, he's into football and was accepted into Elites. Teal and Kim wanted to see him play.

I don't like being within two metres from the football pitch.

I beat you in maths. You owe me, Ellie.

And just like that, Knox had blackmailed me into watching the practice.

Teal, Kim, and I walk towards the pitch together.

"I'm telling you, our team is crazy good. You're going to fall in love at first sight." Kim interlaces her arm with Teal's.

"Love is for losers," Teal deadpans.

"You're funny," Kim laughs.

She thinks Teal is joking, but I doubt she is. Teal has an eccentric personality and the weirdest sense of humour. Sometimes, I don't realise it's a joke until she says it is.

The fact that she's Knox's twin is even stranger.

Kim decided Teal should belong in our circle because she's 'so cool'.

Kim thinks only rock stars are cool. The fact that she clicked with Teal so fast is a miracle in itself. Even Teal seems to like her. She offered her a cup of coffee the other day—and Teal doesn't offer things.

My nerves skyrocket when we approach the wires and the players. It's like I'm walking straight onto the battlefield.

Teal watches her surroundings and stops when a few girls start gushing and squealing—the horsemen's fangirls. "So this is where the youth come to kill their brain cells."

"Don't be a mood killer." Kim's green eyes brighten as she gets lost in the game.

Elites are divided into two teams. Half is wearing blue jerseys and the other half neon yellow ones.

Aiden and Cole are on the blue team. Xander, Ronan, and Knox play for the yellow team.

"Go, Ronan!" Kim shouts when he takes possession of the ball and runs towards the goal.

Cole tackles him with infinite grace and takes back possession. Ronan curses, but he runs like a storm to defend.

Too late, though.

Cole passes the ball to Aiden at the back of the last two defenders without being in the danger of the offside.

He dabbles the ball once then scores.

I can't help but watch his triumphant expression. The ease of his movements. The glint in his grey eyes. The need for more.

He enjoys this. He really enjoys playing football.

It must be because of the challenge. Aiden is the type who loves being tested every step of the way and playing football fixes some of his cravings. Especially if it's against worthy opponents like the horsemen.

Cole ruffles his hair and runs backwards, not taking credit for assisting that goal.

Those who say Cole and Aiden's team play is legendary aren't wrong. That assist was like telepathy. Cole didn't even need to look up before passing the ball.

On his way back to the midfield, Aiden's eyes lock with mine.

His lips curl into a smile. A genuine one that reaches his cloudy eyes.

The world shifts for a second, but I plant my feet wide, refusing to be swayed.

He must think I came for him.

I spot Knox who's wearing number nine. He said it's because he has nine lives, the dork.

"Go, nine!" I scream.

Aiden's smile falls. The darkening of his features is alarming, to say the least.

I never complied to Aiden's requests to attend his practices or his games, but I came today. The moment I shouted Knox's number, he knew I'm not here because of him.

I would've felt sorry if he didn't kill part of my soul.

"Don't mind, Ronan!" Kim yells at the top of her lungs. "You've got this, thirteen."

He grins at us, tapping his chest.

"Go, nineteen, I guess," Teal says.

Both Kim and I gawk at her. She just called Xander's number.

"What?" She glances up from her phone. "Isn't he on Knox's team?"

"Yeah, but there are ten other players on Knox's team." Kim narrows her eyes. "Why him?"

Teal lifts a shoulder. "Why not him?"

Kim gives her an indecipherable look then focuses back on the game.

The blue team is on the attack again. The girls beside us squeal Aiden's number, eleven, and Cole's, seven.

This time, Ronan steals the ball and makes a decisive pass to Xander who gives a one touch in Knox's direction.

The three of us get on our tippy toes as Knox runs at full

speed. He's about to shoot and score when Aiden tackles him from behind.

Hard.

Knox hits the ground head first.

A collective gasp sounds from the audience and even the assistant coaches.

"Knox!" Teal is about ready to tear the wires down and run onto the pitch.

Before she can, Knox stands, appearing non-injured.

He grins at his teammates when the referee whistles for a penalty. Even Ronan ruffles his hair and gathers him in a bro hug.

I glare at Aiden. He stalks back to the midfield with an expressionless face, but I feel the tension beneath the surface all the way to where I'm standing. It's licking at my skin like a vapid, savage animal.

"What the hell is number eleven's problem?" Teal's glare matches mine.

"He's jealous," Kim says.

"Kim!" I hiss.

"What? He is. King doesn't go back to defend. It's not a coincidence he went back after you called Knox's number."

"Whatever."

"You told me not to tell him Knox is your foster brother. Admit it, Ellie. You want him to be jealous."

"No, I don't."

"Yeah, right."

"Don't drag my brother into this." Teal stares between us. "He's a dork, but he's reckless. I don't want him to make enemies with this King bloke."

"Don't worry," I soften my tone when I speak to Teal. "I also don't want Knox involved."

"Sure." She types furiously on her phone. "Eleven is a King and they're Dad's mortal enemies."

As if I could forget the declaration of war between Dad and Jonathan at the Rhodes fundraiser.

"I'm out of here. I'll wait for you in the car park." I pause. "Do you want to join me, Teal?"

"I'm good here."

That's weird. I thought she wasn't paying attention to watching the game with all the typing.

I head to the car park and lean against Kim's car. I retrieve my history book and read through some highlights I made during today's class.

My thoughts bounce back to how Aiden tackled Knox. If he keeps doing that shit, I'll need to have a word with him.

Is he going to bully Knox in the team?

I trust Cole and Coach Larson not to let him, but you never know with Aiden. He's in the habit of proving everyone wrong just because he can.

"Back off," a female low voice reaches me from a few rows of cars on the left. "Don't mistake my silence for weakness."

Silver.

It's her voice.

Curious, I tuck my book in my backpack and head in her direction.

"Do you know how long I dreamt about this?" A male voice.

Adam Herran.

That *bastard*.

"Back off or I swear —"

"Shh, shut up. Shut the fuck up." He lands two blows on the car.

I'm close enough to see Silver's frantic expression. I'm impressed she doesn't flinch as he jams his fist in the car to the left side of her head.

"Adam. If you don't stop, I'll tell —"

"Shut the fuck up, Silver." He hits the car again.

This is none of my business. I should walk away.

I turn to do just that, but then stop as a question barges into my mind.

Am I the type of person who traps people like Ma or the type who sets them free like Dad?

I'm not trapping people, but leaving a person cornered is no different. Even if that person is Silver.

Besides, Adam gives me the creeps.

I approach them and speak in a loud, confident tone. "What's going on here?"

Adam's eyes snap in my direction. They're bloodshot and swollen as if he's drunk. Or high. "Fuck off, bitch. This is none of your business."

"Silver?" I ask. If she tells me it's none of my business, too, I'm out of here.

She discreetly shakes her head and mouths, 'Cole.'

That's it. *Cole.*

She obviously needs help.

I bring out my phone, my muscles tightening with a rush of adrenaline. "Back off right now or I'll call the principal, Adam. Maybe it's his business."

He takes a step forward.

"Come any closer and I'll blind your fucking eyes with pepper spray."

A lie, but I speak as though I do have the pepper spray.

Thankfully, he believes it.

"Stupid fucking bitch," he snarls, pushing off Silver.

I keep my hand in my bag, watching him closely until he climbs into his car and speeds out of the car park.

A deep breath rips out of my lungs.

I jog to Silver who's half-leaning against her car, hugging her midsection with both her arms.

"Are you… okay?" I stop a short distance away.

"You didn't have to do that," she murmurs. "I… I need to go. Forget what I said earlier. Don't mention a word about this to Cole."

"You should tell Aiden." The words feel like acid as I say them, ripping and melting me into nothingness.

"What does he have to do with anything?" She frowns, seeming genuinely confused before she raises her head. "King didn't tell you?"

"Tell me what?"

"Whatever. It's not my place." She opens her car door and flops inside. "I won't say anything until you talk to him."

"About what?" I ask.

"What do you think?" Her expression is unreadable while she shuts the door.

As she leaves the car park, I remain in place for a moment, mulling her words over and over.

I won't say anything until you talk to him.

What the hell is that supposed to mean?

FIFTEEN

Aiden

I stand at the threshold of the pitch, remaining behind the corner.

My grip tightens around a bottle of water. I was supposed to give it to Elsa, but she doesn't need it anymore.

The new boy passes her his sports drink and she gulps half of it down as if she was poisoned and he's giving her antidote. Then, she snorts laughing at something he said.

She's still wearing her track clothes. The jacket outlines her tits and slender waist. She hasn't gone inside, waiting for the other girls to leave before she'd head to the showers.

Conveniently, Van Doren has been keeping her company instead of coming in the football team's locker room.

I found out from Jonathan that the Van Doren twins are Elsa's foster siblings. Still, he's not her biological brother.

It took everything in me not to break his fucking leg during practice three days ago. Or yesterday. Or today.

My blood boils to the point of ignition every time I think Elsa only came to watch practice because of him.

I watch her closely. The slight twitch in her nose as she laughs. The few stray strands that fly all over her face. The flushed skin due to running. The rosy lips.

She's so fucking beautiful.

And she's happy.

The fact that she erased me this fast deepens the dark hole inside my chest.

If she can get over me so quickly, why the fuck has she told me she loved me?

Empty words.

Empty promises.

She was always shit at keeping her promises. Fuck. She didn't even remember me when we first met at RES. For her, I was another boy, while I dreamt about her every time I managed to sleep.

For ten years, she's been a constant in my life, but I was only a stop in hers.

If I want to, I can bring her back.

I can dominate her until she gives in, but it proved useless when she went numb on me in the bathroom.

I can grovel like I've been doing for the past week, but she's not even glancing in my direction.

I can use Reed and the Van Doren twins' weaknesses against her. Blackmail her. Force her to be with me.

And then fucking what?

She'll never be fully mine if her closed-off head doesn't open up to me.

"You look like a creep." A bored voice comes from my right.

"Screw off, Queens."

She stands beside me, crossing her arms over her chest as if she didn't hear a word I said.

I tune her out and continue to watch Elsa. She waves at Van Doren and heads into the locker room.

Fucking finally.

A moment later, he strides in our direction. He smiles at me so wide, I'm tempted to cut his face open. The only reason I don't is because Elsa would hate me even more.

Knight can still do it, though. With the right encouragement.

I tuck that idea for later.

"Nice game." He nods in my direction.

I don't acknowledge him.

He stops and wipes the sweat off his brow. "I hope to get along in the future."

"Not if you keep messing with what's mine."

"Elsa is my foster sister. Oh, and I met her first."

I meet his hazel eyes with my deadliest ones. "Doubtful."

He leans in close and whispers so only I could hear him, "I was kidnapped by her mother first." He steps back with the same smile still plastered on his face. "That means I'll cut you if you hurt her."

Van Doren brushes past me in the direction of the locker room.

I watch his back.

Hmm. So he was a victim of the red woman, too. It makes sense now why Ethan took him and his sister in.

Still, he has no right to threaten me. Not when it comes to Elsa. Especially when it comes to Elsa.

"You have yourself another enemy." Queens studies her pink nails. "Why am I not surprised?"

"Aren't you supposed to be gone?" I stare at the top of her head.

"Charming, as usual, King."

"Don't you have someone else to bug? Oh, wait. He's not speaking to you."

"You're such a twat."

"Could be."

"You know, I was thinking about helping you out, but I changed my mind."

She turns to leave, but I grunt, "Stop. Turn around and tell me your plan."

Spinning around, she shoots me a glare. "I'll talk to Elsa."

"You will talk to Elsa," I repeat to get a better feel of her words.

Queens was completely against this when I ordered her before. She didn't budge even when I threatened to expose everything to Nash.

The fact that she changed her mind now could only mean two things. One: somehow she was persuaded. Two: she's taking revenge against me.

I'm betting on the second.

If she'll do as told, I'd take the bait willingly. Queens is about the only person Elsa would believe.

"Fine, let's go," I say.

"You're not going to ask why I changed my mind?"

"Doesn't matter." For now.

"It's because of her," she huffs. "I might have unnecessarily been a bitch towards her."

"You think?"

"Yeah, but I'm not worse than you." She points a finger at my chest. "At least I didn't hide something so big from her."

"Shut it, Queens."

"Whatever." She walks by my side as we head across the pitch.

"Oh, by the way." She flips her hair back. "You'll do me a favour."

Of course.

She's using my desperation to get what she wants. Just like fucking Nash. I swear they're cut from the same cloth.

Just wait until I have Elsa back and I'll take my revenge against them both.

"Pray tell," I speak in my most detached tone.

"Don't mention a word to Cole about Adam."

Hmm. Interesting.

"I don't have to. He's not stupid and will eventually figure it out himself."

And with that, Queens and I head to the girls' locker room.

Energy buzzes through my veins the closer I am to Elsa.

Alicia used to say that in order to be accepted, you have to bare yourself.

I never understood what that meant.

Until Elsa.

Now, I'll do whatever it takes to be accepted by her.

If it means letting everything go, then so fucking be it.

SIXTEEN

Elsa

I tie my damp hair back then button my jacket.

My movements are mechanical at best. Knox said he'll take me and Teal to some film, but I can't muster excitement about it.

I enjoy their company more than anything else. Being back under my father's wing has given me a sense of comfort I haven't felt in ten years.

Dinner time with Dad, Agnus, Knox, and Teal feels familial, and I'm thankful to have them as a family.

However, something is missing.

At times, I'm certain it's about the past and what I erased from my memory. But the truth is, that's not the only reason.

Even when I laugh and smile and act completely normal, I can still sense the void inside. The terrifying hollowness. It echoes through my empty chest like an old rusty bell.

It hurts.

It really fucking hurts.

The worst part is that I can't even talk about it to anyone. They'd think I'm broken beyond repair. They'll think I'm crazy for tossing and turning all night thinking about the one person I shouldn't be thinking about.

I suck in a deep breath.

You can do this, Elsa. You're strong.

I throw the backpack over my shoulder and step outside.

My feet falter near the door.

Aiden and Silver stand together, appearing deep in conversation.

My lips tremble. The void in my chest claws louder and harder like a trapped animal. That animal needs out. That animal will rip my heart open, run over to them, and shred that scene apart.

Stop. I scream at myself. *It's over, remember? They're engaged. You're nothing.*

Even as I tell myself this, I can barely fight off tears. God, maybe I shouldn't have returned to RES after all.

I don't think I can see them like this for the rest of the year and pretend I'm okay.

My armour has already cracked, and it'll continue to crumble the more I witness such scenes.

I close my eyes for the briefest second.

I can do this.

I'll walk past them with my head held high and pretend they don't exist.

My footsteps are forceful, to say the least, but I jut my chin upwards as I stride in the direction of the exit.

I'm strong. I'm strong. I'm strong…

Their chatter comes to a halt as I march past them. A strong hand wraps around my arm, stopping me in my tracks.

Goosebumps erupt over my skin and my entire body explodes with static.

His scent fills my nostrils. He doesn't smell like me anymore. His scent is mixed with Silver's expensive Chanel perfume.

I grit my teeth to avoid getting lost in his touch. "Let go or I'll scream the whole place down."

"I'd prefer you scream for another reason." The dark, seductive tone takes me completely by surprise.

Is he flirting with me in front of his fiancé? What the hell is wrong with this psycho?

I would've felt sorry for Silver if I didn't feel so bitter and completely out of my element right now.

"Let. Me. Go." I emphasise every word.

"If I do, you'll run away and I can't have that." He tugs and whirls me around so I'm facing him and Silver.

My head is held high, meeting both their gazes.

They won't see my weakness. Not today. Not ever.

"We have something to tell you." Aiden raises an eyebrow. "I would've told you earlier if you'd have listened to me."

"I have nothing to talk about with either of you."

Silver studies her nails. Her beautiful nails all peachy pink and polished. "Remember what I said at the car park?"

I won't say anything until you talk to Aiden.

Her words have been playing in my mind since she said them. I tried not to give them weight, but I couldn't ignore them. Especially at night when I can't sleep.

For that reason alone, I choose to stay.

Seeming convinced that I won't leave, Aiden releases my arm.

"Are you engaged to Aiden?" I ask her.

She nods.

I press my lips together, gather my bearings around me, then speak in a neutral tone that conveys nothing of the chaos running rampant inside me. "Then we have nothing to talk about."

One step is all I take before Aiden grips me by the shoulder and pins me in place. "Listen for once, and stop running away."

Could be because of his intoxicating touch.

Or their engagement that hangs over my head like a guillotine.

Or the fact that he smells like Silver.

Could be all of those combined.

All the pent up feelings I've been repressing explode to the surface. It's ugly, it's irrational, and it's out of control.

"I'm not running away." My voice raises with every word.

"I'm walking the hell away from you, Aiden. You're cancer who'll keep eating me from the inside out until there's nothing left. I'm done being your pawn. I'm done being played. I'm choosing me this time. Not you. *Me!*"

My lungs choke with my breaths. It rises and falls so quickly, I can barely catch my thoughts that scatter all around me like smoke.

"That's smart," Silver says.

"Queens," Aiden warns.

"Fine." She rolls her eyes and faces me. "The engagement is fake."

My lips part. "What?"

"King and I were promised to each other since we were kids. We used it to get into our fathers' good graces. That's it. We never planned to go through with it." She glares at him. "I would rather die before marrying this bastard. He's an unfeeling psycho."

"Mutual, Queens." He smiles at her without humour.

My gaze bounces between them as if they turned into caricatures and I'm trying to grasp a sense of reality.

"Then why…" My voice comes out scratchy and I clear my throat. "Why did you act so territorial about him?"

She hesitates for a beat. "I needed to stay engaged to him for other reasons, but he wanted to end our arrangement because of you. I figured if I pushed you out of the way, he'll keep his side of the deal."

"What other reasons?" I ask.

"I can't say. I mean… It's personal." She meets my gaze with a determined one. "We're ending the arrangement in front of our parents somewhere next week. I'll be completely out of your hair."

No one says anything.

I'm still processing what I heard and trying to categorise it. Aiden has been watching the exchange with that completely detached expression of his. If only I can cut straight through his poker face and see what he's thinking.

"That's all from me." She throws up her hands dismissively. "Good luck with this twat. You'll need a lot of it."

She flips him her middle finger on her way out. Aiden returns the gesture without breaking eye contact with me.

He's watching me with that intensity again. Like a predator. It's as if he's trying to dissect my brain and stick his fingers inside.

Then, I realise he's waiting for me to speak.

"What are you expecting? A kiss or something?"

His lips tilt in a beautifully cruel smirk. "That would be a good start. Although I have dirtier things in mind."

"Do you really think I'll jump into your embrace now?"

"And bed and sofa, and the fucking wall." The sadism shines bright on his face. "I'm taking my fill."

He approaches me with predatory steps. All tall, powerful, and unstoppable.

"Stop right there." I hold up my hand. "If you think what Silver said will let bygones be bygones, you're utterly wrong."

Aiden stops in his tracks and the infuriating poker face straps around his features so tight and mighty. This should mean he's on the defensive. Good. I'm also on the defensive. Let's clash and see who'll come out alive.

"Just because your engagement with Silver was fake doesn't erase the fact that you lied to me."

"I didn't lie to you."

"A lie by omission is still a fucking lie, Aiden!" My voice strains with the force of my words. "You can't stand here pretending you didn't break my trust. Because you did. Every time I decide to give you a chance, you stomp all over my heart and prove me wrong, so excuse me if I have no trust to give anymore."

He takes a step closer. We're nearly standing toe to toe. His scent fills my space, male and clean. No idea if it's because Silver is no longer in the picture. His heat and scent overwhelm me even when I try to numb my senses.

Is it even possible when he already owns them?

"I never lied to you, Elsa. I didn't bring up the engagement because it held zero importance to me. It was a means to an end and a game I played to challenge Nash. It was also long before you and I got together." He pauses. "I don't spend energy on meaningless things, and you know that."

"Meaningless?" I scoff. "How the hell is being engaged to your fuck buddy meaningless?"

"I never fucked Silver," he says in a detached tone.

Wait. *What?*

"Ha. Could've fooled me!" This must be a cruel joke.

"You heard her. We can't stand each other."

"You don't have to stand her to fuck her."

"Yes, I do."

I watch him closely as if he grew two heads all complete with red horns and shit. "But you didn't deny you had her as a fuck buddy."

"I didn't confirm it either."

"Why the hell didn't you?"

"I liked seeing you jealous."

My mouth hangs open, nearly hitting the ground. This fucking psycho will be the death of me.

"Besides, Nash will have my head on a stick if I come within two metres of his stepsister." He lifts a shoulder. "I need my head."

The onslaught of information takes me back by surprise. No, not surprise. I'm floundering with thoughts and memories.

I don't know if I should soften or just hit him across the face.

Can't I do both?

I peek at him through my eyelashes. God, he's so broad and tall and beautiful.

Oh, and a sociopath.

Despite the relief flooding me, my heart can't forget the stabs and the bitter taste of betrayal I felt at the Meet Up.

The humiliation.

The breaking of my heart.

You know, people say you don't feel it when your heart breaks. I did. I heard the cracking sound and felt it tear apart.

Nothing will make me forget that.

At least not yet.

"I still don't trust you, Aiden," I murmur.

His left eye twitches. "Careful, sweetheart. You're pushing me."

"You pushed me first. You started the war *first*. Don't blame me for building my forts."

He touches his finger to my mouth. I cease breathing at the feel of his skin on mine.

His nearness has always been my undoing. Now that I lost the reason to feel numb, all I can do is *feel*.

The rough skin, the lean finger, the tingles, the need to lean in.

"Run and I'll chase. Hide and I'll conquer." He places a chaste kiss on the corner of my mouth. "Time to make your move, sweetheart."

SEVENTEEN

Elsa

Past

I wrap my hand around Grey Eyes'. The freezing temperature shocks my warm skin.

I frown as I stare up at him. "Why didn't you tell me you were cold?"

"It's fine."

"It's not fine. Daddy says children can't get cold or they'll get sick. I don't want you to get sick."

His lips move into a small smile. It's so rare to see him smile. I've even given him my Maltesers and he still wouldn't smile as big as I do.

He watches me closely like Uncle Agnus does when there's something on my face.

I wipe at the corner of my mouth, but there's nothing. "Why are you looking at me like that?

"If you keep your promise, I won't get sick."

I grin and lean my head on his shoulder. It's warm, his shoulder, even though the rest of him isn't. "I will! Absolutely."

Present

A knot squeezes tightly around my heart like a noose, filled with wires and mines.

Sitting up in bed, I wipe the stray tear falling down my cheek. I don't even know why I'm crying.

I didn't have a nightmare, but the stiffness in my chest almost make it seem like one.

Something feral and wild beats beneath my skin, something scary, but also... exhilarating.

I pull my knees to my chest and watch my hands under the dim light of the night lamp. No idea why I do that. It's not like I can reincarnate the feeling of his hand in mine.

Or the warmth of his shoulder when I laid my head against it.

Or how easy our interactions were.

We're like two pieces of the same puzzle, him and I.

He was beautiful even back then—with his boyish features and tousled hair.

He grew up to be lethal.

The words we exchanged play in a loop in my mind. We made a promise. How come I don't remember it?

You're the one who never keeps her promises.

Surely, a promise made by a seven-year-old and an eight-year-old can't be that important.

It's three in the morning, and I probably won't be able to find sleep any time soon. I plug my earbuds in and hit play on my iPod. *Paradise* by Coldplay fills my ears as I retrieve my phone and go through Instagram.

Since Aiden and Silver talked to me on Friday, I went back to stalking him.

What?

I can't control my cravings anymore. I was only able to do that due to my resolve and because I thought I was the other woman.

Now that all those reasons vanished, I'm possessed by this need to check up on him. To just look at him.

He's a drug, Aiden. I'm just a loser on withdrawal.

This is not healthy, but whatever.

I miss him. As far as I know, there's no cure for that, so I'll just scroll through his IG.

He uploaded the last picture about half an hour ago. It's a black and white shot of the surface of his pool. No caption.

Since it's late, he must be having trouble sleeping.

I wonder if he's also thinking about those days in the basement. Maybe he, too, was woken up because of a memory from the past.

A deep longing hits me out of nowhere. It tastes sour, but also delicious.

The longer I stare at his face in the pictures, at his midnight hair and cloudy eyes, at his infectious smile and the devil inside, the harder I'm tempted to reach out to him.

I can hit 'like' and alert him to the fact that I'm online. That I'm awake and thinking about him and our fucked up past.

The song switches to *Things We Lost in The Fire* by Bastille.

I exit his Instagram before I do something I'll regret come morning. I shouldn't be allowed to make decisions this late.

I lie in bed and watch the neon blue numbers on the night-stand, but I can't quite let go of my phone.

Agnus got everyone of us that same alarm clock with blue numbers instead of red. He said it's better for relaxation.

He's always busy making our lives better down to the smallest details. Knox mentioned that he took care of them, the company, and my comatose Dad during the past ten years.

The loyalty he holds for Dad is admirable, to say the least.

Knox says Agnus' only fault is being too quiet.

I disagree. It's such a rare quality. Agnus doesn't speak unless he's spoken to and his answers are always short and straight to the point.

My phone vibrates. I jump.

My lips part and my toes curl at the name on the screen.

Aiden: Asleep?

Holy shit.

Does he have telepathic powers or something? I rush back to Instagram and check if I left a like by mistake.

Nothing. Thank God.

Aiden: You're not.

I mark the texts as read, but I don't reply.

Aiden: Hmm. I like it when you're stubborn, sweetheart. It makes me rock hard thinking about how to fuck that defiance out of you.

My muscles' memory kicks into gear.

I'm thrown back to the times Aiden wrapped his hand around my throat and pounded into me like a mad man in need of his sanity. Like he can't get deep enough or fuck me hard enough.

My core springs back to life at the memory.

It's been a long time—nearly a month. My sexual cravings are going through withdrawals as well. Bringing myself to orgasm doesn't even count. It's pathetic compared to Aiden's intensity.

Of course, I don't tell him that. But I do throw the covers away because it's getting too hot.

Another text pings on my screen.

Aiden: I'm fantasising about how to fuck you next time I see you. Against the wall, on the floor, or in a fucking public toilet. So many choices.

He's so sure I'll let him fuck me the next time.

Arrogant prick.

Elsa: You said you won't touch me until I forgive you. I still haven't.

Aiden: You were given all the reasons to forgive me. Now, you're just playing hard to get.

Elsa: I'm not.

I really am not. I just want him to feel the weight of his betrayal, to recognise how much he shook my trust. That's not too much to ask for.

Aiden: Yes, you are. So I'm changing my tactics.

Changing his tactics? What the hell is that supposed to mean?

I'm still mulling his words over when another text comes through.

Aiden: Are you wearing the rabbit pjs?

Elsa: No.

Aiden: Hmm. Does that mean you're wearing nothing?

I smile despite myself. Aiden and his screwed up mind could be weapons of mass destruction.

Elsa: It means I'm wearing something else.

Aiden: Still, you're naked underneath.

Well, yes. I'm only wearing a cotton nightie and nothing else. But he doesn't need to know that.

Aiden: Do you know what I want?

I see the text but I don't reply.

Still, my nipples tighten against the cloth of my nightdress as the dots appear and disappear.

He's playing with me.

And it's turning me on.

The reply doesn't come through for long seconds. When I think he gave up on replying, another text appears.

Aiden: I want to fuck you so hard in all positions possible and remind you who you belong to. I'll tongue-fuck you and finger-fuck you and come down your throat. Then I'll claim that virgin arse for good measure. You'll be all fucking *mine*. Every. Last. Inch. Of. You. Oh, and you'll scream it for the world to hear. Then I'll bathe you and loosen your muscles just so I can worship your body all over again. When you finally fall asleep it'll be in my arms with your legs tucked between mine. As you rest, I'll watch your adorable sleeping face until morning.

A flush covers me from head to toe, under my clothes and over my skin. A jolt of desire engulfs me like a fog, a halo.

My breath hitches as I read and re-read his words.

And damn me.

Deep down, a part of me wants that, too. That part will be the fucking death of me.

Aiden: I waited for a long time. You know I'm not a patient person.

Aiden: Keep your promise.

I wait for fifteen more minutes, re-reading his filthy words, and rubbing my thighs together, but he doesn't send any more texts.

Hugging the phone to my chest, I fall asleep with a knot in my chest and dissatisfaction between my thighs.

In the morning, Dad drives us to school. He has a meeting with RES's principal about a generous donation.

In this circle, generous donations mean 'my child is made of gold and shouldn't be touched'.

Jonathan does that all the time. That's why both Levi and Aiden are untouchable in the school.

I tried persuading Dad not to do it, but Agnus said I won't be able to change his mind now that he has put his resources into it.

Dad decided to be a thorn in Jonathan's side, and he'll stop at nothing to make it happen.

It's a fight to the death, whether I like to admit it or not.

Rivalling Jonathan's donation to the school is Dad's way to prove his power. One thing's for certain: the board will be thrilled with all the money transferred into their accounts.

Teal, Knox, and I part ways with Dad at the car park. He heads to the administration building while we walk into the eighth tower.

"This is so stupid," Teal sighs.

"I agree," I say.

"It's fun!" Knox smirks. "Think about it. Don't you like the clashing of powers? This is like *Game of Thrones* without the dragons."

I shake my head. Teal rolls her eyes.

"You two are so boring." His face lights up when Ronan appears down the hall with Xander.

Death has Conquest in a lock as he says something in rapid fire. They're probably bickering again.

The girls in the hall flock to them like they're gods walking the earth.

Both Ronan and Xander have the time to wink at one girl and wave at the other even during their bickering.

They're approachable—overly so. If it were Aiden and Cole, they'd be erasing everyone from their immediate vicinity—especially Aiden.

Cole might be polite, but he doesn't go out of his way to make a connection or invite people to parties like the two walking towards us.

"Now, *they* aren't boring." Knox grins, waving at them. "Ro!"

"Oh, please. This isn't the headache I need on a Monday morning." Teal retrieves her phone and scrolls through it.

I'm starting to think the device is her weapon of choice when she decides to erase the outside world.

"Van Doren." Ronan and Xander hug Knox in that awkward bro kind of way.

They have been hanging out since the first practice game. Knox has become a regular at Ronan's parties—to Dad's dismay.

Not sure if Aiden likes it, but the two of them don't seem to care.

"How was my weed?" Ronan points at him with a triumphant expression. "I told you you'd see three girls as six."

Xander nods in our direction.

"*Mesdemoiselles.*" Ronan searches around us. "Where's my Kimmy?"

That earns him a slap upside the head from Xander. Ronan elbows him in the side. "As I was saying, where's *my* Kimmy?"

"She had to drive her brother to school," I tell him.

"I see." He holds my hand. "I missed you during the weekend, Ellie. Why didn't you come to my party? You should've seen my ace performance at the drinking competition. I won, by the way, not to be boastful or anything."

"You know I'm not big on parties," I say.

He waggles his eyebrows. "Unless King is there and you're making babies with him."

My cheeks heat. Ronan won't let me live down that time when he nearly walked in on us.

"Do all your conversations have to revolve around sex and alcohol?" Teal asks with genuine curiosity.

"And weed." He grins, showing his pearly white teeth. "That's the most important part, *ma belle*."

She rolls her eyes and strolls in the opposite direction.

Teal does that a lot—walking away without so much as an excuse—but she does it more often when Ronan is around.

"That's a record, Astor." Xander hits his shoulder, laughing. "Never thought there will be a day where a girl will leave because of you."

"Right? I think so, too." Ronan scratches his jaw. "She must be an alien. No offence, Van Doren."

"Being an alien is cool, mate." Knox grins, but something sinister lurks underneath. "But go near her and I'll cut you, human style."

"Go near her?" Xander laughs. "She'll hang his balls on a stick before you even interfere."

"That's actually true." Knox appears like he just thought about that. "Even my balls aren't safe from her."

"Ellie," Ronan leans in to whisper. "Are they really aliens? Do they do weird twin alien shit at home? Do I have to save you? I have my white horse waiting just outside."

I burst out laughing. He's such a weirdo, but a great one at that.

"Finally." Ronan flings an arm over my shoulder. "I missed that laugh."

The four of us walk to class together, jesting and talking about the Premier League. Knox is the only one amongst us who supports Chelsea. Needless to say, Xander and Ronan give him hell for it.

Their verbal bickering extends to class with everyone watching them as if they're world wonders.

Kim comes in last-minute, grumbling about the traffic and how she barely got Kirian to school on time.

For no reason at all, she glares at Xander before she settles in her seat. He barely glances in her direction, though.

Weird.

Class starts, but neither Aiden nor Cole show up. That's bizarre. They don't skip classes. Ever.

Especially Cole.

I retrieve my phone and check the text Aiden sent me first thing in the morning.

Aiden: Morning, sweetheart. Did you dream of me?

Aiden: I did. Now I have to jerk off all alone while picturing you.

Erotic images fill my mind. Aiden fisting his cock in that rough, masculine way, thinking about me, and bringing himself to orgasm. Aiden's godlike expression when he comes, the tightening of his abs, and the strength of his release.

I squirm in my seat.

Wrong thought in class. Extremely wrong.

I try to focus on Mr Huntington as he reads from the textbook.

"Did you punch the bitch queen again?" Kim whispers from beside me.

"No. Why?"

"She's absent."

I search behind me, and sure enough, Silver isn't here either. Wait. My frantic gaze scans around the classroom.

Someone else is absent.

Adam Herran.

Oh, no.

No, no, no.

I should've known better after I noticed the way he watched her and how he cornered her in the car park.

Would he really hurt her?

Shit.

If both Aiden and Cole are absent, does that mean they're helping her?

My legs bounce during the entire class. I can't concentrate no matter how much I try as all sorts of theories jump into my head.

None of them are good.

What if Adam hurts Aiden? What if something bad happens?

I mean, Aiden is usually the type who inflicts pain, not the other way around, but what if something goes wrong?

What if he's taken by surprise?

I'm going crazy with one pessimistic scenario after the other.

Dread tightens my stomach as time slowly ticks by.

Come back.

Come back.

Come fucking back.

I retrieve my phone and type him a text.

Elsa: Where are you?

I delete it before sending it and choose to instead send him a late reply to his morning texts.

Elsa: I don't dream, remember?

My heart lunges in my chest when my phone vibrates with a reply.

Aiden: I'll dream for the both of us.

The memory hits me out of nowhere.

"I don't remember my dreams," I tell the boy with grey eyes.
He pinches my cheek. "I'll dream for the both of us."
"Promise?"
"Promise, Elsa."

EIGHTEEN

Elsa

Aiden shows up at school during lunch.

I visibly move from my seat the moment he walks into the cafeteria.

To do what?

Hug him? Kiss him?

What the hell, Elsa? Just because I was worried about him doesn't mean I'll jump in his arms.

I sit back down and move the fork in my lunchbox. Telling myself to focus on my food and ignore him doesn't work. There's no getting rid of Aiden. He'll always be there. A constant. A nuisance. A thrill. He's under my skin, flowing in my bloodstream.

Xander, Ronan, Knox, and Kim's conversation fades into the background the closer Aiden comes.

I don't have to look up to feel him. He's in my bloodstream, remember? He flows inside of me. I'm conscious of him whether I like it or not. My senses are tuned to his confident strides, his all-powerful presence, and even his scent. I can smell it, clean and male and all him.

There's no ounce of hesitation about where he's heading. All the people in the cafeteria cease to exist in his eyes. It's cruel, but it's true.

Aiden doesn't and won't ever care about them.

However, he cares about me.

It's in the way his features lighten upon seeing me even though his expression is still vastly unreadable. The way his entire body language points in my direction.

How could I have been so blind not to see it before?

Since we were children and even now, Aiden's features only light up when I'm around.

You're the only thing who breaks the endless vicious cycle.

He told me that once, but I was at a point where I doubted everything about him.

Did I ever believe a word he said? How did that make him feel?

True, he doesn't act like a trustworthy person, and he pisses me off with his manipulations, but it's also true that he never looks at anyone else the way he looks at me.

I was always trapped in my head and never thought of the situation from his perspective. Even when I did, I used it to outsmart him, not to actually understand him.

He stops in front of us. All tall and broad and... sexy.

Yes. He's sexy and I can finally admit it to myself without him having to touch me.

Aiden is the sexiest person I know. Doesn't matter if he's the only sexual partner I had. No one in the world can emulate his intensity and dominance with my body.

The way I react to him has to do with his person as much as his touch.

"King!" Ronan taps the seat beside him. "*Viens par ici.*"

He doesn't even acknowledge him, his entire attention settles firmly on my face. "Come with me."

I stop pretending that I care about the food and glance at him. At how his uniform moulds to his muscular arms and thighs. At how the first button is open, revealing a hint of his tanned skin.

Shaking my head, I ask, "Come with you?"

"You'll understand on the way."

"Hello?" Ronan jumps to his feet and waves in Aiden's direction. "I'm over here."

"Move that pretty arse, sweetheart."

I grab my bag and stand up.

Could be because of hearing him calling me sweetheart again.

Could be because of his damn authoritative tone that has my core all slippery.

Could be both.

Aiden remains motionless for a beat. He probably didn't expect me to agree this willingly. I surprised myself, too, but I can't fight it anymore.

At least not now.

Aiden's pause lasts for a mere second before he wraps his hand around mine and leads me out of the cafeteria.

"Nice talk!" Ronan shouts after us.

I stare at Aiden's hand surrounding mine. It brings back memories of the time when we were children.

Back then, I was always the one who held his hand and clung to him. I also shamelessly snuggled to his side and laid my head on his shoulder.

Who knew there would be a day when our roles would be reversed?

We slide into Aiden's Ferrari and fly out of the school's car park.

"Where are we going?" I finally ask, holding the backpack close to my chest.

Aiden concentrates on the road. "The Meet Up."

"Why?"

"Nash asked to meet us there."

Oh.

I try to fight the wave of disappointment but lose. We're only going to the Meet Up because of Cole. Not that I should be disappointed.

I shouldn't.

"Why did you come with me willingly?" he asks out of the blue.

"I… don't know." And I really don't. I wasn't in the right state of mind.

Maybe it's because I was worried about him and was remembering the past.

Or maybe it's because I miss him. I'm like a beggar, pleading for crumbs and glimpses of him to satiate the thirst and craving inside of me.

I hate myself for missing him. Why is it impossible to *not* miss him?

Tilting sideways, I watch him closely, his black hair and irresistible eyes that could tell a thousand stories. His built and his easy confidence.

He must have something alien in his blood. No. I'm sure he does. Otherwise, how come he draws me in so effortlessly?

"Do you remember the time we spent together ten years ago?" I ask before I can stop myself.

He nods, eyes darkening. "And you don't."

My heart skips a beat. He hates it. Oh, my God. He hates that I don't remember him from back then. It must be why he's been such a dick all this time, calling me Frozen and heartless.

Can I blame him, though? I would've been so heartbroken if he forgot about me.

"It's not by choice." I tuck a strand of hair behind my ear. "Besides, I remember a few things."

"Hmm. Like what?"

"Like spending a lot of time with you and talking. I don't think you ever gave me your name because I kept thinking about you as the boy with grey eyes."

"You spent the entire night with me." He smiles a little. "You wouldn't leave even when I told you to."

"I did not!" My cheeks flame with embarrassment.

"I'm the one with the memories, remember?" His lips tilt with a smirk. "You wiped my face with a wet cloth then covered me with a blanket just so you could slip underneath it with me. Oh, you also held my hand and kissed my cheek. Child Elsa was a stage five clinger."

Is there a hole I can bury myself in it?

Still, I jut my chin. "You're only saying that because I don't remember."

He takes my hand and lifts it to his face. He flattens my palm over his mouth and kisses it so tenderly, a shock ripples through my entire body.

Heat flashes over my skin like rapid fire and shoots straight to my bones.

Oh, God.

I can handle the intense, dirty side of Aiden—sometimes—but I'm completely helpless in front of his soft side.

"You look fucking adorable when you're shy."

He lowers my hand and keeps it on his thigh, tucked in his like it's his most prized possession.

Our fingers interlace. My smaller hand in his bigger one. My feminine fingers against his long, masculine ones.

I'm tempted to remove it, but I love the warmth too much. Besides, I'm still in shock from the way he kissed my palm.

I'm contemplating poking him to stir his ugly side just so I can prove his harsh part always wins. That his soft side is an illusion and a mindfuck.

"You weren't shy before." He tilts his head to the side. "You took and *took* without second thoughts."

"I did not."

"You did, too. I'm telling you, Child Elsa was hardcore."

"God. I can't believe you have dirty thoughts about a little girl."

"You're not a little girl anymore."

"And you're not a little boy."

"No, I'm not. That's why I get to fuck you."

"Do you ever stop talking dirty?"

"Only when I fuck you dirty."

The rumble of his voice sends sparks all over my skin and down to my core.

There's something utterly masculine about his voice, all rough and deep and… dirty.

Yes, dirty. So fucking dirty.

I'm burning up, nearly boiling over at the image of that voice rumbling near my sensitive parts as he whispers crude things to me.

Wrong image for your resolve, Elsa.

"Can't you stop?" I whisper.

"Not when it comes to you."

"Yeah. Blame it on me."

"I blame it on Child Elsa. She made me think of things I never thought about before."

"Like what?"

"Like adult stuff. Told you, she was hardcore."

"You're putting words in my mouth just because I don't remember."

"Oh, you will remember. I can't wait to see your expression when you do."

"Dream on, dickhead."

He chuckles, and the sound echoes around us like a melody. I want to reach for that sound, box it somewhere, and keep it for safekeeping.

For a moment, I just sit there, trapped, mesmerised as his features ease and his shoulders relax.

Now that I think about it, Aiden often relaxed around me. Whether it's his sexual intensity, his maddening possessiveness, or his rare smiles and laughter.

He's at ease with me.

And if I'm honest with myself, I'm at ease with him, too.

Before I can take my fill of his laugh, we arrive at the Meet Up.

Why couldn't the distance be farther?

Cole's Jeep is already parked in the driveaway. I leave my backpack in the car and follow Aiden up the steps.

"Why did Cole ask to meet us here?"

"Don't know."

I narrow my eyes. "You mean to tell me that you came without a plan?"

"I did have a plan." He tilts his head in my direction. "Anything that involves having you by my side is the perfect plan."

My temperature gets ten degrees hotter, but I clear my throat. "Did you spend the morning with Cole? Is that why you didn't come to school?"

"I had a meeting with my consultant about Oxford."

Oh.

Right.

Aiden will go to Oxford. That piece of information has always been tucked into the back of my mind, but hearing it aloud makes it real and… final.

At the end of the year, Aiden and I will go in different directions, whether we like it or not.

The thought feels like stacking bricks at the bottom of my stomach one by each heavy one.

I'm dragging my feet by the time we're inside the Meet Up.

"Not a word, Silver." Cole's steel tone cuts through the silence of the cottage. "I don't want to hear your voice."

"Screw you, Cole."

Silver is here, too? How come Aiden didn't mention that?

On the other hand, this should mean she's not in danger from Adam.

Not that I should worry about her.

"What are you doing here, Queens?" Aiden barges inside without as much as making his presence known.

"Ask Cole," she hisses. Which means Aiden didn't know she'd be here.

I walk inside with careful steps. "Hey."

"Elsa." Cole smiles, but there's no warmth behind it. It's like he has to smile, but doesn't want to. "Sit down. There's something you need to know."

I glance at Aiden with questions written all over my face. He lifts a shoulder and flops down beside me. His arm stretches on the back of the sofa, almost touching my skin, but not quite.

The fucking tease.

Silver sits opposite us in a chair. Her legs are tucked close together to the side. The paleness of her face has nothing to do with her skin complexions and more to do with a wild look in her gaze.

Cole stands beside her like a statue. Unmovable and cold.

If Cole is involved, this must be serious.

My limbs shake despite themselves. If Aiden still has something to do with Silver, I don't know how I'll react.

I'm barely holding on as it is. If Aiden breaks my trust one more time, I won't survive. One thing's for sure, I'll destroy him with me. It's only fair with how much he destroyed me.

"Tell them," Cole orders. He flat out orders Silver as if she's a small child.

I expect her to fight, to be her usual bitchy self, but she just remains quiet.

"If you don't, I will," Cole continues with frightening nonchalance. "Do you want them to hear my version?"

Silver visibly flinches as if she's been slapped across the face.

"Get it over with, Queens." Aiden's impatience shows through his voice. "I don't have all day."

No idea if he's oblivious to the tangible tension between the stepsiblings or he simply doesn't care.

My bet is on the last.

When she lifts her head, her gaze instantly finds mine. "I don't know why we keep getting involved, you and I."

Same.

"This is my final warning," Cole says. "Talk or I will."

"Remember Adam?" she asks.

"Did he hurt you again?" I blurt and she winces.

"*Again*," Cole speaks so low it's terrifying. "So it's happened before, yes?"

Aiden's arm falls on my shoulder, gripping me tight, cutting off my concentration on Cole and Silver.

My eyes slide to his, and I swallow at the tightness of his jaw.

Oh, boy. He's not amused. At *all*.

"How do you know about that, sweetheart? Hmm?"

"He was bothering her in the car park; I stopped him."

"You stopped him," Aiden repeats with a calm, yet terrifying edge. "How did you stop him exactly?"

"I just threatened him with calling the principal and pepper spray."

"You don't have pepper spray."

"He believed I did." I pause. "What are you so agitated about?"

"What am I so agitated about?" His voice is clipped, firm, and authoritative. "Why do you fucking think? He could've taken both of you to God knows where in his state. Do you have no sense of self-preservation?"

"I only did what I thought was right. Okay?"

"Not okay. It's not fucking okay to throw yourself in danger like that."

I meet his glare with mine. Okay, fine, maybe standing up to a buff bloke like Adam wasn't the smartest thing to do. But how can he expect me to just stand there while he clearly meant Silver harm?

A shudder goes through me at the thought of what he could've done to her.

Silver and I may not get along, but I don't wish ill will upon my worst enemy.

I know trauma. I *lived* trauma. It invades your personal space, claws at your walls, climbs them, destroys them, and then dances on the remains.

That shit fucks you up for life.

"Very well, Silver. Very well." Cole stares down at the top of her head, not sure if he wants to choke her or chop her head off. "Tell them why we're here."

Wait. Wasn't it about Adam and that day?

"I only found out yesterday." Silver fixes her already immaculate jacket and stares at her violet nails. "Adam came over and… well, he said a lot of shit."

"Say it," Cole urges—or more like he orders. I've never seen this side of Cole before.

"Adam said that…" She licks her dry lips. "He was the one who pushed Elsa in the pool."

My eyes widen.

"He did, huh?" Aiden's eyes almost turn black. Not sure if he's surprised or merely calculating.

"Go on," Cole urges. "Tell them why he did it."

"He said he did it to get in my good graces, okay?" She meets my gaze. "I swear I had nothing to do with it. I only just found out myself. If I knew, I would've told you."

I don't know why, but I believe her.

Silver is malicious, but she's not a criminal.

"But you knew Adam's intentions," Cole says with a neutral voice. "And apparently, you knew about them for a *long* time."

"Cole —"

"Not a word."

"Cole —"

"Go wait in the car."

She throws her hands in the air and blows out a frustrated breath. "Come here, Silver. Go there, Silver. What do you think I am? Your fucking toy?"

He doesn't move at her outburst and simply repeats. "Go wait in the car."

She flips him off and storms towards the entrance then stops, meets my gaze and whispers, "I'm sorry."

As soon as the door closes behind her, Cole fixates Aiden. "Let's meet later."

"I'll get in touch."

Cole nods once. "And Elsa?"

"Yeah?" I'm still too stunned by the revelation.

"She only learned this information yesterday. Don't beat her up again."

I wince at the reminder.

"Says the guy who watched while she was beaten to a pulp," Aiden scoffs.

"She brought it on herself that time." He smiles at me and strides out of the Meet Up.

A long breath heaves out of me. "I can't believe Adam was the one who did it."

"That daft fucker actually plotted something." Aiden tilts his head, seeming deep in thought. That head of his must be filled with endless methods to inflict suffering and pain.

"How do you know he plotted it?"

"No one went into the pool after Van Doren. For some time, I thought maybe he was the one who pushed you. Now, I'm sure that Adam has been in the pool, and when you showed up, he seized the chance."

"But Knox didn't see him."

"He must've hid somewhere. Under the stairs or in the lockers. There are no cameras there."

Makes sense.

For a moment, we remain silent. I'm trying to soak up what happened and Aiden is probably plotting something sadistic.

After a while, I realise that with Cole and Silver gone, it's only the two of us here.

I peek at him through my eyelashes. I expect him to be deep in thought, and he is, it's just that his entire attention is zeroed in on me.

"What happens now?" I ask.

A wolfish smile tilts his lips. "Now is our time. We'll do whatever you want."

"What if I want to go home?"

"Then I'll take you home."

I eye him suspiciously. "Really?"

He grabs me by the arm and tugs. I land against his chest, arm wrapped around his midsection.

"Later. I'll drive you home later."

"Aiden!" I start to get up.

"Stay," he murmurs, eyes closing. "Just for a moment."

Protests are about to spill free from my mouth, but I say nothing. My ear lands against his calming heartbeat and I do as he asks.

I stay.

NINETEEN

Elsa

I didn't mean to, but I must've fallen asleep.

When I open my eyes, a very familiar scent prickles my nostrils. All masculine and powerful and… hypnotising.

A spark races down my spine and worms its way into my heart. That faulty heart. That messed up, stupid heart.

I'm sprawled all over Aiden's chest. The softness of my breasts mould with his muscles, all taut and hard. Even my legs are intertwined with his like it's the most natural thing to do. Like this is where I always belonged, and it's blasphemy to go anywhere else.

I stir, but I don't change position.

It feels too good to move. His warm skin against mine, the flutter of his breath at the top of my scalp. The cocoon of his strong arms.

After what I learnt about Adam, I'm not in the mood to think about the outside world.

Being here feels right.

It brings back memories from a long time ago when it was only him and I in that basement. When I laid my head on his shoulder and pretended we were in a different place.

His fingers tangle into my hair, massaging my scalp, and

awakening tingles at the bottom of my stomach. The touch is so gentle, I'm tempted to close my eyes and go back to sleep.

My self-preservation is the only thing that stops me. Being close to Aiden is never that simple.

Lowering my guard is about the worst disservice I can do for myself.

He's manipulative and unpredictable and those facts drag me to the edge every time I want to relax.

Yes, my heart and body are itching and breaking to be with him. They're sending all the right signals, too: flutters, tingles, *pheromones*.

Those play for the loser team, though and the strategist, aka my brain, wouldn't let them have their way.

Aiden's fingers pause on my scalp as if he can feel my next move before I make it.

I roll to my side and sit up, inching to the other half of the sofa. Pretending to push my hair back, I compose myself.

The urge to throw myself into his arms overwhelms me. It's like an animal clawing and screeching to be set free.

It takes every ounce of willpower to keep my distance.

"Don't." The harshness in his voice startles me from my thoughts.

I peek at him. The sombre expression on his handsome face takes me aback.

"Don't what?" I'm genuinely confused.

"Don't pull away from me."

"I'm not pulling away."

"I call bullshit. You're going Frozen on me again."

"Don't you think you deserve it?" I glare at him.

"The only thing I deserve is you."

"Newsflash, Aiden. You barely gave me a reason to be all warm and cosy with you. Now that my head is in the game, it's hard to see you in a positive light."

"Is that so?"

No. It's a lie. No matter how much it'd be logical to stay

away from him, I know deep down, in the dark corners of my soul, being with Aiden is the only thing that makes me whole.

He completes me.

And not in a Disney kind of way. His darkness speaks to me on levels that scare the bejesus out of me.

So, yeah, I might be playing my last running away card. What? A girl has to look out for herself.

"You said you'll take me home later." I smother my skirt. "It's later now."

"Fuck that." He grabs my hands in his. A jolt of electricity shoots down my spine.

No, no, no.

He needs to stop touching me if any of this will work.

Before I can pull my hand away, he places my palm on his chest. My eyes widen at his wild heartbeat. I always forget how erratic Aiden's heartbeat can go.

Like thunderstorms.

Deadly, but also alive.

So, *so* alive.

"You owe me from the past, Elsa."

A different type of flutter snakes into my heart. This one is painful and destructive. I stare at my lap. "T-that was my mother, not me."

"She's dead. You're alive." He tilts his head. "I'll take what I can get."

"That's a low blow, dickhead," I mutter under my breath.

He knows how guilty I feel about what Ma did, but like a first-class sociopath, he's using it against me.

Aiden lifts a shoulder. "I'll use whatever I can to get you. I have no boundaries when it comes to you, Elsa."

"Aiden…"

"The scar on my ankle is because she had me cuffed with metal to heavy chains. The scars on my back are because she hit me with a horsewhip over and over again until I passed out. I don't think she stopped even when I lay lifeless on the floor."

"Aiden. Stop."

He doesn't. He digs the shard harder and deeper into my skin with every word out of his mouth.

"She gave me nothing to eat and barely anything to drink. I had to piss and shit where I slept. She treated me worse than a dog, and the funny part was, she never really saw me. She saw someone else when she looked at me. When I finally came back home, the only person who could've made it better was also gone."

Tears stream down my cheeks by the time he's done. My lips tremble and my jaw aches with the need to hold in the sobs.

Aiden speaks so nonchalantly, it's more terrifying than if he spoke with emotions. Now, I see why he doesn't hold feelings in high regard. They were purged out of him a long time ago.

They were whipped, starved, and burned into the fire.

"Do you know how it feels to be hit with a horsewhip until the skin breaks? Until blood drips to the ground?" His jaw tightens, the tiniest bit, before it goes back to normal. "It hurt like a bitch especially for an eight-year-old who didn't know real pain."

The word *stop* lingers on my tongue, but I swallow it.

Aiden lived those horrors, the least I could do is listen. Even if he's using my guilt factor against me.

It's even more tragic he's using his pain to keep me by his side. I would've felt special if my chest wasn't slowly dissolving into a bloodied mess.

"Does it pain you to hear this?" He wipes the tear under my eye with the pad of his thumb. "I can stop if you like."

"You don't have to," the words come out strangled, dying, *weird*.

"I will if you kiss me and make it better."

A tremor shoots through me. Did he do all that just so I would kiss him?

No. Aiden can be an unemotional monster, but I know that Alicia's death affected him more than anything else.

It was the last straw that changed him for good.

"No?" He lifts a shoulder. "Worth a try."

I grab his cheeks and slam my lips to his. Aiden is stunned for a moment, but I don't stop. I nibble and bite on his lower lip like a madwoman.

I want to kiss it and make it better.

No. I want to kiss it and make it go the fuck away.

This shadow that haunted our lives for ten years needs to fucking go.

Aiden opens with a grunt. His kiss is rough, rougher than any other time I remember. He claims me, devouring me whole.

The intensity of his passion ignites and we burn in a perfectly imperfect harmony.

For a moment, it's only him and I in this atrocious world. A world that turned him into a monster and robbed me of my life.

For a moment, he's the most important person in the world. I want to engrave myself under his skin so nothing can separate us again.

I want to be one with him.

The thought of living apart destroys me like nothing else. The thought is torture like being held underwater.

I've been drowning and I'm finally coming up for air.

We pull away for much-needed breath, but Aiden doesn't allow me to leave his orbit. It's like I'm the centre of said orbit.

He rests his forehead against mine. The tips of his fingers stroke my cheek, the curve of my lip, the hollow of my neck, the line of my collarbone.

It's everywhere, his touch. Like he's relearning me and getting his fill.

Our ragged breathing fills the air like two desperate souls clashing only to find refuge in each other.

Everything becomes heightened. The squeak of the leather beneath us. The smell of pine trees from outside. The low whistle of the wind.

And Aiden.

I'm so lost in his masculine beauty and tousled hair. In his skin against mine and the metallic gaze.

In all of him.

He speaks against my skin, rough and unpolished. "There hasn't been a day where I haven't thought about you. Every time I manage to sleep, I dream of you. You were my obsession since we were kids, but now it's way fucking worse. I don't know how I managed to spend eight years without you in my life when now I suffocate if I don't see you for hours."

My eyes fill with tears. "Aiden…"

"Choose me, Elsa. Choose *us*."

There's nothing more I want than to do that. I want to be with him so bad, it's eating me from the inside.

It's driving me insane.

It's ripping at my heartstrings.

His hand slides from my face to my throat. He wraps his fingers around it in a vice-like grip. His forehead disconnects from mine and the clouds in his eyes darken. "I'm being fucking nice here, Elsa. I've been patient, but I'm this *close* to say fuck everything and take you all to myself. Don't. Push. Me." He emphasises as he strokes his thumb over my pulse point. "Even I don't know what I'll do."

My temper flares at that.

"You know what? It doesn't always go as you want, Aiden. If you want to be with me then you'll have to learn a little something called compromise. Google it. I won't be the one who always bows her head while you get your way. That's not how relationships work." I push his hand away and jump to my feet. "Take me home. Dad must be worried."

His left eye twitches and I expect him to drag me back down. He doesn't. He just stands and storms out of the Meet Up.

I watch his rigid back with frustration bubbling in my veins. I was seconds away from melting into his arms, but he had to ruin it by reverting back to his dickhead ways.

I follow him out to his Ferrari. No words are spoken after I give him directions to my dad's new house.

The entire way is spent in silence. The type you taste in the air, bitter and sour.

Aiden keeps a hand on the steering wheel and the other fists on the armrest between us, but he's not touching me.

Screw him. He's not the only one mad right now.

After a few more moments, I contemplate breaking the silence. Finding no words, I remain quiet until the car stops in front of my house.

"Thanks." I grab the door handle.

He continues staring ahead without acknowledging me.

Enough, dammit.

I drop my hand to my lap and face him. "What are you being so mad about?"

No answer.

"So it's the silent treatment now?"

"Go inside before I kidnap and fuck you into oblivion."

My pulse quickens at the image, and my skin turns hot and cold. I wish it was from horror, but it's from damn excitement.

Something is wired wrong inside of me.

Aiden's dirty words ruined me.

When I don't move, he tilts his head to the side. A sadistic smirk lifting his lips. "Or would you like that, sweetheart?"

A knock sounds on the window. I startle out of my stupor.

Aiden straightens, releasing the steering wheel.

I perk up when I see the one waiting outside the window. Dad.

What was I thinking about bringing Aiden over? Oh, wait. I wasn't exactly thinking at the time.

I roll down the window. "Hey, Dad."

"Hey, Princess." He smiles. "Come inside."

I move to open the door.

Dad peers through the window and his smile drops. "You, too, Aiden."

Shit.

TWENTY

Aiden

Ethan Steel is a big man.

Where Jonathan is lean, he's broad. Granted, he's not as big as I remember him from when I was a kid, but that's due to the fact that I grew up not him becoming smaller.

If anything, his strong bone structure is as tall and arrogant as in the past, as if he wasn't in a coma at all.

He sits behind his mahogany desk, watching me with hawk eyes.

His home office is bland with black and brown sofas and bookshelves. He even has a glass chessboard on the coffee table between me and Elsa.

If he isn't a replica of Jonathan, I don't know who is.

Elsa's legs are snapped closed together as she stares at her lap, her shoes, her jacket. Anything but me or her father. Concern radiates off her in waves and prickles my skin.

I meet Ethan's stare with a neutral one. He's trying to intimidate me with silence so when he speaks, I'll have no choice but to fall at his feet.

Jonathan used to do that, too, until he realised the tactic doesn't work on me.

Manipulation affects neurotypical people, not me.

"What are your intentions with my daughter?"

He goes straight to the bullseye. I can respect that about him. I like direct opponents.

"Intentions?" I repeat to get a rise out of him.

"You know exactly what I mean." He plops both his elbows on the desk and leans forward like an emperor planning his attack. "Jonathan must've ordered you to ruin her life."

"How…" Elsa clears her throat. "How do you know that, Dad?"

"I know everything about you, princess." He smiles at her, but his expression hardens when he focuses back on me.

While Ethan and Jonathan are two facets of the same coin, there's one difference. Ethan looks at Elsa like she's his world. He's doing everything to protect her and her legacy.

Jonathan doesn't.

His world has turned bleak and sharp since Alicia's death. Everything he cares about is revenge and power. I doubt he'd bat an eye if either Levi or I fall in the process.

As long as one King remains to carry on with his legacy, he's all good.

"My intentions towards your daughter are simple," I say with the calmest, most determined voice I can manage. "She's mine."

"Aiden!" she hisses.

I lift a shoulder. I won't lie to Ethan. Not about this. He needs to know that I'll fight for her. I'm ready to fight him, Jonathan, and the entire fucking world.

Hell. I'm ready to fight *her* if she doesn't snap out of her stubbornness. It used to be adorable, now it's pissing me off.

I expected Ethan to stand up and throw me out of his house. In all honesty, I wouldn't be surprised if he sics his dogs on me.

However, he just watches me.

The contempt in his gaze would've made me angsty if I weren't brought up to handle these types of situations.

Stressful, intimidating encounters do nothing to those with the King surname. We were taught to overcome them before we learnt to ride a bike.

Elsa shifts uncomfortably in her seat, smoothing her already perfectly pressed jacket.

The twitch in her nose when she's stressed out is too cute for words. Now, I'm itching to touch that nose, kiss it, lick it.

"What does Jonathan think about that?" Ethan's question brings me back from my fantasies about his daughter's nose.

"What Jonathan thinks doesn't matter." I don't miss a beat.

"Does he know that?"

"He knows everything."

A slight smile crosses Ethan's face before it disappears. "You're more like him than you know and for that reason alone, I don't trust you with my daughter."

I'm about to tell him that his opinion doesn't matter, but he cuts me off. "Besides, our families are clashing right now, and everyone has taken a side."

"I couldn't care less about families clashing. I've already taken a side and it's Elsa's."

Her electric blue eyes bore into mine, her cheeks turning a bright shade of red. Her plump lips fall open. Those soft, soft lips. I'm on the edge of my seat, contemplating walking there and kissing the living fuck out of her, devour those lips, rip them in my mouth against my tongue.

I'm so hard, I can feel the pulsing of my dick.

Ethan clears his throat, cutting off my cock's fantasies. "Jonathan will do everything to stop you."

I shift sideways to relieve pressure on my hard-on. Not that it works. See, my cock is a fucking traitor. He doesn't listen to me when Elsa is around. Not to mention he's been deprived of her warmth for a long time, so now it's his time to shine and be a dick—literally.

Thankfully, Ethan's table prevents him from seeing my junk. Otherwise, he would've thrown me out of here about yesterday.

Elsa, however, sees it in all erotic details. Those blues widen even more.

'It's your fault,' I tell her with my gaze. 'If I fucked you earlier, none of this would be happening.'

Who am I kidding?

Beside being a traitor, my dick is an attention whore. Whenever Elsa's in sight, he points at her as if saying, 'Notice me. Suck me. Let me fuck you.'

Yeah, he kind of has a limited vocabulary.

Now, where were we? Right. Ethan and Jonathan. Tale as old as time and as boring, too.

"Let me worry about Jonathan." I pause. "Maybe if you didn't kidnap me ten years ago, none of this would have happened."

"Aiden…" Elsa starts to scold me then decides against it and shakes her head.

Ethan interlaces his fingers. "Maybe if Jonathan didn't burn dozens of people, none of this wouldn't have happened either."

I thought he would fall for the guilt, but he's not like Elsa. He's the tenacious type who can bury the past because, for him, the future is more important.

His phone rings, and he checks it. Standing up, he motions at the device. "I have to take this."

As soon as the door closes behind him, Elsa jumps up and starts pacing. "I should've thought of this. I shouldn't have let you give me a ride. What if he's mad at me? What if he won't forgive me?"

My head tilts to the side, watching her flushed cheeks and how her uniform's skirt rides up her pale thighs every time she moves.

All my attempts to keep my cock down fail.

I'm rock fucking hard imagining that skirt off as I plunge in and out of her warmth for weeks.

No. Not weeks.

Months.

I contemplate bending her over the desk and fucking her raw from behind.

It'd be worth it even if her father walks in on us and murders me. After all, don't they say to find something you love and let it kill you?

"Aiden."

"Hmm, sweetheart?"

Her cheeks are bright red as she hisses, "You're hard!"

I'm sure she can see the lust in my eyes. Am I apologetic about it? Do I care? No and no.

I smirk. "And that's a problem because?"

"You're not supposed to be thinking about that in such a situation."

"*That?*"

"You know." She throws her hands in the air for good measure.

"You mean fucking you?"

She slaps a hand over my mouth and watches her surroundings like she's a spy. "We're in Dad's office."

I kiss her palm.

She removes it with a jerk and turns crimson, if possible.

I love creeping under her skin. I love being the only one who gets to break the ice and slip inside her castle. She might close the door, she might build forts, but I'll always conquer.

"You're incorrigible," she scolds, still fighting off her blush.

"You're the one who brought it up."

She flops into the chair and fiddles with the knight chess piece. Only three moves have been made and the black side is at a disadvantage.

An idea springs to mind to calm her agitation.

If it were up to me, I would fuck her, but I doubt that's the best way to occupy her head in such a situation.

So I move on to the next best thing.

Since the white pieces are in front of me, I push a pawn forward, blocking the knight she's clutching between her fingers.

Elsa raises her head in questioning.

I lean my elbow on the armrest. "Didn't you say you play? Show me what you got, sweetheart."

A spark of challenge ignites in her blue eyes. My dick strains against the confines of my trousers.

That look. That spark. That stubbornness. They're the reason why Elsa is one of a kind.

She moves her knight forward, leaving an opening for my pawn. I raise an eyebrow.

Bold.

I expected her to hold the fort and count her options. She surprised me by going straight to the attack.

Straightening in my seat, I do a quick overview of the board. I consider her options before I think of mine. Elsa isn't the type to hold back, and that'll be the reason for her loss.

While I move a few pawns, Elsa uses her entire battalion.

She's an all-in type of player.

I like that. A lot.

My dick agrees, by the way.

I bring out my queen, and she smirks with sadism. Elsa just gave me a sadistic smirk. "Finally, dickhead."

Her entire body language is sharp and concentrated. Fuck. She's been slowly but surely transforming into a fighter. The challenge shines from her eyes in waves.

Why haven't I played chess with her before?

This is nearly as erotic as fucking her. The power in her body, the boldness in her moves, and the melting of her defiance. Her mind clashing with mine is more euphoric than anything I've experienced before.

"You're keeping your queen hidden, too, sweetheart. Don't think I didn't notice."

She grins, all mischievous and fucking beautiful. "If you're far from the enemy, make him believe you're near."

Sun Tzu. She's quoting her favourite book, *The Art of War*, and yes, I re-read it after she mentioned it's her favourite book, just so I could imagine reading it from her perspective.

Am I too far gone for this girl?

Yes, probably.

"You're such a nerd," I play with her.

"This nerd will bring you down, King." She rolls up the sleeves of her jacket, eyes sparkling and glinting like Christmas lights—and I don't even like Christmas.

The door opens, pulling us away from the vicious battle.

Ethan strides inside and stops beside our board. He watches the game with a critical eye. Elsa lost all her pawns and a knight. I kept most of my pawns, but I lost a rook and a bishop.

"Interesting game," Ethan says. "Too bad someone has to lose."

My jaw clenches, easily reading the hidden meaning behind the words.

Ethan and Jonathan are at war to snatch a partnership with the Rhodes. In the end, one of them will lose.

When that day comes, neither Elsa nor I will ever be the same.

As soon as I arrive home, I head to the shower.

Nash and I agreed to meet so we can put a stop to the fucker Adam Herran.

Once I'm done with him, he'll wish he never looked in Elsa's direction, let alone touch her.

He threatened her life, and for that, his existence will be a payment.

Tit for tat and all that.

He'll wish he was never fucking born.

Out of the shower, I wrap a towel around my waist and another around my neck.

I stop at the threshold to the bathroom. Jonathan stands in the middle of my bedroom, his hands shoved in his trouser pockets.

He's watching the walls as if it's the first time he's in here. It's all squeaky clean. A bed, a desk, and a wardrobe. That's all I need.

I barely spend time in this room anyway, so it doesn't matter. The Meet Up, however, does. That's where I would rather be.

"You went to Ethan's house," he says. It's not a question which means he's still watching me.

Shocker.

"I did," I say, just to be a dick.

Using the towel around my neck, I dry my hair. The black strands fall in front of my eyes, partially obscuring my view of Jonathan.

"What did he say?" he asks.

"Nothing important."

He narrows his eyes but doesn't press the issue. "Keep your head in the game."

Sure thing, Dad.

Only, well, he never earned the right to be called the 'D' word. Other than dick.

"Jonathan?"

He stops but doesn't turn around. "Yes?"

"I'm breaking off my engagement to Queens."

He slowly faces me, his body rigid. "That nonsense is off the table."

"I'm not asking for your permission. I'm informing you that my engagement with Queens is off. Effective immediately."

"Are you choosing to side with Ethan?"

"This has nothing to do with that."

"It has everything to do with that. Sebastian is our ally and a member of the Rhodes' vote committee. He won't vote in our favour if you dump his daughter."

"Then find other allies. Sebastian Queens isn't the only member of the Rhodes' voting committee."

He squints one eye at me. "It's because of that Steel girl. I knew she was rotting your mind."

"She's mine, Jonathan. *Mine.*" I throw the hair towel away and walk to stand toe to toe with him. "Once you accept that fact, I'll accept to be your heir. Until then, you're my enemy."

He stares at me for a beat. It's not intimidation, more like contemplation.

I don't know what he fucking expects. Does he think he can reach me now when he's never made an effort before?

That ship has sailed with Alicia.

"You're an ungrateful fucking brat." His jaw clenches.

"I can't think of a reason why I should be grateful to you."

"Not to me, but to your mother. You have no respect for her memory."

"Stop using Alicia in your mind games."

"Games? Was her death a game? Have you forgotten who caused her accident?" He tilts his head with a manic look in his black-grey eyes. "Have you forgotten how many hours she suffered before she eventually died?"

"Elsa isn't the reason."

"Her father is."

"And so are you."

He pauses for a second, his jaw ticking. "What did you just say?"

"You heard me," I speak in my deepest, lowest tone. "You burnt that factory down, knowing Ethan would retaliate by harming your most precious things. But you know what? That's not why Alicia died. She died because she was trapped in this world when her soul lived elsewhere. All she needed was you and me to root her here. You knew her needs, but you barely spared her your time. Your hunger for power and your ambition came first, and we were an afterthought."

"I did all of that for you." He grits out. "I built King Enterprises for our family."

"Alicia never needed the power or the name, she needed you and you let her down. You killed her slowly, Jonathan. So excuse me if I don't believe in your useless revenge plot. You should've protected her while she was alive." I brush past him to grab my clothes. "I won't repeat your mistake."

Jonathan says nothing. He just turns around and leaves.

The door clicks loud behind him.

Hear that, Alicia? That's Jonathan finally feeling pain. You should rest in peace now.

I know she won't. Her sad expression comes to mind. Her pale cheeks and the constant tears in her eyes.

She hated it when Jonathan was stressed or in pain. She loved the loser more than he ever deserved, and he reciprocated too late.

I won't be my father.

After dressing up, I dial Nash. He picks up after the first ring.

"Are you ready?" I ask.

"Always."

"Are Knight and Astor there?"

"Knight, yes. Astor is too high to move."

Of course. And then he bitches about how we always keep him out.

"King?"

"Yes?"

"Let's leave Adam some hope."

"Why?"

"I want him to think he's safe before we destroy him all over again."

I smirk. I like that idea. "Deal. And Nash?"

"Yes?"

"It's over with Queens, you petty, little bitch."

"Fuck you."

I smile while hanging up.

Time to take care of some overdue business.

TWENTY-ONE

Elsa

The energy in RES is volatile, to say the least. It's been a long time since I walked down the hall and had everyone watch me this closely. Like I'm an animal on display.

Beside me, Teal scrolls through her phone, oblivious to the attention and words said behind our backs.

"It's because of her."

"What do you think will happen now?"

"Is she really all that?"

"Shut up or you'll be next."

Despite my best attempts not to get caught in the drama, curiosity gets the better of me.

This must be about me, not Teal. Not only is she new, but she also doesn't speak to anyone.

Kim runs towards me, shooing the students out of her way. She's panting, her green hair flying in all directions. "Did you… Did you hear what happened?"

I shake my head.

"Adam Herran." She breathes, a smile breaking across her face. "He's quitting the rugby team and the school. He'll enroll in the military academy. Isn't that brilliant?"

On the surface, yes, it is brilliant. However, after Aiden and Cole's reaction yesterday, I'm sure this isn't a coincidence.

I grab Kim by the sleeves and pull her into a corner, away from the crowd of students and eavesdropping ears. Teal follows us, but she's still too engrossed in her phone to pay us actual attention.

"What happened?" I ask Kim.

She closes in. "I heard the horsemen gave it to him good. They threatened to expose his use of performance-enhancing drugs *and* other drugs. Apparently, he has a record."

Aiden.

I can sense Aiden's conniving mind behind all of this.

Since the moment Silver told us that Adam pushed me in the pool, he was up to no good, all lost in his conspiracy thoughts.

To say I feel sorry for Adam would be a lie, though.

He had it coming. Everyone should know better than messing with Aiden King. He's known to destroy his opponents until they can no longer stand.

"Isn't Adam's family powerful, though?" I ask. "Surely they can bring him back."

Kim shakes her head frantically. "I heard there was also pressure from Xander and Cole's parents. They hold some dirt on Adam's father and they used it against him. He already signed the papers for his son's transfer."

Interesting.

Jonathan wasn't involved. I wonder if it's because Aiden kept him out of it or because the older King refused to help.

"Why didn't you tell Dad?" Teal asks without lifting her head.

"I didn't have the chance. Besides, Dad has a lot on his plate."

Teal meets my gaze. "Nothing comes before us for Dad, especially when it comes to you."

Still, I'd rather not bother him. He's been working late with Agnus, pulling all-nighters. The good thing about Dad, though? He's always there for breakfasts and dinners no matter how busy he is.

The three of us walk to class. Kim talks about how cool the horsemen are—except for Xander. According to her, he doesn't count.

In class, Ronan is passing a ball with Xander and Knox. Cole sits at his desk, reading a book titled *Corpse* that appears to be non-fiction. He seems completely detached from his surroundings.

I know better.

It's a façade. Cole is more attuned to his environment than anyone else. He just hides it well.

Silver sits two seats in front of him, earbuds in, and her gaze lost in the distance. Even her minions aren't there. Now that I think about it, Summer and Veronica don't hang around her as much anymore.

Aiden is nowhere to be seen.

I fight the tug of disappointment and fail.

He and I need to talk. A *lot*. He needs to give me a heads-up about the disasters he's planning. I want to hear it from him first, not from the gossip floating around the school.

Biting my lower lip, I contemplate asking the others about his whereabouts.

My phone vibrates in my pocket. I smile when I see the name on the screen. Maybe he has telepathic powers after all.

Aiden: Meet me at the pool.

I don't even think about it. We still have time until the start of class, so I drop my backpack in my seat and take off in the direction of RES's pool.

Upon arriving, the smell of chlorine clogs my nostrils and my feet falter at the threshold.

I was so excited about seeing Aiden that I forgot how much deep water freaks me out.

Since it's the early morning, the place is empty. Taking a deep breath, I cross the last few steps on unsteady legs.

"Aiden?" My voice echoes in the large space.

"In here, sweetheart."

I round the corner and freeze. Aiden stands in front of the deep side of the pool. I would've taken a moment to appreciate his built, his black strands falling over his forehead in abandon, but he's not alone.

Adam is there with him, his eyes bloodshot, puffy, and all wrong. Even his shirt is in disarray like he pulled an all-nighter in a drug cartel.

"What's going on?" I stare between the two of them.

"Herran came to apologise." Aiden pats his shoulder, but there isn't an ounce of camaraderie in it. If anything, he appears on the edge of something sombre and diabolical. "Didn't you?"

Adam remains quiet, his face reddening by the second.

"She's waiting." Aiden grips the rugby team's captain—former captain—by the shoulder.

He's broader and buffer than Aiden, but for some reason, Aiden is the one who appears more powerful. All godlike and invincible.

At this moment, he reminds me of a general who never lost a war. A hero through and through.

Thinking of Aiden as a hero is strange, though. He's not the hero, he's the villain.

But right now, as he grips Adam, after he kicked him out of the school for hurting me, I can't help but think of him as a hero.

Just this once.

"I'm sorry," Adam spits.

"No, no." Aiden tsks. "Repeat it and mean it this time."

"I don't care about his apology," I say. "He's nothing."

"That's true." Aiden's lips curve into a smile. "But he still needs to apologise. You can do it standing or on your knees, Herran. Your choice."

Adam's red-rimmed eyes meet mine, but they're filled with maliciousness more than anything else.

The bastard doesn't feel guilty about what he's done.

"I'm sorry."

"Apology denied." I glare at him. "I hope you rot in hell, Adam."

A sadistic spark ignites in Aiden's eyes. It's as if he summoned his demons and they're now taking reign of the situation.

Or maybe I summoned them. After all, he's doing this for me.

Aiden turns into an unstoppable force for *me*.

"You heard her. Not that I was going to let you go." He circles Adam like a predator before the attack. Smooth, silent... terrifying. "You dared not only to look at what's mine, but you also touched her. Do you know what that means, Herran?"

Adam's throat works with a swallow. I can see him hold his breath, as do I. The darkness in Aiden's metal eyes can only mean trouble.

I'm on my toes, waiting for what he'll say next.

"It means you're out."

One moment, Adam stands there, the next, Aiden pushes him. The rugby player loses balance and splashes into the water, flooding the edge.

Aiden isn't done.

Not even close.

He crouches at the edge of the pool. The moment Adam comes up for air, Aiden grabs his head and thrusts him back down.

No hesitation.

No mercy.

Adam's limbs flail all around, splashing water everywhere. He struggles for breath and only finds water.

Aiden fists his fingers into the rugby player's hair and wrenches him out. He gasps for air like a dying man.

"Were you suffocating in there, Herran?"

Aiden shoves him back into the water. His expression is neutral, serene even. "Good. Now you know what it feels like to drown."

I stand there, my limbs shaking as Aiden holds Adam underwater.

The calmness on his face sends shivers down my spine. I know, I just know, that Aiden would murder Adam and not bat an eye.

He'd do it on school grounds.

He'd endanger his future.

I run up to him, ignoring my fear of the water nearby. "Stop it, Aiden. Let him out."

"Not yet." He uses both his hands to keep Adam underneath the surface. "He hurt you. He hurt what's mine."

"You're going to kill him," I hiss.

"Small price to pay for touching you."

"I hate him, too, but I'm not ready to lose you this way." My voice is loud and clear. "He's not worth it."

Aiden's head tilts in my direction. His steel eyes immediately soften when they meet mine.

I fall to my knees beside him, uncaring about the water soaking my skin, and grip his arm. The tight muscles ripple underneath my touch.

"He's not important, Aiden. You are."

That must've worked.

Slowly, too slowly, Aiden allows me to pull his hands from Adam's head. The latter surfaces, gasping for air.

Neither of us pay him attention, not even when he climbs out, wet and shaking like a dog.

We're too lost in each other's gaze to pay attention to the world surrounding us. We're barely touching, but I feel him all around me, like a constant.

Right now, I'm sure that if I somehow fell into the pool, he'd bring me out. He'd protect me and be my hero once again.

I should probably stop thinking about him as a hero.

"You're a fucking psycho," Adam spits once he's out of the water. He's wet and dishevelled, but I couldn't feel sorry for him even if I tried.

Aiden's left eye twitches as he meets Adam's ashen face. "Fuck off before I finish what I started."

Like the coward he is, Adam limps out of the pool area with his tail tucked between his legs.

And then, Aiden is back to watching me as if I'm the only person in his sights.

What does he see when he stares at me this intently? Is it Ma? Or is he perhaps trying to erase her similarities from my face?

Both Knox and Teal admitted to wanting to hurt me due to how much I look like her, so maybe Aiden feels the same.

Maybe deep down, he wants to hurt me, too.

What if everyone I love hates me because of my genes? It would be tenfold more painful if it's Aiden.

But would he have been willing to commit murder for me if that was the case?

And yes, he was seconds away from killing Adam. If I hadn't intervened, his body would be floating in the pool by now.

Aiden's lack of boundaries should scare me, but for some reason, a halo of calm submerges me.

I stopped him. He allowed me to stop him when he easily could've kept going. That fact fills me with overwhelming internal peace.

"Repeat it," Aiden says.

"Repeat what?"

"The part about how I'm important."

I suppress a smile. Why am I not surprised he only focuses on that part?

Inching closer, my space fills with all that is him. His scent and his warmth. His cloudy eyes and the chaotic emotions swirling inside of them.

Those emotions are mine.

I want to snatch them up, hug them, and somehow insert them into my chest so they can find company with my own erratic feelings.

The closer I am to him, the more the world disappears. The

entire universe is tucked into the small space between us where my knees nearly graze his. "You are important."

He wraps a strong hand around my nape and his lips crush to mine.

I don't resist this time.

I don't stop to think about the consequences.

I just let myself be.

The kiss might've started on my lips, but it possesses my entire body. It pools in my stomach and races down my spine. It paralyses my limbs and awakens my internal organs.

His teeth nibble on my lips, his hand fists in my hair, angling my head back so he can get better access. His tongue finds mine, feeding off me, tasting me, *inhaling* me.

I do the same.

I consume him as hard as he consumes me.

If a kiss had a purpose, this one would be all about finding each other. It's about a connection that existed since the moment I laid eyes on Aiden in that basement.

Everything started then and it's since refused to end.

For the longest time, I tried to fight our connection, but it keeps winning.

Losing never felt so good.

My arms wrap around his neck as I kneel, mirroring him. My fingers run into his black strands, and he groans into my mouth.

It makes me proud, that groan. It makes me proud to bring him pleasure and have this effect on him.

Still clutching me by the hair, Aiden tugs on it. My back hits the cold ground, but my burning skin hardly registers it.

He crawls atop of me, larger than life. His solid body covers mine, his muscles and arms mould to my curves like we're two pieces of a jigsaw puzzle coming together.

He's everything I shouldn't want, and also everything I need.

He shoves his knees between my thighs, and they part of their own accord. He doesn't even have to try twice. I hiss out a whimper at the contact of his trousers against my most intimate part.

Still kissing me, he yanks my skirt up and loosens his belt with the other hand.

The air ripples with tension and heat. I can taste it on my tongue and sense it with the goosebumps covering my flesh.

I curl my nails into his jacket, breathing heavily against his skin. He stole my breath, my heart, and my freaking sanity.

Aiden isn't only a monster, but he's also a thief—the kind who never gets caught.

"A-Aiden… Anyone can walk in." Even as I say the words, wetness shamelessly coats my thighs.

"Fuck them." Aiden grips my chin with two fingers as his other hand yanks my boy shorts down my legs. "I need you, sweetheart. I fucking need to be inside you like I need air."

I need you, too.

But I don't have to say it aloud. Aiden must've read it in my eyes. He really knows me more than I know myself.

He wraps a hand around my throat and thrusts balls deep, filling me whole. I gasp, but no sound comes out.

He stole my ability to breathe, talk, or even think.

He stole my fucking heart and soul, and there's no way I'll be able to get them back.

He's a thief, remember? A damn thief.

"Fuck, fuck!" His entire body tightens with the force of his initial thrust. I can feel his rigid abs without having to touch them.

My eyes brim with tears. Could be due to being filled by him.

Could be because of the way he's squeezing his hand around my throat, barely allowing me air.

Could be because of the intensity in his gaze.

Could be because it's been such a long time that I felt this whole.

Could be all of them.

Being with Aiden is like going through a roller coaster ride in a dark tunnel. There are ups and downs. There's black and danger. But most of all, there's excitement and the euphoric feeling of being alive.

I'm alive.

With Aiden, I never stopped feeling alive.

He picks up his pace, ramming inside me like a mad man, like his body can't contain his passion. Passion that bleeds into me, flaring inside me in the form of sparks and fireworks.

It's slightly painful, and I'll be sore for days, but I revel in that sting of pain. I revel in the way he can't control himself when he's with me.

"I missed you, sweetheart." *Thrust.* "I missed your tight pussy." *Thrust.* "I missed your tiny moans of pleasure." *Thrust.* "I even missed your fucking stubbornness."

Our breaths mingle together, rough and unpolished with raw, unhinged pleasure. Our scents mix and fill the air, killing the chlorine smell and replacing it with pheromones.

Is it weird that pheromones should only be in the brain, but they're now floating all around us? I can inhale them off Aiden's skin, taste them on my tongue.

He angles my thighs up, and I gasp as he hits that sensitive spot inside me. He pulls out almost completely until only the tip remains, then rams back in over and over.

And *over.*

The orgasm hits me with a power I haven't felt before—sharp, deep, and violent. My back arches off the ground as I scream.

Aiden swallows the sound with his lips against mine. He kisses me through my orgasm. He worships my mouth with his tongue and my pussy with his cock.

I can feel myself clenching all around his length, almost strangling him, suffocating him.

He continues his onslaught for a few more seconds before he growls, "*Mine.*"

TWENTY-TWO

Elsa

Past

I strain as I drag the heavy bag behind me. I had to bring everything. The sandwich, my drawings, and *all* the Maltesers. I tricked Uncle Agnus into buying me more behind Daddy's back.

The boy with grey eyes must like Maltesers, too. He's so generous and always shares them with me.

I stop near the basement door and throw a glance around the dark corridors. Them monsters lurk here, you know, but I'm not scared of them. I'm scared that someone—a person—follows me and finds Grey Eyes.

Yesterday, Uncle Reg almost found me. If I hadn't heard him come down the stairs and smelled his pipe, I wouldn't have escaped in time.

I hid in my room and didn't see the boy with grey eyes.

I miss him.

I was counting down the hours until I could see him again, sit by his side, and listen to him talk all night.

He doesn't say much, though. I have to always talk because he's usually silent.

Holding the flashlight under my armpit, I slowly open the basement door.

A smile tugs on my lips. "I'm here!"

No response.

"Grey Eyes?" I drag the bag behind me as I close the door. The creaking is haunting in the silence. It's a little scary, too.

Whenever I come in, the chains would rattle as he'd stand up to meet me.

I direct the light towards the corner. The bag's dragging sound comes to a screeching halt.

He lies in the corner, both arms shielding his face.

But that's not it, no.

Red oozes down his skin and onto the floor.

Red as in blood. So much *blood*.

"Grey Eyes!"

I run towards him, my heart beating so fast like it wants to leave my chest. Once I'm within touching distance, I crouch in front of him, my lips trembling.

He's not moving.

Why is he not moving?

"Grey Eyes..." I shake him with unsteady hands, all sweaty and cold. "Wake up. I brought you Maltesers and your favourite sandwich with cheese and ham. I brought you juice and everything."

The flashlight falls to the ground as I lean closer to his face. Tears soak my cheeks, and I taste salt. "Grey Eyes... P-please, don't go. Don't leave like Eli... Don't leave me."

"I... won't."

"Grey Eyes!"

His lids slowly flutter open, but he doesn't get up. They're black in the dark, his eyes. Like all the emotions have been taken out of him.

His face appears pale and his lips are dry and cracked. The blood has turned sticky around his arms.

It's a mess. I need to fix it before them monsters come here.

Daddy says sharks smell blood from far away, and I think

them monsters do, too. They'll smell Grey Eyes' blood and then attack him.

I run back to my bag and shuffle it across the dirty floor. Perspiration trickles down my temple and down my nose from the effort.

Panting, I search through it. There are napkins and water. Since Grey Eyes always gets hurt, I stole cotton balls and the bottle Daddy uses to clean my wounds. He said an injury needs to be cleaned before it's wrapped.

I wipe the sticky blood away with dry napkins. Blood is gross, you know. It wouldn't go away from the skin.

A deep wound cuts along the side of his arm near his elbow. It must've hurt so much.

The need to cry hits me, my nose tingles and my eyes burn, but I don't cry. I have to be strong for him.

"It's going to sting." Biting my lip, I pour the liquid onto his injury.

A whimper comes from him as he watches me with half-closed eyes.

"I'm sorry it hurts. I'm so sorry." Tears stream down my cheeks even when I tell them not to.

Just because he's not crying shouldn't mean he's not hurt. I'm crying for him, not for me.

Using the cotton balls and the napkins, I wrap it around the wound as tightly as I can. Daddy said it has to be tight and clean so no nasty germs get in there.

"W-who did this to you?" I ask. "Them monsters?"

He nods once.

"I'm going to save you. I p-promise."

His other hand wraps around my arm and tugs me down. I lie beside him, his injured hand remaining limp between us.

"Stay like this," he whispers.

My lips tremble and my nose tingles as I stare at him and cry. I cry for what seems like forever. My tears turn into hiccoughs and then into loud sobs.

It's ugly, snot and tears cover my face, but I can't stop.

It hurts so much.

His thumb wipes under my eyes. "Don't cry."

"I can't stop."

"I don't like it when you cry." He continues gathering my tears and making them go away.

"Why?"

"Because it hurts me when you're hurt."

"M-me, too. That's why I'm crying. I don't want you hurt."

"I'm going to be okay, Elsa."

"Promise?"

He doesn't answer. I jerk into a sitting position, hiccoughing and drawing involuntary breaths. "P-promise?"

"I can't."

"But why?" I shriek. "Does it hurt too much? I'm going to kiss it better."

Leaning over, I place a kiss on the side of his bandage. "Daddy says it heals when you kiss it."

He smiles. It's weak and with no energy, but he smiles.

"You need to eat." I rummage through my bag and bring out the sandwich.

It takes me some time to help him sit up against the wall. Once he's settled, I wrap the blanket around him and place the sandwich between his fingers.

"You have to eat all that to get better."

He munches slowly, not like the other days when he was so hungry, he devoured it.

I crouch in front of him, place my arms on my knees, and watch him. His injured arm lies limp beside him. The bandage around it is ugly.

"I have an idea!" I search in the bag and bring out my black marker. I was going to show him the picture of houses I've been drawing and ask him if he knows how to make one.

Because I told Daddy I'm going to build houses when I grow up.

Grey Eyes watches me closely but he says nothing as I grab his injured arm. Biting down my lip, I lay it on my lap and draw on the non-injured side.

Once I'm done, he studies my drawing. "What is that?"

"An arrow."

"Why an arrow?"

"Daddy says when you feel bad, you should keep that energy inside."

"Why inside?"

"So you can store it for later. Bad things happen for a reason."

"Bad things happen for a reason," he repeats, staring between the arrow and my face before a small smile breaks on his lips.

I love that smile.

I want to kiss it, not to make it better, but because I love it.

So I do just that. I lean over and press my lips to the corner of his mouth.

TWENTY-THREE

Elsa

Present

I startle awake. My hair sticks to the side of my face with sweat. Sitting in bed, I pull my knees to my chest like in that dream.

Only it wasn't a dream. It was a memory of when Aiden got the scar on his forearm.

Raw emotions creep under my skin like creatures from the night, rough and mysterious.

The tattoos.

His arrow tattoos are inspired by what I drew back then.

He's right. I've been under his skin for such a long time just like he's been under mine.

Even though I don't remember everything, I clearly remember that potent connection we shared in the basement.

Our story started there whether I like to admit it or not.

Back then, it was children finding friendship in each other. Truth is, we were and still are lost souls finding refuge in one another.

I check the time and it's a little after midnight. Retrieving my phone, I type.

Elsa: Are you there?

Aiden has been absent from school since the scene at the pool three days ago. Apparently, Jonathan didn't like the way he ended the engagement with Silver and he's making him pay in the only way Jonathan knows how—taking him away.

They've been on some business trip to China. Aiden has been texting me sporadically whenever he finds the time.

To say I miss him would be an understatement and an insult to my feelings.

Just when I thought we could talk about our differences and have a real conversation, Jonathan has to ruin it.

No reply comes through.

It should be around eight in the morning in China right now, but he could be too busy to reply.

I'm about to try to go back to sleep when my phone vibrates in my hand, making me shudder.

Aiden: I'm always here for you, sweetheart.

My heart does that flip-flopping thing like it's having a crush on Aiden all over again.

Aren't we over that phase already, heart?

Before I can reply, my screen lights up with another text.

Aiden: Did you have another nightmare?

God. He knows me so well. Under normal circumstances, I would be fast asleep at this time.

Elsa: Half-nightmare. Half-dream.

Aiden: Do tell.

Elsa: It was about you.

Aiden: I told you, one day you'll dream about me like I dream about you. Was it kinky?

Elsa: No.

Aiden: Half-kinky?

Elsa: What does half-kinky even mean?

Aiden: It means I tied you to the bedpost and fucked you for an entire day.

I bite the inside of my cheek, my temperature rising.

Elsa: No. It wasn't like that.

Aiden: It wasn't, huh? Funny because that's what I dreamt about. We need to synchronise our dreams.

I suppress a smile. What type of magic does Aiden possess to make me feel better even through texts?

Elsa: If I ask you to tell me about the past, will you?

I expect him to think about it, to tell me I'm not ready, but the reply is immediate.

Aiden: Whenever you wish.

A stuttering breath heaves out of me. The type of breath which lifts some weight off my chest. Not all the weight, but the relief is there, as tiny as it is.

Elsa: Thank you.

Aiden: Don't thank me until you know all the facts.

My hand turns clammy around the phone. In the back of my mind, there's a giant box titled *The Truth Isn't Easy*, but his words magnify that box, it's becoming wider and bigger than what my head can contain.

Dad and I talked about my missing memories, alone and with Dr Khan. My shrink recommended that I remember it on my own without hearing retellings, and Dad complied.

The truth is a sneaky thing. Like a witch, it demands a high price before setting you free.

Life as I know it can go up in smoke—including my relationship with Dad and Aiden.

I squash that scary thought and type the question I've been asking since he left.

Elsa: When are you coming back?

Aiden: Less than a week.

Aiden: Why? Do you miss me?

I don't even think as I type. I don't listen to my paranoia anymore. Denying my feelings for Aiden only destroyed me from the inside.

Elsa: I do.

The phone brightens up with his name and the picture of our first kiss.

Shit.

I didn't think he'd call.

Clearing my throat, I answer, "Hey."

"Say it. I need to hear it." The raspiness in his tone sends tingles racing down my spine. That voice is made to say dirty, authoritative things.

"Say what?"

"That you miss me."

"I miss you." My voice is low, sultry. I didn't even know I had that range.

"Fuck, sweetheart. I'm hard."

A wave of longing grips me by the throat. It tingles at the bottom of my stomach, pooling there. "You are?"

"Fuck right, I am." His growl is rough, animalistic even.

God. I love his voice when he lets his real self shine through.

"You drive me fucking crazy, Elsa."

"How crazy?" I ask because I can't help myself.

"Crazy enough to jerk off in the bathroom when I should be downstairs."

My cheeks heat as if they've been set on fire. My entire body is.

The desire in Aiden's voice is contagious. It's the type that grips you by the neck and never leaves.

"Talk to me, sweetheart. Let me hear your voice." He pauses. "Scratch that. Touch yourself as if I'm there with you."

My free hand is already travelling under my shirt, caressing the soft skin of my breasts. They're heavy, aching.

"How do you want me to touch myself?" I ask.

"Remove your clothes." His raspy order travels through my ear and hits me straight in my core. "Do it slowly as if I'm watching."

Manoeuvring the phone between my shoulder and ear, I push down my cotton shorts. Despite their soft material, they create maddening friction across my heated skin.

I place the phone on the pillow and drag the T-shirt over my head, letting it fall beside me.

The cool air in the room creates goosebumps that cover my

burning flesh. My nipples pucker, straining, demanding to be touched.

"Done," I murmur as I hold the phone again.

A groan cuts through the other line. "Are your nipples hard?"

"Yes. T-they…"

"They what?" I can almost imagine the tightening of his jaw.

"They hurt."

"They hurt, huh?"

"Yeah."

"Why do they hurt, sweetheart?"

"Because they want your hands on them," I blurt out, sucking in a sharp breath.

"Touch them as I do." So much authority. It's the most erotic thing I've ever heard.

I wrap my thumb and forefinger around one nipple and squeeze. A whimper slips from between my lips.

"That's not how I touch you," he grunts.

"N-no?"

"No. Pinch them savagely as I would."

Suppressing a moan, I squeeze my sensitive nipple harder, torturing it as if Aiden's doing it.

I imagine him here with me, his lips wrapped around my other nipple, sucking it into his hot mouth. He nibbles on the perky bud sending tingles straight between my legs.

"Aiden…"

"Hmm, sweetheart?" I feel his grunt on my skin instead of hearing it.

"More. I want more."

"Are you wet for me?"

"Yes." A hundred times, yes. My arousal coats my thighs and permeates the air.

"Open your legs and dip your middle finger inside that soaking pussy."

I don't need to be told twice.

The moment my finger rests inside, I buck off the bed. It's as if Aiden is here, thrusting that long finger in me, sampling me.

"Add another one."

"But…"

"Do it."

Oh, God. Why are his orders such a turn on tonight? They're more than words and straight up torture devices.

Carefully, I add another finger. My eyes roll to the back of my head with how tight I feel around them.

"Move them for me, sweetheart. Let me hear those noises you make."

I thrust my fingers in and out. The entire time, I imagine Aiden scissoring his fingers inside of me. His body overpowering mine. His strong muscles tightening with each movement.

"Touch your clit."

My thumb grazes the swollen nub. Pleasure rushes through me in torturous bursts. I hold the phone between my cheek and my shoulder and use my other hand to twirl my hard, aching nipple.

Closing my eyes, I surrender myself to the overwhelming sensations. I might be the one touching myself, but I'm not the one behind this pleasure.

Aiden's raspy orders are.

It's almost as if he's the one thrusting in and out of me, teasing my clit and playing with my nipple. He's bringing me closer to the edge with every single touch.

"Aiden… Oh, my God, Aiden."

"Fuck right, your God."

My pace escalates, ears buzzing, and stomach tightening. The sheets underneath me feel harsh and painful against my overheated skin.

"Harder," he orders on a grunt. "Faster."

I follow his command, my heartbeat jacking up with every move.

"Fuck." His breathing deepens on the other end. "Fuck!"

The thought that he's touching himself to my moans and whimpers drives me insane.

I can imagine him standing in the bathroom, his trousers and boxers pooling at his feet. He's fisting his cock in that rough, masculine way and jerking up and down like he's angry. Like his body yearns for mine the way mine does. Like his soul needs mine to be whole.

My movements turn more frantic and out of control at the thought.

I can taste the release on my tongue.

"Oh... Aiden... I'm s-so close..."

"I'm going to come." He grunts. "Are you ready for me, sweetheart?"

"Yes... Yes..." I gasp as the wave hits me like sparks in a starless night.

I cry out then hide my face in the pillow to kill the sound.

My fingers are still seated deep inside of me, slick with arousal. It's almost as if Aiden has been filling me—not my own hand.

It would've been more euphoric if he was here in person, though.

A deep growl fills my ear as Aiden reaches his own climax. I pant into the phone. I wish he was here so I'd see his sex God face when he comes.

"That was..." I breathe. "Amazing."

"We're not done," he rumbles.

"No?"

"Remove your fingers."

I do. "Done."

"Now suck. Let me taste you."

My cheeks flame at the thought, but I shove my index and middle finger into my mouth.

Tasting myself is intimate, but the fact that I'm pretending to be Aiden is even more intimate.

I lap my tongue around my fingers, making small noises.

"You know what I'm fantasising about?" His low, deep voice makes me suck harder for some reason.

I make a negative sound without removing my fingers.

"I'm fantasising about those pouty lips wrapped around my dick as I fuck you with my tongue."

A jolt of pleasure shoots through me, and I'm tempted to touch myself again. That's the type of effect Aiden's dirty words have on me.

"Soon, sweetheart. I'm claiming all of you."

I release my fingers with a pop. "Promise?"

A dark chuckle fills the other end. "Oh, I promise."

TWENTY-FOUR

Aiden

For the past week, Jonathan has been parading me around China for his investors and fuck knows what else.

If I have to sit down for another meeting like a puppet, I'm going to destroy something around here.

This is Jonathan's revenge for breaking it off with Queens. In his words, I put a smudge on his immaculate relationship with Sebastian Queens, and I'll have to do something in return.

Truth is, he's still petty about how I called him out about Alicia.

I only agreed to play along because he threatened to take it out on Elsa.

While I'm fine with declaring war on Jonathan, I won't watch him use her as a subject of destruction.

He'll have to go through me first.

Still, I need to go home—like yesterday.

Nash, Knight, and Astor have been filling the group chat with texts that pissed me the fuck off.

Knight: So King is no more, huh?

Nash: Looks like it.

Astor: Fuck yeah. My threesome dream will come true.

Astor: On a scale of 1 to 10, how likely do you think I can convince Kimmy and Ellie to wear bunny outfits?

Nash: Elsa, 0. Kimberly, 6. If drunk, 9.

Astor: I better get Kimmy drunk then *grinning face*

Knight: Do you want to die?

I'm surprised that little shit Astor even showed up in the group chat. He sometimes acts like the thing doesn't exist then bitches about how we keep him in the dark.

Bottom line is, I need to go back and fuck the three of them up for even thinking I'd leave Elsa.

That will only happen after death. Even then, I might make a deal with the devil so I can haunt her from afar.

What? I have to protect her.

We've been texting for the past week—or more like sexting. I came to the sound of her voice more than I can count.

After our momentary—and fucked up—separation, Elsa has become more liberated about her sexuality and pleasure. She even texted me she's been thinking about me in class.

Little fucking tease.

Other times, she'd tell me about the snippets of memories she's been having lately. Like my tattoo and the nights she spent with me in that basement.

However, she never mentioned her mother or the promise she made me.

A huge chunk of her memory is still missing, and I think I know exactly how to get it back. It's a drastic method, but it's all I have. She asked me to tell her everything, and I will. Just not in the traditional way.

Elsa will never be whole unless she remembers what happened that night. She'll never fully accept me unless she remembers our bloody past.

After all, it was all because of me.

She might have erased her memory due to all the trauma she lived through, but I was the final nail in the coffin. If she hadn't done what she did, maybe things would've been different.

No.

I won't allow myself to think of that option. Everything is said and done. I just have to find the best way to tell her.

After the 10th meeting of the day ends, Jonathan's Chinese investors shake hands with him and me. As the door closes behind them, I flop onto the sofa.

Jonathan's Chinese office is more grandiose than the one in London. It has grey and blue decor, a glass desk, and a large window that overlooks Shanghai's endless buildings.

I twirl the phone in my hand. "I'm booking a ticket to England."

Jonathan smiles from behind his glass desk.

Well, fuck.

It's never good when he's smiling with triumph as if he scored the deal of the century.

"You know." He interlaces his fingers at his chin and leans back in his tall leather chair. "As indestructible as you were, I knew you'd self-destruct one day."

I tilt my head to the side.

He's been pissed off since the reality check I threw in his face about Alicia's death. I knew he'd find retribution in some way. I thought the trip to China was it. After all, he kept me away from Elsa—even if temporarily.

I should've known better.

Jonathan's temporary solutions are usually a camouflage to a bigger plan that concocts in the background.

"What have you done?" I rise to my feet. "I swear if you hurt her —"

"I don't need to hurt her. I only need her away from you."

My left eye twitches. "What the fuck did you do, Jonathan?"

"You're right, Aiden. I have other allies beside Sebastian. There's another member of the Rhodes' voting committee who promised to be my way into Ethan's corporation."

"Do you seriously think Ethan Steel would let anyone close enough to spy on him? He's more private than you."

"He'd let his future son-in-law."

My muscles go rigid as I hiss, "What did you just say?"

"If I can't keep you away from her; I'll keep her away from you." He motions ahead. "Ethan has just accepted to marry his daughter to Earl Edric Astor's son. You can go back to England now. Congratulate Elsa on my behalf."

Earl Edric Astor's son.

Fuck no.

A heavy weight settles on my chest as I slip out of the office without a word.

Elsa is mine.

Fucking mine.

It's time the world learns that fact.

TWENTY-FIVE

Elsa

S omething is wrong.

I sense it in my bones the moment I walk inside our house.

The air is stuffy, suffocating even.

Knox and Teal sit with Agnus and Dad in the lounge area. The chesterfield sofas appear like a battlefield.

Dad and Agnus sip their coffees in silence. Knox appears thoughtful. Teal's brows are pinched together in… confusion? Anger?

She's wearing a pullover, with the words, *If you see me jogging, kill whatever the hell is chasing me* written on it.

Usually, I'd smile at her sarcastic quotes, but the mood is completely off today.

I inch closer, fingering the strap of my backpack.

"Princess," Dad smiles as soon as his light brown eyes meet mine. "You're finally here."

"Sorry, I spent time with Kim and Kir. We promised him to watch a film together." And I just finished a run in the rain. It's been too tense lately and only running allows me to relax. Of course, I changed my soaked clothes at Kim's or Dad would give me grief. Like Aunt, he's strict about endangering my heart condition.

"It's okay." He stands. "Let's talk in my office."

He walks ahead of me. I throw one last glance at the other three. Agnus encourages me to follow Dad with a nod.

Knox sighs. "I hate this whole shit."

"You…" Teal clears her throat, peeking up at me. "You have to think about it."

Okay. That makes the situation even more ambiguous than when I walked in. Better follow Dad and find out what's going on.

Dread tightens my muscles as I take the steps two at a time. When I'm at the top, I check my phone.

My stomach falls when I find no texts from Aiden. For some reason, I want to talk to him right now.

I've been barely keeping myself sane this entire week. With him gone, RES is empty and fucking depressive. I see him in every corner and every hall. Hell, I even went to the football practice, imagining him scoring a goal in that perfect posture.

I didn't know how much I needed Aiden in my life until he was gone.

With the time difference, we could only text at odd times of the night. It's not nearly enough.

The thought that we'll be permanently separated at the end of this year brings a taste of nausea to my throat.

It steals my breaths, that thought.

To distract myself, I've spent nights at Aunt and Uncle's, doing yoga. I went out with the horsemen, Knox, Teal, and Kim, but nothing and no one can take up Aiden's place.

He's been a constant in my life since the beginning of the year, and now that he's gone, it's pure torture.

Tucking my phone back in my pocket, I hug my backpack to my chest and follow Dad into his office. We sit side by side on the black leather sofa in the centre of the room.

"How was your day?" he asks.

"Good."

Dad always asks about my day and if I need anything. While

that makes me happy on most days, I'm not the least bit joyful right now.

Bricks of anxiety pile at the bottom of my stomach with every second he remains silent.

"What's going on, Dad?"

"You know that your opinion matters to me more than anything else, right?"

I nod once, unsure where he's going with this.

"As you know, the Rhodes have a voting committee in place. Their members will decide whether Jonathan or I get the partnership."

"I do."

While I've been butting out of Dad and Jonathan's war, Agnus has been keeping us in the know. Each company has been recruiting members of that committee to vote in their favour.

Sebastian Queens, Silver's father, is a member, and Jonathan is pissed off at Aiden for breaking off the engagement at a time like this.

Still, I'm sure Sebastian will vote in Jonathan's favour considering they've been long-time allies.

I heard Agnus talk about how Dad has been recruiting some of the aristocratic members. If they manage to convince one of them, all the other ones would follow. Those noble folks are loyal to each other.

"I found a possible strong ally within the voting committee," Dad says.

"Really?" My face lights up. "Who is he?"

"Earl Edric Astor."

"Oh. Ronan's father. I'm happy for you, Dad."

His expression isn't the least bit joyful, though. "There's a catch."

"A catch?"

"Earl Astor only agreed to form an alliance if we become in-laws. My daughter to his son."

The information hits me like a hurricane with all the lightning and thunder.

"Do you mean… I have to marry Ronan?"

The idea doesn't even sit straight before my brain completely revolts against it. Ronan is my friend and I really like his goofiness, but that's it.

That's *all.*

He's not the one I dream about. He's not the one I've been yearning for, feeling all empty and miserable.

"Ronan wouldn't agree to that," I whisper. He's a player and loves his freedom more than anything in the world.

Dad remains cool and calm. I don't know how he does it. "Earl Astor said Ronan will agree to anything he asks of him."

Oh, God.

I'm going to be sick.

"And…" I meet Dad's gaze. "What did you tell him?"

"I said I'll talk to you." Dad takes my hand in his, strong, warm, and safe. "I'll never force you to do anything, you know that, right, princess?"

Oh. Thank God.

I want to help Dad, but I'll never agree to an arranged marriage. I want to marry someone I love. Someone who flips my world upside down by just being there.

Someone like Aiden.

Wait… no. Where did that idea come from? I don't want to marry Aiden… right? It's too early to even think about marrying Aiden.

Stay the fuck down, heart. Don't even think about celebrating that thought.

"Think about it," Dad says. "I'll go with whatever you decide."

I'm tempted to tell him 'no' straight away, but the look in his eyes stops me. It's not pleading, but it's close to… desperation.

Dad needs this alliance.

It hurts me to think about killing all his hopes at once. I need a lot more courage than I have right now.

After agreeing to think about it, I retreat to my room.

I throw my backpack on the chair and flop onto the bed. I hit play on my iPod and *Another Place* by Bastille fills the air.

What's the best way to refuse Dad's offer without being a complete bitch? Either way, he'll lose Earl Astor and might even be categorised as an enemy by the upper-class community.

Dad spent a lot of energy on this come back. Hell, he returned from the *dead*. I can't just destroy his efforts.

Ugh.

This is so confusing.

I need a cup of hot chocolate to calm down. Oh, and my meds. Aunt will call me in a few and give me a lecture if she finds out I didn't take them.

My heart palpitations have turned up in intensity these last couple of days. I'll have to cave in and visit Dr Albert.

Please don't have the doctor suggest a surgery. The thought of another one terrifies the bejesus out of me

My phone vibrates on my way to the kitchen.

My heart beats loudly at the thought that it might be Aiden. What would he say if he found out? Actually, I know what he'll say.

He'll ask me to refuse and if I can't, he'll do it for me.

Aiden doesn't care about Dad's well-being or how much losing Earl Astor's support would devastate him.

Aiden is shameless about what he wants and isn't above flipping the world the middle finger.

My stomach sinks when the caller ID doesn't turn out to be Aiden.

Speak of the devil.

I swipe the screen. "Hey, Ronan."

"Hey, fiancé." His playful tone releases some of the dread perched on my chest.

"This isn't the time to joke around."

"Who says I'm joking? Father just said I'm getting married to you. I hit the jackpot! Think about the number of threesomes we'll have, Ellie. Even Kimmy will be game to join if you're my wife. *Le paradis est juste ici.*"

I narrow my eyes as if he can see me. "Why do you sound so happy?"

"Because I am! I've been imagining the look on King's face when he finds out you're my fiancé." He hums. "You think I'll be able to catch his expression on camera before he chops my head off with an axe?"

I smile despite myself. "Probably not."

"I'll ask Knight or Nash to film it, then. I'm leaving a legacy behind. Oh, and a fortune. You'll be one of those lethally rich widows who dresses in black and has three black cats."

I laugh, stopping near the corner. "You're such a twat."

"See? Marrying me won't be so bad. We'll have so much fun."

"Be serious, Ronan." I sigh. "Why don't you tell your father you don't want to get married?"

"I can't tell my father anything. His word is law in this household."

"So you'll agree?"

"Already done. I'm an earl's only child and heir, Ellie. It's written in my birth certificate that I'll have an arranged marriage. I'm lucky it's with you and not with some snob that will suck the life out of my bones. You know how fucking scary that is?"

I pause, thinking about his point of view. I never thought Ronan would have these types of worries. He's always so playful and carefree, no one sees the weight he carries on his shoulders.

"But I —"

"I know." He cuts me off. "King, that lucky bastard, came first. *Fucker.* However, I'm not allowed to refuse the engagement from my side. You have to be the one to stab your sword straight to my virgin heart."

"You're such a dork." I laugh.

"And you have such an awful taste in men," Ronan mocks with an edge of drama. "Now if you excuse me, I'm going to nurse my broken heart with some weed and a girl—or two."

I hung up with a smile.

The smile falls when I realise that Ronan's completely out and I have to be the one who ends this. I groan. Is there no other way aside from hurting Dad?

"Are you going to agree?"

I jump at Teal's quiet voice. I didn't even notice she was there.

"You know about it?" I ask.

"Agnus mentioned it." She studies her black nails, not meeting my gaze. "Thirteen already agreed to marry you."

Since that practice football game, Teal often calls the horsemen by their jersey's numbers.

"I thought you were with Eleven?"

"I am… sort of," I say. "I won't marry Ronan. I just have to find the appropriate way to tell Dad."

Teal meets my gaze, but she remains silent. "Dad needs that alliance with the Astor family. Earl Astor has the best title amongst the voting committee and if he pledges to Dad, everyone else will follow his lead."

"I know that." That's why it hurts so much, and my brain is working in overdrive.

"If you know, why don't you act?" she asks with genuine curiosity as if all of this is too easy.

"I can't do an arranged marriage when I already have someone else in my heart."

"That's why it's better to have no one in your heart. Those who show weakness lose."

"It depends on who you show that weakness to, Teal."

She gives a sharp nod and sidesteps me to walk towards her room.

I'm tempted to follow and ask her why she's been in such a pissed off mood today—more than usual—but I choose to give her space.

Besides, I'm too caught up in my own head right now.

My phone vibrates.

My heart jumps with joy at Aiden's name.

Aiden: Come out the back entrance.

I don't even think about it. I jog down the hall and straight to the back door used by the staff.

The moment I step outside, a strong hand wraps around my mouth. I gasp, but the sound is drowned into the skin.

The hard, strong skin I recognise.

My gaze meets Aiden's for the briefest second, and excitement whirls into my bones.

I barely get a glance before he picks me up and throws me over his shoulder like a caveman.

Squealing, I hold on to his back with both hands. "W-what are you doing, Aiden?"

"I'm kidnapping you, sweetheart. It's been long overdue."

TWENTY-SIX

Elsa

I'm being kidnapped.

How does someone react when they're kidnapped?

It's not like I have the manual or something. Considering my relationship with Aiden, I should've probably bought the thing.

Deep down, I knew he'd do this someday. I knew he'd give the world his middle finger and whisk me away on his black horse.

Like an old-fashioned kidnapper, Aiden tied my hands in front of me so they're lying on my lap. He also covered my hands with a blanket so no one would see what he's done.

I should be thankful he didn't strap my mouth with duct tape. But then again, that will draw people's attention and Aiden is too smart for that.

The car speeds into the distance like a wrecking ball. Aiden's complete concentration is on the road. There's no tick in his jaw or a twitch in his left eye.

If I didn't know better, I would say he appears serene. Peaceful even.

Oh, who am I kidding? There's no such thing as peaceful with Aiden. Not when I'm sure he heard all about the engagement.

For the past hour or so, I've been thinking about what to say, but I'm distracted by his scent and sheer presence.

I'm lost in how his dark jeans tighten around his muscular thighs and how his grey pullover brings out the metal colour of his eyes. His hair is dishevelled in a sexy bedroom kind of way, though some tiredness is wearing down his expression.

I heard the flight from China to England is more than twelve hours. He must be exhausted. Still, I relish in the fact that he came to me first.

He crossed the seas for me.

Despite the circumstances, the breaths I take are deeper, cleaner, and so damn liberated.

The itch to hug and kiss him writhes inside me like I'm possessed. I want to run my fingers through his hair, feel his slight stubble against my cheek, and let him own me.

All of me.

I had an epiphany during this separation and the subsequent marriage proposal with Ronan. I've always belonged to Aiden and he's always belonged to me.

It started ten years ago and has been ongoing since.

I was just too stubborn—and scared—to admit it.

The fact that Aiden's not saying anything about the engagement is putting me on edge.

Aiden's silence is a lot worse than his words. His silence is the calm before the storm and the wind before the hurricane. It's feeling your limbs shake right before an earthquake.

The road becomes deserted the longer we travel. I thought he'd take me to the Meet Up, but we left London altogether.

"Where are we going?" I ask.

"A kidnapper doesn't tell their victim where they're going."

I resist the urge to roll my eyes. "You know I had nothing to do with the engagement."

Silence.

"Dad only asked for my opinion."

"What was your response?"

"I haven't told him yet."

"So you're considering it."

Shit. I didn't want him to get to that conclusion. "Of course not."

"You know what's the difference between you and me, Elsa?" His voice is rough, commanding, and hard. "I'm all in, but you always have a foot out. Even when we're together, that brain of yours is always thinking of an escape plan."

His words hit me harder than they should.

That's it.

All this time, I've always fought the idea of Aiden and me — even subconsciously.

"You didn't give me strong reasons to trust you," I whisper. "It's not like I resisted you without a reason."

"Are we playing that game? Because I had a stronger reason to hate you." The calmness of his voice draws chills over my skin and down my spine. "You reminded me of the woman who destroyed my childhood, but I didn't let my hate win. You let your distrust win every fucking time."

"Aiden —"

"I chose you, Elsa." He cuts me off, gripping the steering wheel so tightly, his knuckles turn white. "I chose you over my mother's memory, my father, and everything I fucking know. But you never chose me."

"I wasn't going to agree to the engagement." My voice trembles despite my best efforts to remain unaffected.

"You didn't refuse either. If it were me, I would've done it on the spot."

"Like you did with Silver?"

"That was fake and it happened long before you came along. It meant fuck all and you know it." His eyes meet mine, dark, hard, and almost black. "But you were biding your time. You are thinking about something that should be non-negotiable."

"I was thinking about a way to refuse without hurting my dad. I finally have him back, and I can't cause him or his company any harm."

He barks a humourless laugh that scrapes over my skin like

daggers. "Your father, the company, your new family. They all come first. Where do I fit into your list of priorities, Frozen? Am I a fucking afterthought?"

"That's not true."

How the hell do I tell him that my world revolves around him when he's so frustrating right now?

Damn him and the way he gets under my skin.

"While I was on the other end of the world, thinking about ways to come back to you sooner, you were thinking about your *engagement*," he hisses the last word as if it leaves a foul taste in his mouth.

"I was thinking about you, dickhead! I was thinking about how my life is an empty shell without you in it. I was re-reading your texts in class because I couldn't stop missing you. I had to run in the rain like a lunatic because of thinking about *you*. So don't sit here telling me that you're an afterthought, Aiden. If you were, I wouldn't be in so much pain right now."

My chest heaves with the raw breaths and the strain of my words. I turn my head in the other direction, not wanting to look at him.

The car swerves into a dirt road. We bump for a few seconds before coming to a screeching halt underneath a tree. If it weren't for the seatbelt, I would've toppled over.

Still refusing to acknowledge him, I stare out into the distance. The flaming of my cheeks spreads to my entire body like a rapid-fire.

Aiden places two fingers under my chin. His touch is rough, yet gentle at the same time.

I jerk away. "I'm mad at you right now."

"I told you. We can be mad at each other while I touch you."

When he grips my chin again and turns me to face him, I'm ready to give him a piece of my mind. The hunger on his face stops me. It's tangible and raw, so raw my own hunger responds in kind.

A jolt of want zips through me and deep longing grips me in its merciless clutches.

"You missed me, huh?" His metal eyes shine, almost becoming black.

"Maybe."

"Maybe is good enough." He pauses. "For now."

His thumb grazes my jaw, and I feel it straight in my peaking nipples and slick core.

My breath catches, but that's not the only thing abnormal. My heartbeat is palpitating like crazy. I'm not sure if it's because of my illness or Aiden's touch.

His fingers tilt my chin up and he captures my lips in a slow, soft kiss.

This isn't the time to be soft.

I don't want him to be gentle and take his time with my mouth. I want him to *own* me. I want him to fuck my brains out like he can't breathe without me just like I can't breathe without him.

Manoeuvring my bound hands, I loop them over his neck. My fingers grip strands of his hair as I push my tongue up the roof of his mouth, demanding more.

With a groan, Aiden is on top of me. His hard muscles flatten my chest, nearly suffocating me.

He's too much.

Too raw.

Too… real.

He fiddles with something on the side of the seat and we both topple backwards.

My eyes flutter closed as I kiss him, my fingers toying with the hairs at the back of his neck. Our breaths mingle together, rough and unrestrained like a symphony. I arch my back and slowly roll my hips against his pelvis.

That earns me a groan. Deep, and animalistic.

"Fuck, sweetheart. I need to be inside you," he grunts and yanks at his belt, nearly ripping it off.

"I'm going to hurt you." His blackening eyes slam into mine like a challenge.

"Y-you will?" I ask in a small, trembling voice filled with excitement and thrill.

"Oh, I will." He grins, but it's still intense. "And you'll like it."

He yanks my skirt up and my underwear down. I don't know how he's made it inside of me, but he has. The brutal thrust stretches me open. I don't only feel the fullness in my pussy, it's ramming straight to my belly, all deep and hard.

I grip the back of his neck for balance, my body arching off the seat.

His thrusts turn merciless, and true to his words, it does hurt. It hurts so good. It's the pleasurable type of pain only Aiden can give me.

Like last week when I continued feeling him inside me for days. Every time I moved, every time I sat down, or ran, he was a constant reminder inside me.

"I'm addicted to you. I'm obsessed with you. I'm mad about you." With every word, he hits my most sensitive spot.

My whimpers and moans tremble and vibrate off his throat with every pound and every touch of his lips against my heated skin.

He feathers kiss after a kiss to the curve of my jaw, the corner of my mouth, and the tip of my lips. He licks them, devours them, *feasts* on them.

My ears ring and my limbs quiver with the force of my pleasure. The orgasm rips through me like a heatwave, violent and uncontrollable. It's not about the pleasure of the body anymore. It's about the one who's bringing me said pleasure.

The damning realisation hits me.

I'm screwed.

There's no way I'll be able to live without Aiden King.

Tears barge to my eyes as his body stiffens and his cum coats my inside. He collapses atop of me, his entire weight covering mine

It's not tears of sadness. No. They could even be tears of happiness. They might as well be tears of acceptance.

Aiden props on his elbows, breathing heavily atop of me, the rise and fall of his chest vibrating on my skin. He licks my tears. One by each one.

"Don't cry."

He said it a long time ago, didn't he? That it hurts him when I'm hurt.

I stroke the hair on the back of his neck and we remain like that for what seems like forever.

For a moment in time, it's just me and Aiden shielded from the world.

I even forget that we're in public and some passing cars might have seen what happened in full detail. Hell, even if they didn't see, they would've noticed the shaking of the car due to Aiden's rough thrusts.

Truth is, I couldn't care less about what they saw.

The only thing I care about is the person atop of me, protecting me from the world.

"Now what?" I murmur after a while.

"Now we go back to where it all started."

TWENTY-SEVEN

Elsa

Now we go back where it all started.
It turns out to be here.
My home in Birmingham.

The scent of pine and copper fills the air like a thick fog. The cold, punishing wind whistles in the distance and blows blonde strands in front of my face.

A shiver claws down my spine, causing my limbs to quiver. It's not due to the wind or the cold.

No.

It's the fact that I'm standing here with Aiden which hits me with a strange type of terror. The type that bleeds under your skin and forges wires around your bones.

I'm shivering like a leaf in the pounding rain.

This brings back a horrible feeling from a long time ago. I can taste the pungent taste on my tongue. Back then, I stood at the shore, my toes soaked by water as Eli dove into the lake and never surfaced.

One second he was within touching distance, the next he was gone.

Just like that. He was *gone.*

That sensation burns through me and grips me by the throat, its nails scratching and scraping the skin. That sensation tells me without words that the past will repeat itself. This time, I'll lose Aiden just like I lost Eli.

"Why are we here?" I ask.

"You said you want to know the truth." Aiden touches my elbow. "You can do that where it all happened."

I'm tempted to shake my head, grab Aiden, and tell him to drive me to the nearest hotel.

A part of me wants to run as far away as possible from this place and my dark, fucked up memories.

But then again, what did running ever do for me aside from nightmares and unanswered question?

If I keep being a coward, a large chunk of my life will be missing. I'll always stare back at my reflection with confusion. I'll always keep wondering about what-ifs and whys.

Enough is enough.

I'm done running.

I'm done being a coward.

It's time I unravel my past. The good and the bad.

Aiden stares down at me with a perfectly raised eyebrow. "You said you're ready."

"I am." I peek at him through my eyelashes. "Is this what you want to do?"

"What I want to do is tie you to my bed and fuck you until you can no longer move. What I want to do is feast on your pussy instead of food and fill you with my cum."

The explicit images assault my mind and core. I feign anger. "Aiden!"

"You asked." He clutches my hand and interlaces our fingers together. "What I want can wait until you find out what you need."

A smile tugs on my lips. He can be so dreamy sometimes— the keyword being *sometimes*. It's rare as hell.

"Let's take a detour." He tugs me behind him as he tiptoes towards the back entrance.

"Why can't we use the front entrance? This is my house after all," I whisper, somehow sensing we need to keep quiet.

"Your father's people will be at the door and immediately notify him of our arrival."

That must be why he parked the car far away from the property's gate.

"Why shouldn't Dad know we're here?"

He grins. "I'm kidnapping you, remember?"

"That's not the only reason, is it?"

"We can't be interrupted." His gaze roams the back entrance before he pushes the ajar door open.

We slip through the storage room. No one is here. Agnus mentioned that since we don't live in Birmingham for the moment, most of the staff was transferred to London.

However, there are a few security men and a housekeeper.

I pull on Aiden's hand. He throws a glance over his shoulder in question.

"We shouldn't go through the kitchen. The housekeeper and her husband will be there." I tug him in the opposite direction. "Follow me, there's a secret path."

Aiden doesn't protest as I guide him through a tight hallway leading straight to the eastern tower.

I don't hesitate as I take the twists and turns. I've been here countless times before.

Due to the absence of windows, the only light coming through is from the tower's opening. The walls are renovated, but they emanate the same darkness as before.

Wait.

I've taken this path from the storage room to the basement every day. I can imagine a little girl with pale skin and hair, walking through these tight, long halls alone at night, carrying a flashlight and struggling to drag a heavy bag.

"This is how I came to find you every night," I whisper.

His lips twitch into a small smile. "I figured. Told you, Child Elsa was hardcore."

"It used to be scary back then, all dark and silent," I blurt. "I always sang to myself so I wouldn't get captured by monsters."

"Did it help?"

"No. The fact that I'd find you at the end of the tunnel is what kept me going." I glance at him over my shoulder. "*You* kept me going."

"You kept me going, too." The smile still lifts his lips, but there's no joy behind it. If anything, he appears a bit sad.

We arrive at an intersection. I take the right one without thoughts. After a few more minutes of walking, we stop in front of a metal door. It's fingerprint protected.

The basement—or more specifically, the stairs that lead to the basement.

"This is it," I murmur, fighting the trembling in my limbs.

"Whose fingerprint opens it?" Aiden asks.

"Mine, Dad's, and Agnus." I exhale. "Dad told me I can come here whenever I'm ready."

"Who's Agnus?"

"Dad's right hand."

"So that's him."

"You know him?" I ask.

"Jonathan mentioned him a time or two. Besides, you always talked about him back then."

I raise a shaky finger and miss the screen. A red light blinks back at us.

Aiden cradles my hand in his and slowly places the pad on the fingerprint-recognising screen. It lights up in green.

Both of us take a deep breath as we start to step inside.

This is it.

We're taking a trip into our past.

"Wait." He holds up his hand. "Your phone."

I blink. "Why?"

"Just give it to me."

Frowning, I reach into my pocket and hand him my phone.

Aiden brings out his own, powers off both devices and places them in front of the door.

"Why are you doing that?"

"No interruptions, remember?" He takes my hand in his again and we resume walking inside. An automatic light goes on in the stairs. This is new. There were no lights aside from my flashlight back then.

The metallic door clicks closed behind us.

I jump at the small sound, and Aiden strokes the back of my hand with his thumb.

To say I'm not scared would be a lie. I'm actually terrified.

Every step down the dark stony stairs is like those I took in my subconscious during my sessions with Dr Khan. What I find when I reach the bottom won't be pretty.

Then Aiden's touch registers, his warmth, his silent support. The fact he's here with me fills me with a strange type of peace.

I can do this.

If I want to have a future with Aiden, I need to figure out the past first.

"Are you okay?" he asks.

"Kind of." I breathe out. "Aren't you scared?"

"I'm not scared, I'm cautious."

"You should be. This place must bring back horrible memories."

"No, I'm not cautious about this place or the memories associated with it. I'm cautious about how you'll react after you learn the truth."

If I was anxious before, then my state of mind is skyrocketing right now.

We arrive at the bottom of the stairs. I'm sucking air into my lungs as Aiden pushes the metallic door open.

Both of us freeze at the entrance.

The basement appears a lot smaller than in my memory. Back then, it was a large pitch, all dark and dirty and... horrid.

But that's how people react to traumas. Everything is magnified, becoming bigger and scarier than it actually is.

The basement is in fact the size of a room, perhaps three to four metres length.

An automatic light shines on the dark grey walls and ground. There are no chains in the corner. Dad probably got rid of those. A lavatory takes their place.

Other than that, the entire basement is empty. Neither the walls nor the floor have been renovated; they look just how I remember them.

It's clean now, though. There's no smell of piss and vomit.

The air contains residual humidity and cigarettes. Who comes down here to smoke?

"Bring back anything?" Aiden's questions pulls me back from my observations.

I shake my head and step inside. The door closes behind us.

Standing in the middle, I study my surroundings closely, trying to commit anything to memory.

This place is crowded with memories, but that's not all they were for me. They were precious pieces of my childhood. I've been incomplete since I erased them.

Aiden releases my hand, and I feel the emptiness before I can see it. He strides to the corner with purpose and stops in front of the wall.

A shiver races down my spine and creeps into my soul.

Even though he's facing away, I can almost see that small boy chained to the corner, hungry, thirsty, and bleeding.

God. I don't think I can do this. I'm tempted to grab him and run away from here.

I want to protect him.

Actually, I wanted to protect him since that first time I laid eyes on him.

I walk towards him on unsteady legs and wrap my arms around his waist from behind.

His warmth seeps straight to my shrivelling heart. I rest

my cheek on his tense back, the back full of welts and scars. The strong, *strong* back that never bowed down.

The onslaught of tears nearly take over. If I give in to it, and to those destructive emotions, I'll be sobbing all the way to Sunday.

I won't be that girl.

I'll be the seven-year-old Elsa who brought Aiden food and made sure he was okay.

I'll be strong.

"We can do this, Aiden. We owe ourselves that much."

His hand wraps around mine. "I don't care as long as you're with me."

We remain silent for a moment. He doesn't move to turn around and I don't attempt to release him.

"Tell me what happened that night," I murmur.

"That night?"

"The night of the fire. The night I lost you." I blow out a shaky breath. "I want to hear it from you."

TWENTY-EIGHT

Aiden

Past

Elsa didn't show up.

I waited all day, but there's no trace of her.

The chains clink behind me as I pace the length of the room.

I stare at the arrow she drew on the side of my arm and it's starting to fade. I want to keep it. Every time I see it, I recall the focused expression on her face when she drew it. The line between her brows. The twitch of her nose.

Maybe she won't come anymore.

Maybe the red woman hurt her.

I'll save you. Her soft voice echoes in my head. *I promise.*

My pace quickens. She promised not to leave me here and I know she won't.

I sit back down, my gaze locked on the door.

The wound hurts, and I'm warm and hot. Perspiration coats my temple and back. I don't know if it's because of the wound or the weather.

My head rests on the cold wall, eyes fluttering closed. Just a second. I'll remain like this for a second.

I shake my head.

What if Elsa comes when I'm asleep?

She can come now…

Or now…

I must've fallen asleep because someone is shaking my shoulders. I tense, thinking about the red woman.

No.

Her hands aren't soft and small. She doesn't smell of cotton candy and Maltesers.

The moment I force my lids open, Elsa's grinning face greets me. Her missing tooth is starting to grow.

She leans down, wraps her arms around my shoulders, and hugs me. Her joy runs in spades between us. Even though it hurts and I'm about to collapse, her energy is contagious. I can't help but smile despite not knowing what she's so happy about.

Is it weird that her happiness makes me happy?

"Daddy came home!" She gushes. "I'll wait till Ma goes to bed and then I'll tell him about you. He's going to help you!"

My smile falls.

She frowns. "Aren't you happy?"

"I am."

"Then why do you look sad?"

Because if her dad helps me, I won't see her again.

Mum never spent a day without me, and now that I've been away for a long time, she won't allow me to go outside again. My father will do that, too.

Meaning, I won't see Elsa any time soon.

"Smile." She places her index fingers on either side of my mouth and pulls.

"Do you want me to go?" I ask.

She nods frantically. "I don't want to see you bleeding and cold."

"If I go, I won't come back."

"Why not? You can come back. We're friends." Her bottom lip trembles. "Right?"

"I don't think I'll be able to come back."

"I'll tell Daddy to take me to you."

"Your dad doesn't like my dad."

"I don't care. I like you. Daddy gives me everything I like." Her fingers run in my hair. "Tonight, you won't be hurt anymore. Wait for me, okay?"

She reaches into her dress's pocket and I'm not surprised when she retrieves a small bag of Maltesers and stuffs it in my hand. "I'll give them to you."

She stands, then crouches back down and places a peck onto my cheek. "Wait for me."

I do.

After she's gone, I sit on the filthy floor, watching the door and the Maltesers she left in my hands.

I'll eat them when she returns. Maltesers are too sweet and I don't like them much, but I haven't told her that. Elsa's so enthusiastic about them and I like watching her eat them. Besides, she loves it when I share the chocolate balls with her.

My eyes flutter closed and my skin turns warm then cold, but I don't sleep. I think about Mum and how happy she'll be when I go back. Maybe Jonathan will take us somewhere and make Mum happy.

The door barges open.

I jump to my feet. It's not Elsa.

The red woman strolls inside, clutching a horsewhip in her hands.

She's wearing a long, sleeveless, red dress. Her golden hair falls to her shoulders and her lips are painted in bright red. Even her heels are red.

Like blood.

Mum used to tell me about the power of the darkness. She said the real monsters look more beautiful than angels.

The red woman is as beautiful as the angel in our garden.

I shrink into the corner, tightening my hold on the bag of Maltesers. The sound of the red woman's shoes comes closer.

"Eli… Mummy is back."

Her voice is calm and black like winter nights. At times like these, I wish I can feel Mum's warmth and hear her soft words.

If I pretend to be Eli, she won't hurt me.

"Did you miss Mummy, Eli?" She stands in front of me, a serene smile on her face.

"I did." *I miss my mum, Alicia.*

She crouches in front of me and runs her red nails down my face. Goosebumps erupt in her wake. "I told you not to swim in the lake. Why did you?"

"I-I'm sorry."

"You won't repeat it, okay?"

I nod, twice.

She smiles and stands up.

Phew. She didn't get angry this time. I'm about to sit back down when she stops and whirls around so abruptly, I jerk against the wall.

"What is *that?*" She shrieks, pointing at my hand.

The Maltesers.

I hide them behind my back. "N-Nothing."

"I told you not to lie to me!" Her voice echoes around us. She grabs my hand, her nails digging into the skin.

I try my hardest to keep the bag of chocolates, but she snatches it away.

"Give it back." I glare at her. "It's mine."

"You ungrateful little bastard." She slaps me across the face.

I fall to my side onto the hard floor, my cheek stinging.

"I gave you everything, everything! But all you do is lie and play at the lake when you shouldn't!"

The first lash of the horsewhip lands on my back. Something rips at my skin, and I scream.

"Mummy will fix it, Eli. Mummy will fix everything."

Crack.

I wail. The pain is unlike anything I've felt before. It hurts more than when she cut my arm or when she chained me with the cuff.

"Stop…" I crawl to the corner on all four, shaking all over.

Crack. Crack. Crack.

She goes on and on… and on.

A sticky warm liquid travels down my spine and drips onto the floor.

Drip.

Drip.

Drip.

My eyes flutter closed and a tear falls down my cheek.

I'm sorry, Elsa. I won't keep my promise.

TWENTY-NINE

Elsa

I listen to Aiden's retelling of that day.

Every word and every sentence is like being stabbed in the gut. It's like being cut open and left bleeding on the ground beneath us. It's like being in the middle of an earthquake, buried alive.

We sit side by side on the cold ground without touching. Aiden hasn't looked at me once since he started talking.

His gaze is lost in the distance as if he's seeing the events play out in front of him. As if my mother is right there, whipping a small child until he bled and passed out.

He's watching the corner as if he can see himself; weak, small, and defenceless.

The moment he stopped talking, heavy silence engulfs the room.

Frightening silence.

Earth-shattering silence.

I pull my knees to my chest and resist the urge to hide and cry.

I won't do that.

This is Aiden's memory, not mine. He was the one who suffered, not me.

I turn away from him because I know I won't be able to hold on for long, and I don't want him to see me breaking.

"Then what happened?" I ask in a small voice.

"That part belongs to you," he says. "I won't force you to remember."

"Okay." A long breath heaves out of my lungs. "Okay," I repeat because apparently, my mind is caught in a loop.

"Elsa?"

I'm still facing away from him, so my expression isn't visible. Is there a way to dig a hole to bury myself in?

"What is it, sweetheart?"

My chest thunders with explosions and sparks when he calls me that. How can he call me that after what happened? How can he look at my face, let alone be with me when I'm so much like her?

His tormentor.

His torturer.

"Elsa, look at me."

"I can't. I just can't, Aiden." I choke on the words. "What if you eventually hate me? What if one day you wake up and realise you're sleeping next to a monster?"

"That will never fucking happen."

"How do you know that? How can you be so sure?"

"Look at me," he repeats, but this time it's a low, deep order.

I wipe my cheeks and turn to face him. The depth of longing in his eyes takes me by surprise.

Oh, God.

"Aside from the first time you stepped into RES, I never saw you as your mother." He takes my hand and cradles it between his strong ones. "You're the little girl who brought me food and drinks and her annoying Maltesers. You're *not* the red woman."

A sob tears from me, hanging in the air like an axe. "What about in the future? What if you change your mind?"

"Never, sweetheart. Do you know why?" He wipes the tear under my lid and strokes the corner of my eye. "While you look so much like her, you don't have her empty gaze or her haunting voice. As long as you have this spark in your eyes, I'll always recognise you as *my* Elsa."

Something lifts off my chest even when my heart is being ripped open, bleeding about what happened to him.

I peek at him through my wet lashes. "Can I ask you something?"

He makes an affirmative sound.

"Was I violent back then? I mean, don't some children that age show signs of antisocial behaviour?"

"Hmm. You weren't violent per se, but you didn't forgive injustice. You were obviously a lonely child like me, and that's precisely why we connected. The difference between us is that you found trouble in controlling and directing your energy. It's like you were trapped in a reality you couldn't accept."

"And you figured all that out back then?"

"No. I studied over the past years." He taps the side of his head. "This one isn't empty."

"Obviously." I smile a little. "I bet it's crowded in there."

"You're welcome to take a tour any time." He winks. "Just know it's not free."

I smile at the amusement in his tone. "What currency do you accept?"

"Something simple. Sex."

I push my shoulder against his jokingly. "Does your mind always go there?"

"With you, yes." He lowers my hand to his trousers and wraps my fingers around an unmistakable bulge. A groan escapes his throat at the contact.

"Here?" I gasp, lowering my voice as if someone can hear. "This is like a torture chamber."

"We had good memories in it, too." He grins and his cock hardens beneath my hand. "We can make them better if you open that mouth for me."

I can say no.

I mean, even he would understand. We were supposed to come here so I'd recoup my memories not so I would suck him off.

However, my mouth doesn't act as my brain thinks.

There's this overpowering need to bring him pleasure after all the pain he experienced.

I scramble to my knees in front of him and cup him harder through his jeans. The grunt of pleasure is all I need to carry on. I remove his belt and flip open his jeans with frantic movements. The moment I free him from his boxer briefs, Aiden captures both my hands in one.

"What?" I pant, confused. "I thought you wanted my lips around your dick?"

"And I still do. First, lie down."

"Why?"

"Do it," His authoritative tone is hard and raspy.

The air around us ripples with static and pent up desire while I do as I'm told, not sure where he's going with this.

"Remove your underwear. Do it slowly so I can watch."

The way he orders me makes me all hot and tingly. Why do his commands turn me on this much?

Hooking my fingers on either side of my boy shorts, I drag them down my legs as slow as I can, getting drunk on the sinful way he watches me. He's like a predator, ready to jump and feast on my flesh.

Once the underwear hangs from my fingers, Aiden extends his hand. "Now, give them to me."

I do, and he places them in his pocket like they always belonged there.

Why on earth is that so hot?

Still keeping eye contact, he yanks down his jeans and boxer briefs.

The view of his hard, throbbing cock causes my own thighs to quiver.

He runs a hand from the base of his dick to the top. I'm so enchanted by the view, my mouth parts.

"You're going to wrap those lips around my cock, aren't you, sweetheart?"

I nod absentmindedly, watching the streak of precum glistening at the tip of his cock. I want to lick that, suck it, and swallow it whole.

He lies on the ground opposite me, his dick in front of my face.

"Put your mouth on it."

I don't think twice.

With a deep breath, I take him into my mouth as far as I can. I lick and suck him off, my fingers cupping his balls.

I'm barely getting used to his size when cold air tickles my most intimate part. Aiden's head disappears under my skirt and his lips find my soaked folds.

The intimate contact leaves me breathless for a minute.

"Don't stop," he rasps against my entrance, his slight stubble creating harsh friction over my soaked folds.

"I promised you'll come over my lips while you're sucking my cock."

A shiver shoots down my core, making it all slick and sensitive. I use both my hands and lips to lick and stroke his cock.

Aiden feasts on me, teasing the delicate nub before he thrusts in and out of my opening. He's literally tongue-fucking me.

I'm so full of him it becomes unreal. I don't stop sucking him, giving it my all despite the amount of stimuli he's pushing through my body.

The pre-cum coats my tongue, salty and tantalising. I fasten my pace and only stop when he nibbles on my clit.

A full-body shiver takes over me as the orgasm sweeps through me from the inside out.

I open my mouth, letting Aiden thrust his hips a few more times. He comes so deep in my throat, I hardly taste anything. There's only an aftertaste when he pulls out of my mouth.

I'm so boneless, I can barely move or think. My lids flutter with the intensity of the orgasm he wrenched out of me.

"Come here, sweetheart."

I crawl and land in Aiden's embrace. Our clothes are all over the place, both of us half-naked and dishevelled, but it feels right.

It feels *so* right.

He pulls my skirt down and tucks himself in ever so effortlessly. His strong arms surround me and I know I'm going to be all right.

Just like back then.

A flashlight explodes in my head like fireworks.

Just like back then.

The memories flood my brain so fast, so hard I don't know how to stop them even if I could.

Just like back then…

THIRTY

Elsa

Past

I stand hidden in the balcony, not making a sound.

Daddy is talking to Uncle Agnus about work and stuff. When he's done, I'm going to tell him about Grey Eyes.

After Daddy helps him, I'll visit his home and we'll become best friends.

Uncle Agnus stands beside Daddy, who's sitting on the sofa. That uncle doesn't like sitting around much. He doesn't like to talk much either.

Daddy's jacket and tie are thrown on the table; his face appears tired.

Everyone has been saying Uncle Reg is no more. I asked Uncle Agnus what 'no more' means since he's Uncle Reg's brother, and he said it means he went to Eli.

I hope he'll take care of him in that place called heaven.

Uncle Agnus squeezes Dad's shoulder. "It'll all work out, Ethan."

"It will, Agnus." Dad staggers to his feet. "It will."

Uncle Agnus lets him go. "Where are you going?"

"To Elsa." He smiles. "I haven't spent time with my princess in a long time."

"Before that, there's something I need to tell you."

Dad stops, but doesn't turn around. "About?"

"Abigail. It appears she has been hiding Jonathan's son."

"*What?*" Dad whirls around so fast, I flinch.

Uncle Agnus remains unaffected, his expression as serene as always. It's like he's a rock, a solid rock Daddy can lean on. "Reginald kept him under her order."

Dad's jaw works. "Why am I only finding out about it now?"

"Because I just found out myself. One of the staff heard sounds near the basement area."

"Sounds," Daddy repeats slowly. "What type of *sounds?*"

"Whimpers. Cries."

"Fuck." Dad kicks the table. "Fucking fuck!"

"She's hurting children again, Ethan. You need to do something about it this time." He pauses. "If you don't, Elsa will be next."

"Don't you think I fucking know that?" Daddy's shoulders rise and drop with harsh breaths. "I'll send her back to the psych ward."

"And this time, don't get her out for Christ's sake."

"You want me to tell you were right all along, Agnus? Is that it?"

"I'm always right, Ethan. You wouldn't be in this predicament if you listened to me and didn't marry her."

"If I didn't marry her, I wouldn't have Elsa. I would repeat it all over again if I was given the choice. Only this time, I would lock her in for her and everyone else's sake."

Uncle Agnus' expression doesn't change. "I'll be downstairs if you need anything."

"Go home. Check on Knox and Teal and get some rest." Dad sighs, running a hand over his face. "Reginald was a backstabbing traitor, but he was your brother."

"I have no brother who betrays you. I'll check on the staff and security before I go." Uncle Agnus nods and heads outside.

Daddy is leaving, too.

Shoot. He can't go and not find me in bed.

Besides, he has to help Grey Eyes. I *promised* him. He must be waiting for me.

"D—"

The word dies in my throat when Mum barges inside.

She's wearing her beautiful red dress with ribbons that flutter over her waist. Her cherry perfume smells good even all the way here. Tears stream down her cheeks, but she doesn't appear sad. She appears… lost.

My fingers dig into the curtains as I hide behind the patio door.

"Abby." Dad steps back in the room letting her in.

"Ethan… I-I think I hurt Eli."

"You hurt Eli, how?" he asks slowly.

"He… he wouldn't stop bleeding." She shows him her hands soaked in red. "He wouldn't stop bleeding, Ethan. He wouldn't talk to me anymore… I only wanted him to be strong. Is it wrong to want my children strong? That's why I take Elsa to swim in the lake, you know."

"You take Elsa to swim in the lake?" Dad grinds his teeth.

Oh, no. He'll be angry and them monsters will come out.

Ma's eyes become clear, almost haunting as she saunters to Daddy's desk and sits behind it. Placing one foot over the other, she speaks in a determined tone, "Of course, I do. She doesn't know how to swim. I have to teach her so she doesn't drown like Eli. She can't be a Steel if she's weak."

"Abby…" Dad grits out, but he turns away from her to take a deep breath. "We'll go somewhere tomorrow, okay? Now, I'll go check on the boy. Jonathan would go berserk if something happens to him."

Yes! I knew Daddy would help him.

He takes two steps in the direction of the door.

"Stop…" Mum calls in a trembling voice. "S-stop it, Ethan. I-I won't forgive you if you take Eli away from me."

"He's not Eli, Abby. He's Jonathan's only fucking son." He marches to the door. "I'll come back once —"

A loud bang echoes through the air.

Dad staggers backwards and falls against a chair. A large spot of red explodes on the back and the front of his white shirt.

D-Daddy?

His face morphs into utter confusion as he looks behind him.

Ma stands there, holding Daddy's gun while crying. She's crying so hard, her body shakes and the weapon nearly drops from her hand.

"W-why… Abby?" Dad croaks. "Why?"

"You c-can't take Eli from me. Not even you, Ethan. Not even you…" She strides out of the room, the gun in her hands.

"D-Daddy?"

I run inside. My little feet skid to a halt.

Blood.

A pool of blood and Daddy lies in it.

My ears ring as I approach him. "D-Daddy! You p-promised you won't leave me like Eli."

"E-Elsa…" He breathes harshly, flopping down against the floor. "I… need you to do something for me, princess."

"Anything, Daddy."

"Run to your uncle Agnus the fastest you can."

"No," I sob. "I won't leave you."

"R-Run!"

"Daddy!"

"RUN!"

Suddenly, harsh hands pull me by the hair and the strands rip at the roots.

Ma's manic blue eyes bore into mine. "Elsa! What did you give Eli? What did I tell you about not going to the basement?"

"M-Ma… Daddy is hurt." I cry. "He's hurt."

"You'll end up like him if you don't do as I say." She drags me behind her.

"Daddy! Daddy!" I screech and wail in her hold.

"A-Abby…" he breathes, his face pale and lifeless—like Eli's. "Leave her alone. She didn't do anything."

"She gave Eli chocolate when it's bad for his health! That's why he wouldn't wake up," she snarls. "Don't worry, Ethan, I'll make her a good girl."

"Abby…" Dad holds out his hand in my direction. It's all red. So, *so* red.

I reach out my hand to him as well, struggling against Ma. "Daddy!"

"L-Leave her… Abby…"

She smiles even though her face is full of tears. "We'll be right back, honey. Love you."

Ma drags me behind her. I struggle against her hold, fighting and crying. Them monsters in Ma's eyes are laughing at me. They're going to take Daddy just like they took Eli.

Then, they're going to come back for me.

"Now, Elsa." Ma's grip tightens around my hair. "We're going to fix Eli, okay?"

"Daddy!" I cry, my voice is so thick, it's hoarse.

If I lose Daddy like I lost Eli, I won't be able to stay here anymore. I can't stay with Ma and them monsters in her eyes.

She hauls me down the stairs towards the basement. My feet shake the longer we walk down.

The door swings against the wall as she kicks it open. My feet turn into stones.

Grey Eyes.

There's a large patch of red on the back of his shirt. He faces the wall and he's not moving.

Why isn't he moving?

"Wake up!" I shriek. "You have to escape them monsters in Ma's eyes."

He doesn't even stir.

"Eli, your sister is here." Ma coos in a soft voice, reaching into her dress's pocket and retrieving a set of keys. "Come on, baby, let's go outside. You love it outside."

I stare at the keys in Ma's hands and then back to Grey Eyes.

"Eli, if you don't wake up, Ma is going to be mad, okay?" Her voice hardens, eyes darting back and forth.

"I'll wake him up." I wipe my cheeks with the back of my hands. "Give me the keys and I'll wake him."

"Very well, darling." She places the keys in my hands. "You're such a good girl. Daddy's girl. I was Daddy's girl, too."

I don't listen to her. As soon as I have the keys, I jog to the boy who added colours to my days and free the cuff at his ankle. His skin is covered in red like his back.

"Grey Eyes." Big fat tears fall on his pale face as I clutch his cheeks. "Grey Eyes, please… You… You promised…"

Why does everyone keep breaking their promises? First Eli, then Dad, and now him.

His skin is on fire. Sweat beads down his forehead and brows.

"Are you done yet?" Ma asks from the entrance, her voice growing impatient. It's bad if Ma loses her patience. She'll let them monsters do as they like.

"Please… Please…" I stroke his black hair back. It's sweaty and damp.

He stirs, his eyes slowly fluttering open. Blinking twice, he mutters, "Elsa?"

"Yes, it's me!" I grab him by the arm. "Come on, we have to go."

He staggers to his feet, slightly leaning on me.

We slowly reach my ma. She watches us with a serene look on her face. "My babies."

Aiden glares up at her even though he only reaches her waist.

"Go first, Eli." I smile at him. "Ma and I will follow. Right, Ma?"

She nods slowly.

He stares at me and hisses, "What are you doing? We have to leave the red woman. She has a *gun*."

"Go, Eli!" I push him towards the entrance.

"No." He digs his fingers into my arm. "We'll go together."

"I'll meet you outside," I murmur. "Once you get help, I'll find you."

"Elsa…" His expression is pained, and the plea in his voice almost makes me cry.

I don't.

I have to be strong.

"Remember." I grin. "You promised you'll marry me."

When he doesn't move, I push him out and slam the door shut behind him.

My chest heaves, rising and falling so fast as I lean against the door. A bang comes from the other side, then another and another.

He's trying to come back inside, but I won't let him. I won't let them monsters take him away.

I'll protect him.

Ma frowns, fingering her gun. "What are you doing? Let's follow your brother."

"He's not my brother, Ma. Eli went to heaven."

Her face contorts, nostrils flaring. "I told you not to say his name."

"Eli! Eli! Eli!" I scream. "His name is Eli, Ma! And I want to say his name. I want to talk about him. I want to —"

I hear the bang before I can feel it.

The pain goes through my body all of a sudden like fire-works. It's burning me on the inside.

"M-Ma…"

She's pointing the gun at me, her face filled with tears. They fall down her beautiful dress as I drop to the floor.

My bones feel like they're crushing beneath me.

"Elsa… B-baby… I'm so sorry, Ma is s-so sorry. Oh, God! Oh, God! What have I done?" She crouches beside me. The gun hits the floor as she presses her hands over my chest.

Blood flows from between my lips and I taste metal as she becomes a blur.

The pain takes me over and seeps under my skin. It hurts,

but maybe it's fine now. Because them monsters are gone from Ma's eyes. They disappeared, giving me back my ma.

She's crying loudly as she fumbles over me, pressing her hands and tearing her dress to cover my chest.

"DAAA!" She screams, her voice hysterical. "It's all because of you, Da. You made me like this. You *killed* me."

"M-Ma…"

"Hush little baby, don't you cry. Everything is going to be all right…" Still pressing a hand over my wound, she retrieves the gun and puts it under her chin. "Ma is coming, baby. Ma will make it all right, Eli."

And then she pulls the trigger.

THIRTY-ONE

Aiden

Present

I wrap my arms around Elsa as she cries softly into my chest. She's been crying for such a long time. When I think no more tears will come, out a new wave hits her and she succumbs to it all over again.

I knew there would be repercussions when she remembers her past.

That day was the darkest day of her life. She lost both her parents and a large chunk of herself.

Back then, I thought she was gone, too.

I thought it was all over.

The memory of that time when I no longer heard her voice has been a constant part of my nightmares.

It's even worse than the red woman and her torture.

When you have a light in the middle of the darkness and that light dims to nothing, it fucks you up.

That's why my world became black after that.

I stroke her shoulder as she weeps quietly. My hand glides over the curve of her throat and stop at her pulse. Her beating, throbbing pulse. It's a constant reminder that she's alive, not dead.

Her scar is proof she doesn't have that gush in her chest.

Her bright blond hair isn't soaked in red like when she lay there lifeless.

That's why I'm obsessed with those three parts of her.

I gather her close to me and her body trembles.

I'm ready to do anything to stop her from crying and hanging on to pieces from the past. However, having her hold on to me as if I'm her lifeline stirs the beast inside me.

For the rest of our lives, I want to be the only one who witnesses her breaking and support her through the storm. I want to be the one who soothes her ache when she needs soothing. The one who wipes her tears when they need wiping. The one who lifts her up when she needs lifting.

I want to be there for her, full stop.

She's mine. Fucking *mine*.

It's not only her body or her heart that I'm interested in, I want her entire soul so she'll never be able to leave me.

Some would argue this isn't the right thing, but fuck the right thing.

Elsa and I didn't meet under the right circumstances. We just met, and then we re-met, and then we became inseparable.

Maybe there'll come a day where I don't need her as much as I need air. There will come a day when I wake up in the morning and the first thought won't be about her.

Though, I doubt it. That day will only come with death.

I run the pad of my thumb under her swollen eyes, wiping the moisture away. Elsa leans into my touch, slowly closing her eyes.

Fuck *me*.

Her small methods of showing affection get me every fucking time. I like it when she stops fighting our connection and snuggles into me like I'm her world.

Like she also can't live without me.

One day, she'll be more open about her feelings and how much she wants me. One day, she'll wake up beside me and see me, not our past.

It'll take effort and a lot of persuasion, because Elsa's brain is wired differently from mine. While I don't give a fuck about what happened and only see our future together, Elsa is plagued by the past and won't be whole unless she makes peace with it.

She has been chained to invisible trauma and demons for ten years. Knowing her, she must feel guilty about erasing her memories.

It'll take her some time to come to terms with what happened, pick up the pieces and move on.

I'll be with her every step of the way.

"Do you…" She hiccoughs over her words, drawing unsteady breaths. "Do you think it would've been different if Dad put her in the psych ward?"

"We can never know. The decision wasn't ours to make."

For some reason, this makes it worse, not better. Truth is, if Elsa and I were in Jonathan and Ethan's shoes, we could've probably made the same wrong decision.

The human mind doesn't work based on theories or what-ifs. It's heavily chained to circumstances. We were children back then. We knew nothing.

Jonathan and Ethan's mistakes are their own. Elsa and I will make sure to never make the same ones.

Resting her head on my bicep, she stares up at me with teary, blue eyes. "What happened to you after that?"

"I heard the gunshots."

She gasps. "You… did?"

"I hit the door and called your name, but you never answered."

It was the last time I called her name. I can almost feel the ache in my chest as I hit that door until my knuckles were bloodied.

"Then I finally managed to open the door. You and the red woman were lying there"—I point to a spot near the entrance—"in a pool of blood. You were on your side with a dark hole in your chest. Half of the red woman's face was gone, spluttered all over the wall and the floor, but I didn't look twice in her direction. You know why?" I dig my fingers into the flesh of her scar over her shirt. "You weren't moving."

She places her hand over mine. "I'm so sorry you had to see that."

"I thought you were dead."

"I'm not. I'm here, Aiden."

She is. This isn't a dream or a nightmare. She's right here with me.

Like she promised.

"Did you find your way out of the mansion?" she asks.

"No. I think I fainted or something. The next thing I knew, I was in a hospital and Jonathan was sitting beside me. One of his insiders or security guards must've gotten me out." I smile with no humour. "The moment I opened my eyes and saw him instead of Alicia, I knew something was wrong."

She surrounds my arm with her small hand. "I'm so sorry about Alicia."

"Stop apologising." I lift her chin so I'm staring down at those hypnotic eyes. "You're not to blame. You were a victim as well."

Her bottom lip trembles like when she was about to cry as a child. "You didn't see me as a victim, Aiden. You told me you'll destroy me the first time I stepped into RES."

"That day, I saw the ghost of the red woman. And yes, Elsa. I was angry at you for not keeping your promise. I was even more pissed off that you didn't remember me, so I wanted you to pay." I grin. "Then I decided you're mine."

Her adorable features light up. "That's a drastic change."

I lift a shoulder. "Could be."

"And you've been such a dickhead."

"You still love me."

Her cheeks redden, but she remains quiet.

"Say it," I grip her chin tighter.

"Aiden..." I can see hesitation in her eyes, hear the quivering in her voice. Soon, she'll be hiding in her frozen castle, refusing everyone access.

"Say it, Elsa," My tone becomes harsh and non-negotiable.

A sigh rips from her. "I love you, Aiden. No matter what."

"No matter what, huh?"

"Yes, dickhead. No matter what."

She wraps her small arm around my midsection and buries her face in my chest. I rest my chin on the top of her golden locks and inhale her coconut scent.

"You used to smell like cotton candies and summer," I tell her. "And fucking Maltesers."

"Hey!" She pushes at my chest. "Don't go insulting my Maltesers. I love them, okay? Besides, you should be honoured I shared them with you. They're delicious."

"Not really. I only ate them because you kept shoving them down my throat."

"You ungrateful arsehole."

I chuckle, running my fingers through her hair. "I haven't eaten them since back then."

"Me neither. I remember wanting them when I was a kid, but Aunt's strict diet didn't allow me regular chocolate and sweets. I never asked Uncle for them, though." Elsa pauses. "I guess deep down, I knew I shouldn't eat them alone."

"I'll buy them for you." I smile.

"I'll share."

We remain like that for a few minutes. For a moment, I forget that we're in the basement where the red woman tortured me and then died.

I forgot the sight of Elsa lying motionless in her own blood.

For a while, it's just me and her finding our roots.

When I kidnapped her here, all I wanted was to give her back the connection to her past. Not knowing what would happen was dangerous and left me with no backup plans—except for really kidnapping her and never returning.

I'm not comfortable with the unknown. I thought if she

remembered she saved me on the expense of her mother's death and her own metaphorical death, she'd hate me.

"Do you regret saving me?" I ask in the quietness of the room.

It's the only vulnerable question I've allowed myself over the years. Her mother would still be alive if she didn't save me.

Her electric blue eyes bore into mine with a deep sense of affection. "I regret many things, but saving you was never one of them. You were my light and I had to protect you."

"Even if the cost was your mother's life and your memories?"

"That's mental illness. It's neither yours nor my fault."

I nod once.

I doubt she truly believes that, but I'll let it pass. We have the entire future to revisit this.

"Who do you think saved me?" she asks.

"I don't know. I was already passed out at the time."

She bites her lower lip like she does when in deep thoughts. I lean down and kiss it, making her blush.

"I remember how Ma pulled the trigger, but I don't remember hearing your voice," she muses. "Then… Someone held me and —" She gasps. "Oh, my God! There was someone else."

THIRTY-TWO

Elsa

Past

I'm moving.

The ground shifts from underneath me and someone holds me in their arms.

Daddy?

No. Daddy needs help.

It's dark in here. I can't open my eyes. I can't speak.

I can only remain motionless as someone carries me. The faint shuffling of footsteps is the only thing I hear.

"You'll be fine. You're Steel's legacy."

The voice is distant, almost from another room. Or maybe is it from another place?

My head lolls against the arm carrying me.

Daddy. Save Daddy, too.

Did Grey Eyes leave safely?

I want to ask those questions and more, but my mouth doesn't move. Nothing moves.

A small whimper reaches me from the ground. The sound is so haunting and pained, it rips through me.

Ma?

Am I imagining it?

The sound comes again like a howl in the winter.

This time, the one carrying me stops and turns around.

"You just wouldn't die, would you?" The voice sounds disapproving, angry almost. "You don't deserve this life, Abigail and we both know that. It'll all end today."

And just like that, they march ahead. The whimpers grow far and quiet the more he walks. We're leaving Ma behind. Why?

I'm trapped in and out of the darkness as if we're playing hide-and-seek.

The person strides on and on.

I want to call for Daddy or Ma, but I can't.

When I think they'll never stop walking, they halt and place me on something soft. "Take her to the hospital. Call Blair and Jaxon Quinn, then watch from afar. Don't interfere, and only make sure she's safe."

Daddy. Daddy. Save Daddy.

"Burn the whole mansion down," the voice says in a sure tone.

"Are there any survivors inside?" Someone else asks.

"No," the voice says. "We're leaving. Now."

Daddy.

Daddy is still in there.

And Ma, too.

My eyes flutter open the slightest bit. Two men climb into the back of a black van. One of them is Dr Shepherd, Dad's personal doctor.

He leans over a body wearing a bloodied white shirt.

It's Daddy.

Don't leave me.

The other man sits on Dad's other side, watching him closely.

"Burn it," he tells a man in black standing near the van.

The man speaks into his hand and the mansion catches on fire.

I stare at the man beside Dad through blurry eyes. He watches the house being eaten by flames with a neutral expression as if there isn't a person inside. A person whimpering and asking for help.

"Let's go," he commands and the van flies down the road with other black cars following it.

His voice.

It's him.

The one who told my ma she doesn't deserve this life and that it'll end today.

The one who's currently burning my ma inside.

The one who's taking Daddy away like heaven took away Eli.

The one without emotions as he does it all.

Uncle Agnus.

THIRTY-THREE

Elsa

Present

I jump to my feet, my heart thundering viciously in my chest.

Agnus.

Uncle Agnus.

He's the one behind the fire and the one who killed my mother. Well, she shot herself, but she wasn't dead yet. He burned the mansion down while knowing she was in it.

He was by my father's side all this time, and he kept an eye on me.

For what?

All this is completely abnormal.

Aiden stands and wraps my jacket around my shoulder. "What is it? Did you remember something crucial?"

My eyes bore into his darker ones, and my breathing calms down a little. "It was Agnus. He saved me and Dad, but he killed my mother."

A frown etches between his brows. "Your mother was already dead."

"No! I heard her whimpers and so did he when he carried me out of the basement, but do you know what he did? He just walked the fuck out. He wanted her dead, Aiden. He burned the mansion while she was in it."

I'm shaking, my entire body going into some sort of shock and anger all at once. "He killed her… He killed my mother."

"Calm down, Elsa." Aiden rubs my arm, his voice strong but soothing.

"I can't calm down! He killed Ma, Aiden!"

"She shot herself," he grinds out, holding on to patience he doesn't own. "She wanted to die."

"Just because you wanted her to die doesn't mean she wanted to die."

His left eye twitches and I regret the words as soon as I say them. What the hell is wrong with me?

Ma is a monster in Aiden's eyes. She was a monster to me as well, but I keep holding on to the fact that at some point she was my ma. Sweet and caring and with a blinding smile.

"I-I'm sorry, Aiden. I didn't mean —"

"I never wanted her to die. I only wanted her to leave me the fuck alone." He squares his shoulders. "You're better off without her. She shot you and your father. What else do you need to let her go?"

My lips tremble and I fight the need to hit and scream at him.

I don't because he's right.

Ma was messed up, but maybe I'm messed up, too, if I can't completely hate her.

Once we return, I need to talk to Dr Khan.

What if I eventually become like her? What if my trauma will take over my life like her trauma has taken over hers?

The door clicks open.

Both Aiden and I stand side by side as the newcomer steps into the basement. My hands ball into fists on either side of me.

Agnus.

Remaining at the door, he places both hands in his pockets.

He appears different now, more monstrous and vicious.

Agnus, Dad's right hand man, Knox and Teal's caretaker, our saviour, but he's also a murderer.

That knowledge makes his features sharper, younger and harsher.

His light hair is styled back and his pale blue eyes appear serene. Confident. Just like when he ordered his men to burn down the mansion while Ma whimpered in it.

I start towards him, but Aiden wraps his hand around my arm protectively.

Agnus retrieves a cigarette from a pack, but he keeps it between his thumb and forefinger without lighting it.

That must be the source of cigarettes' smell in the basement.

"How did you know we'd be here?" I ask.

"I get a direct notification when this door is opened."

"Does Dad know about this?"

"He doesn't need to." Agnus pauses. "Yet."

The thought that Dad trusts him burns at the back of my throat like acid.

"I assume you remember now," Agnus continues. "I told Ethan you'd remember if you come down here, but he's stubborn when it comes to emotions."

"You killed my mother," I breathe, my face going up in flames.

"Shut up, Elsa," Aiden whispers harshly, but only I can hear him. "Don't provoke him when we have no exit plan."

He digs his fingers into my arm, keeping me in place. He's watching our surroundings, probably searching for a way out.

"What will you do?" Agnus asks with that infuriating confidence. "Tell Ethan?"

I swallow my rage even though I want to poke his eyes out. It kills me that this man has been on Dad's side after he erased Ma from the face of the earth.

However, Aiden is right. I have to be rational about this.

"What if I do tell Dad?" I ask slowly.

Agnus twirls the cigarette between his fingers. "You saw Abigail dead."

"She wasn't dead. She was whimpering and pleading for help."

"And I helped her."

"By burning her?"

"By offering her a way out, yes. Half her head was gone. She was going to die either way." He watches the floor as if she was still lying there, moaning in pain. "Besides, Abigail has been the living dead since Eli's drowning. I respect her choice of finally putting herself and everyone else out of their misery."

"You don't regret it, do you?"

"The only thing I regret is not forcing Ethan to send her to the psych ward sooner. A miscalculation on my part, unfortunately. If he did, neither Knox nor Teal nor Aiden would've been hurt. If he did, both of you wouldn't have been shot and separated for ten years. So no, Elsa. I don't regret purging Abigail from the life she didn't want in the first place."

He's a psychopath, isn't he?

If he's so detached after killing someone, he must be some sort of a psycho.

However, as I hear his argument, I can finally see why he did it. I can finally see why Aiden thinks it was the right thing.

Ma wanted to kill me and Dad.

Ma stopped being my mother the moment Eli died. She drowned with him in that lake and since then, she tried everything to bring us all down to her hell.

The fact I wanted her to live isn't only an insult to Dad and I, but it's also an insult to the three children she traumatised; Knox, Teal, and Aiden.

It's an insult to the promise I made to Aiden ten years ago.

I had hoped to have everything, but it was impossible.

One way or another, Ma would've ended our family just like her family ended.

"If you think you're so righteous," I ask Agnus. "Why didn't you tell Dad about what you'd done?"

"Like you, he has irrational feelings towards Abigail. He would've wanted her to live even after she shot you both." He pauses speaking, still twirling the cigarette. "I've been by Ethan's side since we were ten years old. I know from experience that if he stops trusting someone, he'll cut them completely out of his life. I can't afford that."

"What if I tell him?" I try to keep the challenge out of my voice.

"You won't, Elsa. Ethan lost so much. First Eli then Abigail and then ten years of his life. He finally thinks he can start anew with you, Knox, and Teal. If you tell him unnecessary things, he'll cut me from his life, but he won't cope well with it. If you want to be the reason behind that, then by all means, go right ahead."

"Are you threatening me?"

"I'm simply stating facts."

I narrow my eyes. "Sounds like a threat to me."

He smiles without humour. "Believe me, this isn't how I issue threats. You're lucky to be amongst the few people I'll never threaten."

We maintain a war of gazes for what seems like an hour. Agnus doesn't flinch or even blink.

A stone. He's a damn stone.

"He's right." Aiden faces me. "Steel Corporation remained standing because of Agnus. If he leaves, it'll backfire on your father badly, especially with the competition between him and Jonathan."

"You're supposed to be on my side." I glare at him.

"I am, sweetheart. That's why I'm telling you to disregard your emotions and give free reign to your brain." He strokes my cheek. "Deep down, you know this is the best thing to do."

"I'll give you time to think about it." Agnus places the cigarette to his lips. "It won't be long before Ethan finds out you're missing. I disabled the ability to open the door from the inside. Stay here and process everything carefully, Elsa."

The door clicks shut behind him.

Aiden runs to the entrance and up the stairs, but it's too late. The metal door is already blinking red.

I stand by his side and press my finger on the screen. It continues blinking in red.

"Fuck," Aiden curses.

"Did he just lock us in?" I murmur in astonishment.

"The phones are outside," Aiden curses again.

"I can't believe he did that. Dad will never forgive him."

"He wants you to think carefully about what to say to your father." Aiden glances at me. "He probably doesn't want to hurt you. If you give him what he wants, he'll let us out."

"How? He locked us in." I contain a frustrated yell.

The psycho.

I can't believe I've never seen the signs before. I thought his quiet nature was because he preferred helping Dad from the background, and while he did, he also plotted chaos.

Even back then, Agnus didn't seem sad about Uncle Reg's death, his twin brother and only family.

He only cared about the fact that Uncle Reg betrayed Dad by siding up with Jonathan and helping Ma.

A scary thought whirls into my brain.

"What if he..." I gulp, the idea hitting me like a hurricane. "What if he hurts Dad?"

"He didn't save him to hurt him," Aiden says. "Besides, think about it. All of Agnus' motives lead back to Ethan. I say he'd never hurt him."

"How do you know that?"

He grins, a sadism so deep ignites in his cloudy eyes. "I know my kind when I meet one."

"Your... kind?"

"Agnus and I are the same. We don't mind creating anarchy if it gets us what we want."

"So he's planning anarchy?"

"He already did with that fire."

"This only means he's unstoppable."

He raises an eyebrow. "Am I unstoppable, sweetheart?"

"You are."

"How about when it comes to you?"

"You still are… sometimes. I mean, I know you care about me, but that doesn't mean you're politically correct."

"And I'll never be." He dismisses ever so casually. "In your mind, do I want to hurt or protect you?"

"Protect me." I don't even think about it.

Aiden might've wanted to hurt me at the beginning, but that's changed. He doesn't want to inflict pain on me anymore—except during sex sometimes, but that's part of our foreplay.

Aiden is my number one protector now, and I can admit it out loud.

"Agnus is like me," he emphasises every word. "He's just like *me*."

The realisation hits me like an eruption of a volcano. "He wants to protect my dad."

"Exactly."

I gasp. "Do you think he has feelings for him? Is he… gay?"

"Could be. Could be not."

"I mean I didn't notice anything between him and Dad, but…" I trail off, raking my head for any suspicious moments but come up with nothing—at least from the outside looking in.

"He could only care about being his right hand and best friend," Aiden says. "With people like Agnus, you'll never know unless he says it out loud."

I ponder on his words. Now that I think about it, Agnus took Knox and Teal in because Dad asked him to. He saved and watched me from afar because he knows how much I mean to Dad.

All his actions lead back to my father's well-being.

Well, all except for locking me in a basement with no way out.

That reality of things hits me hard when Aiden pulls and pushes the door with no result.

We're trapped.

THIRTY-FOUR

Ethan

When I think back on my life, I'm left with the bitter feeling that I accomplished nothing.

It doesn't even have anything to do with the nine years I spent sleeping while the world moved on around me.

I dreamt a lot about normal family life during those years. About Abby's angelic smile, Eli's laughs, and Elsa's giggles.

Little things. Impossible things.

Because the truth of the matter is, Agnus was right. I started a family with a mentally unstable woman, and I was too smitten to think straight.

I started a family with a woman who shouldn't have given birth.

Elsa will never know this, but it was because of Abby's neglect that Eli drowned. She removed his swimming jacket and asked him to go into the water. She told him to be free.

She confessed all that to me at his funeral.

Perhaps that's why Abby lost all her bearings after his death. Her notion of freedom is different than any of us.

Abby was damaged since a young age. She was broken but smiled. She was innocent but wanted to be wild.

She was different, and that's exactly why I was attracted to her. I was a moth drawn to a flame that eventually burned me.

If I could redo the past, I would lock Abby away the second Elsa was born. I would've followed the therapist's recommendation and kept her away from children.

The truth of the matter is, I was selfish, and there's no way to fix my selfishness now.

That's why it feels like I accomplished nothing in my forty-four-years-old life. Business ventures and economic success don't count. I couldn't even protect my employees from the fire ten years ago.

However, as I stare at Teal and hear her words, I can't help the smile that breaks across my face. I might not have accomplished much, but I at least saved her and Knox. They're the best thing that happened to my life after Elsa.

And Agnus.

I let Teal finish talking. She's speaking fast, skipping over words, and blurting out what's inside her.

Teal isn't talkative, but when she does speak, she doesn't know how to stop. I let her get on with it, because if I interrupt her flow, she'll lose her chain of thoughts.

"You don't have to do that," I tell her once she's finished. "I'll find another way."

"No." She stomps her foot while standing up. "I'm in, Dad. I made my decision."

"Think more carefully about it, Teal."

"I have. That's why I'm talking to you. I want to do this."

"Do what?" Knox barges in, dropping on the armrest of Teal's chair.

I shake my head. The kid is a headache. He's so lively and energetic, it drives me bonkers sometimes.

He always goes around saying he wants to be my best son, threatening both Elsa and Teal so they don't step the line. He already is, I just don't tell him that so he doesn't lose his energy.

Knox has an infuriating habit of losing interest once he gets what he wants.

"What are you gonna do, T?" He pulls on his sister's strands. "Don't tell me Dad agreed to let you pierce your belly button."

"Pierce your belly button?" I stare at her.

She elbows Knox, cheeks flushing.

"Uh-Oh. You didn't know that?" He grins at me. "Forget I said anything."

"Piercing your skin is off the table, Teal," I tell her in my stern voice.

They still suffer trauma from sharp objects, Teal more than Knox. She puts on a brave façade, but I won't let her go on with that idea.

"Screw you, Knox." She glares at him and he merely lifts a shoulder.

"Where's Elsa?" I ask her. "We need to tell her about your decision."

"Ah, she went out yesterday evening." Knox offers.

"Went out?" I thought she was in her room all this time. That's why I didn't want to disturb her.

"Aiden King took her away in his car." Knox waggles his brows. "I saw them when I was flirting with the neighbour. Eh, I mean greeting the neighbour."

Aiden King took her.

My muscles tense. Where could he have taken her for the entire night?

I call her. No answer.

Fuck.

"Do you have his friends' numbers?" I ask Knox.

"One second." He takes out his phone and types something in it then puts it to his ear. "Hey Ro, have you seen Aiden?"

Silence.

"I see, I see. Hide well. Talk to you later, mate." He hangs up and faces me. "None of them have seen him. He's not picking up either. Ronan said he's hiding in his home because Aiden will come for his head any second now."

This is bad.

If Aiden is not picking up either, this could mean two things.

They ran away.

Or they were taken.

I scratch my chin, thinking about the possibilities. Despite the fact that Aiden's character is too infuriatingly similar to Jonathan's, he wouldn't hurt Elsa. Not with the amount of care and possessiveness I've seen in his eyes in my office.

And Elsa wouldn't leave without informing me first.

This leaves one option: something happened to them. With or without consent.

Bloody hell.

I scroll through my phone and find the one name I didn't want to contact until the day I die.

Our friendship morphed into a rivalry for a reason. Both of us hate losing and do everything in our power to become number one.

But fate has a funny way of messing with our lives.

I hit his number. He answers after two rings, "Are you ready to admit defeat?"

"We have a problem, Jonathan."

THIRTY-FIVE

Elsa

We sit in here for what seems like days.

According to Aiden's watch, it's only been one day.

We've been here for exactly thirty-five hours and counting.

We did all. We tried the door, we screamed—or more like, I screamed. However, there was no sign anyone would come to help.

There was a reason why Ma chose this place. It's on the far eastern side, no one wanders here, and I'm pretty sure it conceals sounds somehow.

My energy has been waning over the past hours. We have nothing aside from water from the tap.

No food. No blankets. Just like ten years ago.

It's not cold per se, but a slight tremor has been going through my limbs since the door closed behind Agnus.

There's a tightness in my chest, suffocating and bruising. Now that I think about it, I flew out of the house without taking my meds the moment Aiden texted me.

Please don't act up now, heart. It's super bad timing.

Aiden's sitting, his back against the wall as I nestle between his long, powerful legs. My back rests against his chest and my head lies on his hard shoulder.

It's weird how such a hard muscle can be so comforting.

"Maybe he won't come back for us," I whisper into the silence. "Maybe he decided it's better if I'm out of the way?"

"He will."

"How do you know that? What if he has an accident and dies and no one will come for us?"

"Now you're being dramatic, sweetheart."

"It's a possibility."

I lift my head and watch him closely; his neutral expression and undisturbed eyes. How can he be so calm about this? While I've been losing hope, shaking, and pacing, he's been sitting here as if we're on a picnic or something.

Granted, he's more cool-headed than me, but this is a life or death situation. My head's crowding with horrific images about how they'll find our corpses months from now, decayed and stinking.

Tears fill my eyes. I don't want to die. Not now.

Not when I'm ready to overcome my trauma. Not when I'm finally getting control over my life.

"Hey." Aiden's lean fingers cradle my face and stroke my trembling chin.

"I can't stop thinking about dying."

"Then let's occupy that head of yours with something else." He grins, and my aching heart flutters with sparks.

"Like what?"

"Since you're a curious little kitten, I'll let you ask me any question you like."

My eyes widen. "Any question?"

He nods.

Whoa. That's some commitment for the devil.

I straighten so my back is propped up against his bent knee. "And you'll answer them all."

We need to get that straight, because 'you can ask me any question' in Aiden's manipulative words can also mean he'll choose not to answer.

His grin widens as if he can read my mind. "And I'll answer them on one condition."

Of course.

I huff. "What?"

"You'll remove a piece of clothing for every question I answer."

"Hey! That's not fair."

He lifts a shoulder. "Take it or leave it."

I should've known the deal would end up playing in his favour.

My jacket lies on his lap. I try to retrieve it. I need all the clothes I can get.

Aiden snatches it away. "This was already off. It doesn't count."

Dickhead.

Since my underwear is already somewhere in his pocket from the earlier sixty-nine, that only leaves me with three pieces of clothing; my shirt, my skirt, and my bra.

Three items, three questions.

I glare at him.

The arsehole must've thought this through.

Still, I'll play. He's right. I need to get my head off the dark thoughts swirling inside it.

My mind crowds with all the questions I wanted to ask, but he always deflected his way out of them. The first one is easy.

"Do you miss Alicia?" I ask.

He appears deep in thought for a second. "Sometimes, I walk inside the house and wonder how it would feel if she was there, but then I recall she'd still be married to Jonathan because she was so helplessly in love with him, and I stop wondering."

That's interesting.

Aiden's lack of empathy is like being in a logical, emotionless state of mind twenty-four seven. That state of mind even forbids him from missing his mother properly because he thinks she would've suffered if she lived her life as Jonathan's wife.

"Take the shirt off," he orders in that delicious deep tone. "And make it sexy."

With a sigh, I unbutton my shirt. I don't really know how to make it sexy, so I just do it without rush, slowly revealing the swell of my breasts covered by the simple cotton bra.

Aiden watches me the entire time with a dark, predatory gleam. His head tilts to the side to get a better view.

My nipples harden under his scrutiny, throbbing for attention.

Not now.

I let the shirt fall to the floor, ready for the next question. I've been burning to ask it since the time I heard about it.

"Who was the girl you and Cole had a threesome with?"

He raises an eyebrow. "Let me guess, Astor said he walked in on our 'kinky shit.'"

I frown. "You know."

"Typical Astor running his mouth about something he saw when high. Nash and I never had a threesome. Neither of us is the sharing type."

"But Ronan said he saw you."

"The fucker was so high that he got her hair colour wrong. Astor saw me fiddle with the ropes and he thought I was binding her when I was actually unbinding her and saving her from Nash's crazy kink. See? I can be a gentleman when I want to ruin something."

Aiden and Cole never had a threesome. I was being all green with jealousy over an imaginary person.

"Who was she, anyway?" I ask.

He smirks. "Nash's damnation."

Nash's damnation.

Interesting. I wonder why Aiden worded it that way.

"Now," his voice deepens with perverse lust. "Take the bra and skirt off."

I cross my arms over my chest. "Why both? I only asked one question."

"Two, actually." He grins with mischief. "You asked who's the girl I had a threesome with and then even after confirming I didn't fuck her, you still asked who is she."

Damn it.

I should've known Aiden will set me a trap somewhere.

"A deal is a deal, sweetheart. Your curiosity is adorable."

"Oh, shut up." With a huff, I unclip my bra and let it fall to my side.

Aiden's eyes feast on me like I'm his favourite meal, the one he'll have before a death row.

I shimmy out of my skirt next and kneel naked in front of him.

For long seconds, Aiden just watches me. His brows draw together over darkened eyes as if he's a predator sampling his prey.

"Hmm." He reaches a finger and traces it over my hardened nipple. "Are you cold, sweetheart?"

Even if I were, his touch is making me all tingly and warm.

"No," I say.

"Then I shouldn't warm you up, huh?"

Ugh. Is there a way to take back my words?

"Aiden…"

"Hmm, sweetheart?" He twirls both my nipples between his fingers, twisting, and torturing them.

A zap of pleasure shoots to my core until I'm almost sure he can see my pussy glistening with arousal.

He pinches my nipple hard. I throw my head back in a whimper.

"I'm waiting." His voice turns husky with lust. "Was there something you wanted to say?"

I meet his eyes reluctantly, pleading for him to take me already. "I… I…"

"What do you want?" He leans over and sucks a nipple into his mouth. His tongue laps around the peak, licking and twirling.

My stomach flutters with a thousand butterflies.

"Say you want me." He speaks against my soft flesh, his stubble tickling my skin.

"I want you." The words come out in a tortuous breath.

I was always such a mess when he teased my breasts. They're throbbing and aching, but I still want more.

I want all of him. The good and the bad and the ugly.

He drags his pullover over his head, messing up the black strands. I barely register the emptiness on my sore nipples before he goes back to sucking on them, torturing them with his tongue, lips and teeth.

At the same time, he yanks down both his jeans and boxers. The thickness of his cock nestles at my thigh, hot and ready.

"What else do you want, sweetheart?"

I'm distracted by the perfection of his cock and the tautness of his abs. Those hard, powerful muscles of his arms and thighs can snap me in two if he chooses to.

Maybe I would've believed that a few months ago, but not now. I trust Aiden now.

I trust he won't hurt me.

I trust he'll bring the world to its knees for me.

"I want to be your queen."

"You already are." He grunts against my skin, and I briefly close my eyes at the sensation.

My fingers trace along his forearm and arrow tattoo. The one I'm sure he got for me. It's a reminder of our past on his skin. Just like his scars and mine.

Proof we both survived.

We're survivors.

"What else do you want?" he murmurs, fluttering kisses all over the curve of my breasts, the hardness of my nipple, and the softness of my tummy.

It's barely enough.

Scratch that. It's *not* enough.

I want to feel his raw strength right now. I want to get lost in him and his intensity; it's the only thing I have.

"Fuck me, Aiden." My words end on a moan when he thrusts two fingers inside me. I'm so wet, he barely finds any resistance.

"Hmm. I love it when you're soaked for me, sweetheart." He kisses his way up to my ear then nibbles on the shell. "I love that you're mine. Now, say it."

"Say what?"

"That you're mine."

"I'm yours, Aiden." The words leave me in a hushed murmur like I'm divulging my deepest, darkest secrets.

Because that's the truth, isn't it? Admitting to be so whole-heartedly his is both liberating and scary, but I'm ready to take that step.

I'm ready for everything with him.

Aiden curls his fingers inside me, bringing me pleasure but also touching my soul and making a permanent place for himself.

"There hasn't been a day where you weren't fucking mine, Elsa. You've been mine since that first day you walked in here."

"Yes, yes."

His lips find my ear and he whispers in husky words. "And I've been yours."

My chest vibrates with the sparks and explosions going off all at once. Those words are my undoing. I might've had some sanity before, but now it's poof. Gone.

My lips find his and kiss him with abandon. I kiss him until my lungs burn, demanding breath. I kiss him until my air is saturated with his scent.

Aiden removes his fingers, and my walls clench with the need to keep him there. Before I can protest, he manoeuvres me so I'm sitting on his lap and slides his cock inside me in one ruthless thrust.

I cry out, holding on to his shoulder for balance. If my nails were any longer, I would've scraped his back.

He fucks me like never before. His rhythm goes from slow, lazy strokes that touch my damn soul to fast, ruthless thrusts that make me bounce off his lap. With every rock of his hips, I'm thrown into a delirious state of pleasure, rough and consuming.

My space is filled with him. His scent. His strength. His intense gaze.

My muscles tighten around him with the force of my build-up.

"Fuck, sweetheart." He curses without slowing his fast pace. "Your tight pussy is strangling my dick."

How does he do that? How does he stimulate my body even more with his dirty words? Sweat covers my brows as I grind against him, trying to match his pace.

"Are you going to come for me, sweetheart?" He nibbles on my shoulder and neck, most likely leaving hickeys. "Are you going to clench all around my cock?"

I nod several times as the pleasure mounts to heights I can't control.

I cry out at the violent waves hitting me. It's a madness, I'm sure of it now. Just like I'm sure that I don't want it to end. My fingers stroke his brow as I ride the high. I run my fingertips over that small mole at the corner of his eye, needing to engrave it and this moment to memory.

Aiden slides a finger into my wet folds, coating it with my arousal, then trails it to the crack of my arse.

It could be because I'm in the middle of an orgasm, but the moment he thrusts his finger inside my back hole, I scream louder, tightening around his dick like never before.

Oh, God.

What is happening to me?

Aiden doesn't stop. As his finger stretches my virgin hole, his cock thrusts deeper and harder. I can almost feel the thin wall between his finger and his cock as he fills me from both ends.

I hold on to his shoulders while he picks up his rhythm. He angles me forward so his cock brushes against my clit with each of his thrusts.

A different type of build-up starts at the bottom of my

stomach. The pressure from his finger in my arse eases the more he teases my clit.

The friction fills me with sparks, all bright and blinding.

"Fuck, you feel like sin." He moves his finger in and out of my arse before he eases another one in.

I gasp, feeling stretched whole.

God.

Oh, God.

Why does it hurt so good?

"You're so fucking tight. Hmm. I might break you if I use my cock."

My breath hitches at the thought, but my arousal coats him, dripping down my thighs.

"D-Do it," I whisper.

He pauses thrusting in and out of me. "What was that?"

"Fuck me. All of me."

His chest shudders with a groan that fills the space around us, masculine and so damn hot. "You'll be mine? All *mine*?"

"Yours. All yours."

I don't get a warning. Aiden slips out of my pussy and arse. Before I can concentrate on the hollowness, he flips me around.

"On your elbows and knees."

I scramble into the position in front of him, my heart pounding in my chest.

Thump.

Thump.

Thump.

Aiden places a hand at the top of my back and lowers me further so my arse is in the air and he's behind me. Not too long ago, I would've felt self-conscious about being so exposed to him. Not now.

Now, a burn covers my skin, yearning for more.

Two of his fingers thrust inside my pussy. I moan aloud as his cock traces my wetness to my back hole over and over again.

It's then I realise he's using it as lube.

"It's going to hurt," he muses. His voice holds a sadistic, dark edge.

This is my chance to escape this, but the truth is, I don't want to.

Deep down, I want it to hurt.

If Aiden is open about admitting how much he perversely wants me and can't get enough of me, I can be the same.

"Do it," I murmur.

"Even if it hurts?"

"Especially if it hurts."

He growls and slowly eases into my tight hole. I remain motionless, not breathing.

"Relax," he groans. "Ease into me. Don't fight me."

I try as hard as I can to lose the tension in my shoulders. Aiden's cock is barely inside and it stings.

He pumps his fingers inside my pussy, scissoring them, and the pleasure loosens my muscles.

Aiden's free hand grips my hip and he rams inside me in one go.

I scream, the pain ripping me open from the inside out. Tears spring to my eyes.

Oh, God.

It hurts. It hurts like hell. It's even worse than when he took my virginity.

I'm about to change my mind, to tell him to stop, but then he starts moving. Both in my pussy and in my arse. His fingers meet his cock through the thin wall, and his thumb grazes over my clit.

"Oh... Aaaah..."

"You like that, huh?" Aiden's deep voice turns me on even more.

I move my arse against his thigh, needing more.

He reaches over and pinches my nipple. I cry out at the torturous sensation.

"Answer me," he orders.

"I..." I gasp. "I do."

"You do, huh?"

"Y-yes…"

"Do you like my cock better in your pussy or in your arse."

"I… don't know."

"Hmm. I love your arse as much as your pussy." He picks up his pace. "I never thought that would be possible."

"Aiden…"

"You're so fucking tight in here, sweetheart. I can barely move. Do you feel how much you're strangling my dick?"

Aiden's dirty talk must be contagious because all I can say is, "Yes."

He pumps inside me in a long torturous rhythm that wrenches pleasure out of me. "Do you like it?"

"I-I do."

"Then come for me." His authoritative tone hits me in the core.

A whirlwind of pleasure sweeps me over like a hurricane. My nerves are so stimulated I come twice, at the same time. Or maybe it's one long orgasm that bleeds into the next.

I don't even get to control it. It takes me over like a possession, like an otherworldly power.

I arch my back, chanting Aiden's name like a prayer. He might as well be touching my soul instead of my body right now.

"Tell me you love me," he grunts near my ear as his thrusts turn animalistic.

"I love you," I pant.

He follows me over the cliff with a ravenous growl. "Mine. You're all *mine*."

I am.

It's useless to deny it anymore.

If we never find a way out of here I'll die happy knowing I'm with the person I love the most.

The boy I loved since I was seven.

THIRTY-SIX

Aiden

"Are you on Viagra?" Elsa pants as she lays her head on my arm.

She just finished putting her clothes back on—all of them—so I don't ravage her anymore.

It's cute that she thinks mere clothes will keep me away from her.

Nothing will.

"Viagra, huh?" I grin down at her.

"I mean, your sex drive is endless even under extreme circumstances. I'm so sore." She blushes, and unable to stop myself, I pull on her cheek.

It's impossible to stop craving her.

Maybe one day when we're older, and I have fucked her all the ways possible, I'll be able to get enough of her.

But even that is a slim chance.

"What do you like the most about me?" she asks with a red hue covering her cheeks.

"The most?"

"You know, what do you find most sexy about me?"

I chuckle. "Are you trying to seduce me again, sweetheart?"

"Just answer me." She plays with the hem of my pullover.

I try to think about the things that turned me on the most

about her. The smell of coconut in her hair when she's freshly showered. The fluttering of her eyes when her head rolled back in an orgasm. The shape of her mouth when she called my name. The softness of her touch when she clung to me.

There were too many things I find sexy and utterly irresistible about her. From the twitch in her nose to the slight bite of her lip and straight to the twinkle in her eyes.

So when it comes down to a specific answer, it's easy. "Everything," I say.

"Everything?" she asks, voice laced with confusion.

"Your passion, your darkness, your fire, and even your damn stubbornness. I find all of them sexy and there isn't a thing I would change about you. So yes, everything."

Her lips part and her eyes soften with deep affection before she turns her gaze away as if hiding her reaction.

"You're touched, aren't you?" I poke her arm.

"Shut up." Her cheeks turn crimson.

I smile. "Pay me back, sweetheart."

"Pay you back?"

"Yeah. Tell me what you like most about me."

"No."

It's my turn look at her twice. "No?"

She lifts her chin in defiance, eyes glinting. "It's a secret."

"You don't get to keep secrets from me."

"Yes, I do." She lay her head on my arm. "I can't have you lose interest in me."

"Believe me, that will never happen."

"Still no. You need a challenge, remember? I'll be that challenge and more."

I smile to myself. This is why Elsa is one of a kind. This is why she'll always be mine.

No one understands me as much as she does.

Her breathing calms down and she yawns. "I'd kill for something to eat right now."

And then her eyes flutter closed. Her slender body snuggles onto my side and her chest rises and falls in a steady rhythm.

I probably exhausted her. It was my goal since the beginning.

The only way to stop Elsa from thinking about the dark reality is to distract her. That's why I claimed her virgin arse, came one more time in her pussy, and then I ate her out to relax her even more.

She whined, saying she has to go back to yoga if I continue fucking her all the time in different positions.

I stroke the blonde strands off her forehead and place a kiss onto the top of her head.

Her stomach growls so loud. She winces, groaning softly.

I said Agnus would return, but it's been nearly two days.

My initial reasoning is that he won't do something that will throw him completely out of Ethan's grace. Leaving us here for two days is extreme even if he wanted to teach Elsa a lesson and force her to not talk about her mother's death.

I'm still sure he wouldn't risk Ethan's wrath, though.

Did he somehow miscalculate something?

While I kept Elsa distracted with sex, we're both losing our energy. We can only survive on water for so long before it becomes a problem. We're lucky this place isn't freezing like the outside, but I can feel the cold seeping through my bones from the ground.

"Do you regret it?" she murmurs, her tiny hands gripping my arm.

I like how she's holding on to me with all her might. Her entire body clings to mine like it's the most natural place to be.

"Regret what?" I ask.

"Getting to know me. Pursuing me. All of it." A stuttering breath chokes out of her. "If you stayed away from me, you wouldn't be here."

"I regret nothing, sweetheart, least of all knowing you."

"You said you regretted two things from the past and I'm the third."

"Hmm. Do you store everything I tell you?"

"Yeah," she says wryly. "I guess I do."

I consider not telling her, but it's useless to build a wall between me and Elsa. Besides, it's better to keep her distracted.

"When I was a child, I always wanted to tell Alicia to leave Jonathan. I didn't because I saw how much she loved him, and I regret not speaking up. My second regret is not fighting to stay with you when you pushed me out of this room. My third regret is believing you were dead and not searching for you."

She remains silent, but nods.

"How about you?" I ask slowly. "Any regrets?"

For a second, I believe she went back to sleep, but then her quiet voice drifts around me. "I regret not telling Dad about the subtle way Ma abused me. She took me to swim in the lake Eli drowned in and kept me underwater until I thought I would die. She hit me when I didn't listen to her. Back then, I didn't say anything because I was scared Dad would be mad at her and they'd fight. It wasn't the right thing to do. If Dad knew about the way she treated me, he would've sent her to the psych ward. She wouldn't have hurt Knox, Teal, and you."

"You were a child and loved your mother."

"Do you think love gives you the right to compromise?"

"I don't know. Do you?"

"Sometimes, yes."

She grips me tighter as she talks about her childhood and the memories she repressed for so long. Most of them are happy memories about her older brother and her father and even her Uncle Reg and Uncle Agnus.

Talking is her way of distraction.

I force myself to focus on her words instead of how much I want to spread her legs and fuck her once more. The only reason I stop myself is because we need the energy we have left.

Survival is such a fucking bitch.

"I'm glad I met you back then," she says after a while. "You were my light in the darkness."

My chest expands with a mixture of strange feelings. I never thought there would be a day Elsa would call me her light, even in past tense.

I was always the shadow to her darkest desires and I thought I was fine with that. Turns out, I'm a selfish bastard who wants it all. Both her light and her darkness.

Her best and her worst.

Her *everything*.

"And now?" I ask.

"Now you're just you." She sighs.

"Meaning?"

"Meaning you drive me fucking crazy, but I love every second of it."

I grin. "You love every second of it, huh?"

"Yes, dickhead." She shoves me, but then digs her fingers into my pullover and draws me closer to rest her cheek on my arm. Her skin is warm.

"I meant it the other day, loving me is a one way road. You can't go back."

"Oh, I know…I won't…" Her voice is quiet.

She falls back asleep. We remain like that for half an hour until she starts mumbling something in her dreams.

"Elsa?" I cradle her cheeks and pause at the burn in them.

I thought the flush and the heat were only because of how thoroughly I fucked her.

Is she having a fever?

"Elsa, open your eyes."

"I love you, Aiden. I really, *really* do." She tightens her small hands in my pullover one more time before they fall on her side.

Fuck! Fuck!

I take her hand in mine; they're feverish, too.

"Have you been running in the rain again, Elsa?" I curse under my breath.

Why the hell does she have this weird habit of running in the rain when she has a fucking heart condition?

The hunger and exhaustion must be making things worse.

My muscles tense and my brain fills with a thousand scenarios.

First of all, I need to keep her body temperature down.

I carefully place her on the ground and put her jacket under her head. She pulls her legs to her chest and bends into a foetal position.

Yanking my pullover off, I soak it with water from the lavatory and wrap it around her head.

A moan rips from her colourless lips. The flush on her face has been reddening by the second.

Sweat beads on her forehead and down her temples.

I place a hand on her heart. The beat starts slow then turns hard within a second.

That's not good.

This isn't a simple fever. Her heart condition is acting up and I'll bet my life she didn't visit her heart physician after she left with her father.

When she collapsed that day after running in the rain, our family doctor said she should visit her specialist as soon as possible. Knowing Elsa, she probably didn't want to worry her father as soon as she reunited with him.

"Fuck, Elsa. Fuck!"

We need out of here.

Fucking now.

If not treated properly, a simple fever can be lethal to someone with a heart condition.

I know because I've been studying the shit out of it since I learnt of her illness.

That's why I've been even stricter than her aunt about her special food. I brought her water with the highest concentration of minerals because I read it's good. I've been watching her while she runs, looking for tiny clues about her breathing.

However, I couldn't stop her from running in the rain since she often does it behind everyone's back.

I snatch my pullover, soak it with water again and then wrap it around her head.

My lips touch her forehead one last time before I stagger to my feet.

Adrenaline shoots through my veins and fills me with one purpose only. I'll open that door even if I have to dislocate my shoulders in the process.

Elsa and I will get out of here.

We're not losing our lives in this basement another time.

THIRTY-SEVEN

Jonathan

Unlike common belief, villains aren't evil.

Villains are simply people who go after what they want even if it means walking all over the crowd.

I might be considered the villain of this story, and I'm fine with that. My beliefs are my own and none of anyone's fucking business.

Like an Italian politician once said, it's better to be feared than loved.

Fear brings efficiency and gets things done.

Love is for masochistic fools.

I was in love once. It's irrational and out of control.

Perhaps that's why I'm trapped in my own head, scheming one revenge plot after the other.

I know full well it won't bring Alicia back, but I go on with it anyway.

Why?

Because it's irrational and out of fucking control.

If I focus on revenge I won't feel the emptiness. If I focus on revenge, I direct the pain outwards instead of inwards.

I was at the airport, ready to put Aiden back in his lane when Ethan's number flashed across my screen. I thought we were back to playing our old games. However, everything changed when he told me Aiden and Elsa are missing.

It's been fifty-five hours since they were last seen.

Aiden is a little fuck, but he's my son and the only thing I have left of Alicia. I have to bring him back.

Ethan's security team and mine have been going through all the places Aiden and Elsa could disappear to.

We interrogated their friends and came up with nothing.

Ethan and I sit in the back of a van speeding to where the signal of their phones was last detected, somewhere near Northampton.

"The bank?" Ethan asks. His composure is a mere mask just like mine.

"Negative. He hasn't used his credit card."

He sighs. "Neither did Elsa."

Aiden is smart enough not to use credit cards if he wanted to escape. However, neither Ethan nor I are considering that option.

One. Elsa would never leave her father after their reunion, even for Aiden.

Two. If Aiden planned to escape, he would've made small withdrawals from his bank account over the past few months so they'd have cash handy.

Which means they were taken against their will.

"Aiden took her," Ethan grits out. "If he didn't, none of this would've happened."

"She went with him." I rub my temple. "Stop pretending as if your daughter is a saint. She was glued to his side all this time no matter what I did."

He glares at me but says nothing.

I go back to reading the text from my security team. Aiden's car hasn't been located yet.

Fucking brilliant.

"Where's your dog?" I poke Ethan. "Have you lost the leash?"

"Watch it, Jonathan. I won't allow you to disrespect Agnus."

"Touchy, aren't we?"

"He saved Aiden that day," he says with an edge of smugness. "If it weren't for Agnus, you would've lost your only son."

"Agnus the saviour," I mock. "I should've known he'd bring you back to life. If there's anyone capable of that black magic, it's him."

"Unfortunately for you."

"It's a waste you returned, Ethan." My shoulders tense as black memories hit me. "I'll make your existence hell for every second Alicia spent in that car slowly dying."

"Are you blind?"

I pause, his reply taking me by surprise. I don't do surprises.

Usually, Ethan would rise to the challenge and tell me my plot for the Birmingham factory is the reason everything is ruined. He'd tell me, like Aiden, that the car accident might've been Alicia's cause of death, but she was dying for years.

"Blind to what?" I ask slowly.

"To Aiden and Elsa, fucker. You've been observing it longer than me, so how come you're still blind to it? Those two have been sharing a connection for the past ten years. Neither you nor I will be able to break it."

"Let me worry about that."

"Have you seen them play chess?" He raises an eyebrow. "You should. It might change your mind."

"My son won't be with your daughter and that's final."

"Does your son know that piece of information?"

My jaw ticks.

"I thought so. You're losing control of him, if you haven't already. Do you know what that means, Jonathan?" he asks, but it's clearly rhetorical since he continues, "It means if you continue to push him, he'll leave you and your entire legacy behind."

It takes all my self-control to remain calm and focused.

While I hate to admit it, Ethan is right. Aiden is slipping away. I can lock him out like I did in China, but that's a one-time thing. If I want to keep him by my side, I need a change of tactics.

"Does that mean you're okay with their nonsense?" I tap my chin.

"No, I'm not. Aiden is so similar to you and I would rather he stays the fuck away from my daughter. But do you know what's the difference between you and me? I consider Elsa's well-being before my own."

"Something must've broken in your head while you were sleeping all those years."

I look through the window at the trees passing us by.

"We fucked up, Jonathan. Both of us. I'm brave enough to admit it."

I glance at him. "How about you leave me that deal with the Rhodes, then?"

"That's a business deal; the best one will win." He pauses. "The past is in the past. Our children shouldn't pay for our mistakes."

Sappy fuck.

His phone vibrates before I can say anything.

"Agnus, where have you been? I've been trying to reach you all day." Ethan listens to the other end. "This isn't the time for your phone to die. Elsa is missing."

His brows scrunch. "You sent me a text? Fine. Let me check. And return to London immediately."

He hangs up and checks his phone then his jaw tightens.

The emptiness I felt since Alicia's death strikes me again. Only now, it's sharper and harder.

Something is wrong with Aiden.

"What happened?" I ask in a voice I don't recognise.

Ethan shows me his phone.

Agnus: There's been activity at the basement's lock in Birmingham's mansion.

"Elsa went back to the basement," Ethan murmurs. "It doesn't make sense. If they went more than two days ago, why haven't they returned?"

"Aiden is a survivor," I say with finality.

"So is Elsa."

I bark at the driver to change the direction to Birmingham.

It all ends where it started.

THIRTY-EIGHT

Aiden

I've been slamming my shoulder against the metal door for the past hour or so.

My dominant left shoulder is safely dislocated, so I switch to my right one.

I tried everything from pushing to pulling and even kicking. They're all useless against a fucking metal door.

Logically, I recognised that, but I still didn't stop. It's the only way we'll get out of here.

In between, I've been soaking my pullover with water and placing it around Elsa's head.

She's been slipping in and out of consciousness, mumbling feverish things about her brother, her mother, and her dad. She was even having a conversation with Eli in a language that doesn't sound like English.

The worse her state becomes, the harder I kick the damn door.

Bang. Bang. Bang.

The bitter taste of desperation is reminiscent to how I felt when I hit the door ten years ago. Back then, I thought she died. Back then, I lost hope.

But not now.

She can't fucking die.

"Aiden…" Her croaked voice is like a rush of adrenaline, tightening my muscles.

I leave the door and descend the stairs two at a time to reach her. She's sprawled on her side, eyes closed and face pale. It's even paler than earlier. I touch her cheek and it's on fire—even worse than before.

Fuck.

I grab my pullover, pour cold water on it, then place it back on her head.

"Aiden…" she mumbles in her feverish haze.

Her pupils move rapidly behind her closed lids. She must be dreaming.

I sit on the floor and let my dislocated shoulder fall limp. It hurts like a bitch when I move it. My attempts to push it back were it belongs have failed miserably.

Pain doesn't matter, though. The girl lying helpless in front of me does. I lean over and place a chaste kiss on her dry lips. "I'm here, sweetheart. I'll always be here."

"I love you, Aiden." It's barely a whisper, but it hits me straight to a sombre corner in my soul.

She loves me.

Elsa fucking loves me.

I'll never get enough of hearing those words out of her mouth.

I take her hand in mine and place a kiss on the palm. "Stay with me, Elsa. You promised, remember?"

"Do you love me?" she whispers.

I capture her cracked mouth in a quick kiss, nibbling on her bottom lip longer than needed.

"Tell me, Aiden… T-tell me…"

"I will when you open your eyes."

"I said it many times. You're not fair."

I chuckle at the lines forming on her forehead. She's frowning and being stubborn even when feverish.

"What I feel for you isn't only love, obsession, or addiction.

It's all of those and more. Do you know what that means, sweetheart? It means I can't live without you, so don't you fucking dare leave me."

A small smile tugs on her lips before it falls flat. Her hand grows heavy in mine.

I check her pulse. It's been jumping in and out of synch for the past hour. Her skin has turned alarmingly white for someone with a fever.

After one last kiss to her lips, I start to stand up. I'm getting her out of here if it's the last thing I do.

Even if I have to lose a limb in the process.

The click of a door echoes in the air.

My head snaps upright as fast footsteps come down the stairs. I never thought I would be happy to see Jonathan's face.

Ten years ago, when I woke up in the hospital and saw his face instead of Alicia's, I became black. But now, it's the complete opposite. He's not bearing bad news this time, he's come to help us.

He stops at the threshold of the basement with Ethan by his side.

I can almost imagine what they're seeing.

I'm half-naked, my left shoulder drooping to one side. Elsa's head lies on the floor as she mumbles gibberish.

"She needs a doctor," I order. "Now."

THIRTY-NINE

Elsa

Eli smiles down at me.

His face is as clear as glass. He has dark hair, a shade darker than Dad's and his eyes are the same as our father's, too.

He always said he's Dad's favourite and I went crying to Dad so he'd tell me that I'm his favourite, too.

Dust of freckles cover his cheek, adding a boyish charm to his face.

Eli is so pretty.

The only difference is he's small. I am not.

I'm wearing my RES's uniform as I stand with him in our back garden with all the tall trees and the wires.

"Why did you leave, Eli?" I whisper.

"Come on, crybaby." He holds out his hand for me. "We're going to have fun."

"Fun?"

"We'll go to a place where we'll be free."

Free.

Eli and I. Free.

"Hurry, crybaby."

I'm about to place my hand in his when voices slam into my head. Firm lips press a kiss after a kiss against my dry ones.

"Stay with me, Elsa. Don't you dare fucking leave me."

That voice.

That touch.

"Crybaby?" Eli's eyes water with tears. I hate it when my brother cries.

"Stay with me, Elsa." The voice…

"Please, crybaby. Don't leave me alone."

"Elsa!"

"Eli and Elsa together forever, right?"

The onslaught of both voices hits me over and over again. Tentacles of pain wrap around my heart. I can't breathe.

I can't fucking breathe.

"Bring her back!" The voice shouts. "Bring her back before I smash this whole fucking place."

There's so much pain in that voice. So much passion. So much… care.

Hearing him fight for me is like being lifted into the clouds. It's peaceful but scary.

"Crybaby?"

Eli's hand is still stretched in front of me. His expression is drawn downwards as he pleads.

"I'm not a crybaby anymore." But as I say that, a tear streams down my cheek. I recognise the finality as I pull my hand. "Goodbye, Eli."

He turns to smoke, fading into the distance.

I'm tempted to try and catch him, to spend more time with him, but I recognise, deep down, this isn't where I'm supposed to be.

Someone is waiting for me.

And I have a promise to keep.

The moment I open my eyes, a headache assaults my temples.

I'm disoriented for a few seconds. It takes several blinks to focus on the walls surrounding me.

White walls. Antiseptic smell.

The hospital. I'm at the hospital.

"Elsa, you're awake."

Dad's voice filters through my consciousness. He sits beside me, his five o'clock shadow appears a few days old.

"Oh, hon." Aunt takes my hand, Uncle standing by her side with a relieved expression plastered all over his face.

"What happened?" My throat is all scratchy and dry, but the words come out clear.

"You had a fever," Aunt speaks in rapid-fire. "Dr Albert said you had palpitations. Depending on the test results, changing your dose of pills can be enough for now, but if there are any further complications in the next few months, he might have to operate. I can't believe you haven't told us your heartbeat rate has been acting up."

"Blair." Uncle shakes his head at her.

"Fine." She points between Dad and I. "But you bet I'm going to hound you about your appointments from now on."

"How long have I been out?" I ask in a small voice.

"Two days," Dad says.

Two days. Woah. That's a lot.

Aunt goes on to tell me about the tests and the doctor's recommendations. She has it all written in her planner and both Uncle and Dad's schedule so no one forgets.

I'm listening to them, but something doesn't seem right. I search my memories about what actually happened.

Aiden kidnapped me. Check.

We went to Birmingham. Check.

I remembered the past. Check.

Agnus showed up and locked us in. Check.

We had lots of sex. Double-check

But after that, it's a blur of mismatching mosaic colours.

I search my surroundings, but there's no sign of Aiden. A jolt of panic grips me like those tentacles from the dream.

"Where is Aiden?" I interrupt them in a choked voice.

"He stepped out with Agnus for coffee," Dad says.

"A-Agnus?" I all but shriek.

Why would Agnus have private time with Aiden? Is he planning something else?

Oh, God. What if he decides to hurt Aiden because Dad doesn't like him? What if he thinks, like ten years ago, that's the best solution for everyone?

After all, he has no moral compass stopping him from eliminating people who don't fit into his bigger picture.

My brain goes into overdrive. It's impossible to see clearly, let alone think.

"Yes, Agnus." Dad smiles. "He's the reason we found you. If I checked his text earlier, we could've avoided all of this."

So Agnus did tell Dad.

I'm confused. Was what Aiden said true? The part about how Agnus wouldn't hurt us.

"If we look at it from the other side." Uncle squeezes my hand. "Maybe it's for the best you got stuck in there. If you didn't, we might've found out about your recent condition too late."

"Oh my God, you're right." Aunt's eyes widen. "The next appointment is months away. It could've been too late then."

I can't help thinking about what I told Aiden a long time ago.

Bad things happen for a reason.

The door opens. Aiden and Agnus walk into the room, appearing deep in conversation.

Deep in freaking conversation.

They stop when Aiden's metal eyes meet mine. Those eyes that are never a void when he's around me. His left arm is in a sling and he's holding a coffee in his non-dominant hand.

Despite the fact that Agnus stands beside him, my heart flutters.

Aiden is here.

Everything is going to be okay.

He slams the coffee on a nearby table, not caring that it splashes on his hand and runs towards me.

I try to sit up.

Dad and Aunt start to protest. Aiden beats them to it and places a hand on my chest, gently forcing me to lie back down.

"What are you doing?" His voice is firm and non-negotiable. "You're still weak and need to rest."

I want to say I'm completely fine, but I doubt I'll get the majority vote—if even just one—here.

Even Aunt who's not Aiden's biggest fan is nodding along with him.

"We'll be outside," Dad addresses my adoptive parents. "Blair. Jaxon."

Uncle places a kiss on my forehead and stands up.

Aunt strokes my cheek and covers me to the neck. "Just so you know, I won't be out of your hair, hon. I don't care what your father and Uncle say."

I nod with a smile as Uncle wraps an arm around her shoulders and leads her outside.

Agnus gives Dad an indecipherable look. It's strange how they can communicate without words. I guess it's possible if they've been best friends since they were ten.

Dad stops at the entrance. "Right. Elsa, Agnus said you have something important to tell me?"

My heart hammers in my chest as I glance between Agnus and Aiden. The latter lifts a shoulder, adjusting the blanket and appearing oblivious to the whole thing.

Agnus' expression is completely blank.

Why the hell would he tell Dad that? Does he want me to disclose what happened in the past? Is he ready for the consequences?

I meet Dad's eyes, and the decision is easier than I ever thought it would be.

"I do, Dad." I smile. "I remember the past."

Agnus doesn't move and his expression remains the same. He really is ready, isn't he?

"You do?" Dad's face hardens. I don't think he wanted me to remember.

Like Aunt, he doesn't like me exposed to all that trauma. However, I think they understand that in order to overcome the trauma, I needed to have a recollection of it.

"I remember that night." I nod in his right hand's direction. "Agnus saved us all."

"That he did." Dad appears almost proud. "He really did."

Agnus raises an eyebrow in my direction. Aiden simply smiles, shaking his head.

I meet Agnus's unfeeling eyes with my own.

"We'll talk later, princess." Dad smiles at me then at Agnus and exits the hospital room.

Agnus nods at me. "Thank you."

"I'm not doing this for you. I'm doing it for Dad."

"My gratitude still stands. Ethan deserves a daughter like you."

And then he's out of the door.

"Ethan deserves a daughter like you," I repeat with mockery. "Can you believe that shady man?"

"I can, actually." Aiden strokes my hair back like he can't stop touching me, a small smile lifting his lips.

"Hey, what do you keep smiling about?"

"Well, Agnus was certain you'd tell Ethan the truth because you're righteous like your father. He was actually wrapping up things at the company. I told him you wouldn't."

"How could you be so sure?" Even I wasn't until earlier.

"Because you love your father, and you're the type who sacrifices for those they love. You know how much Ethan suffered by losing his family and that it would destroy him to lose his best friend of thirty-four years. Even though you don't agree with what Agnus did, you understand why he did it and you know he'll never hurt him. Deep down, you're comfortable that there's someone like Agnus protecting your father."

I groan. "How the hell do you know me so well?"

"I stalk you on Instagram." He winks.

I can't help but chuckle. The sound soon turns into a cough.

"Hey, take it easy." He strokes my cheek, his thumb caressing my lips. "If you give me such a fright one more time, I swear —"

Lifting my head, I close the distance between us and seal my mouth to his. I was dead for a moment, but he brought me back to life.

I can only feel alive if he's touching me.

If he's saying my name and calling me back to life. If he's telling me things—

What I feel for you isn't only love, obsession, or addiction. It's all of those and more.

I pull back from his lips with a jolt. "Did you… Did you by any chance tell me you love me while I was feverish?"

A gleam sparks in his eyes. "Maybe."

"Aiden! That's not fair. You're supposed to tell me that while I'm conscious."

"Hmm. Like now?"

I nod frantically. "Yes, totally like now."

"Hmm. I'm not really feeling it, but we can fix that if you bring me back to the right mood."

"Aiden!"

"What? This is your punishment."

"Fine. I'll do it."

As if possible, the spark in his eye ignites further. "What did you have in mind, sweetheart?"

"Guess you have to wait until I'm out of the hospital."

He smirks. "Sneaky."

"I learnt from the best."

His lips come back to mine and I breathe him in. The hospital smell fades in comparison to his scent and his warmth.

My fingers thread in his jet black hair and I let him ravage me. I let him show me just how much I mean to him.

Aiden and I aren't the darkness and the light. We both have tarnished minds and souls.

But we're not soulmates.

We're lost souls that fit in perfectly imperfect harmony.

And I'll do everything I can to protect what we have.

"Wait," I say against his mouth. "What were you and Agnus talking about earlier?"

"We're planning something. It's going to be fun."

Aiden and Agnus are planning something.

What on earth could two psychopaths consider 'fun'?

FORTY

Elsa

I spend a few days at the hospital.

The sheer number of tests exhaust me and I can't even complain.

Dad and Aunt stand next to me like grim reapers, not allowing me to say anything.

Turns out Aiden is a lot worse than them when it comes to my health.

He's been there for every test, wheeling me from one department to the other. When I told him I could walk, he ignored me and continued his path.

At night, though, he'd sneak inside my room, spread my legs, and eat me for dinner. He said I'm too weak to be fucked, but he can still relax me with his tongue.

Relax me. As if.

I had to cover my face with the pillow so Dad and Aunt don't hear my moans of pleasure from the other side of the room.

Aiden is a sex God. He doesn't have to stimulate me for long and I'm soon screaming his name.

His dislocated shoulder has been healed. Since they removed the sling, he doesn't allow anyone else to touch me. Not even the nurses.

One of them told me he has it bad, and I kind of agree.

I never thought I would like this side of Aiden, but I do. My chest flutters at witnessing his care and concern for me. It makes me feel special and loved.

This is Aiden after all. He never shows this side to anyone, not even his family.

When Levi and Astrid visited me yesterday, they kept asking me what type of voodoo spell I used.

Everyone else came by as well. Knox and Teal were waiting outside that first day I woke up and spent the night.

Today, they're here again with the three horsemen and Kim.

Aiden lurks in the corner, cutting an apple for me, his face calm. However, the darkness beneath the surface radiates off him in waves. I can feel it without looking at him.

I know exactly why his demons are contemplating to come out and play.

Aiden is possessive—like over the top. He's not so pleased that Ronan, Xander, and Knox are sitting on the bed, surrounding me, laughing and jesting about mundane things.

If it were up to Aiden, they'd all be thrown out—except for Kim and Teal. Actually, even the girls are debatable.

However, since he knows I'm happy about their company, he's trying to control that side of him.

Thus far, he's succeeding.

I act oblivious as I listen to Knox tell me about their last game and his 'heroic' performance.

"I'm telling you, Ellie." Knox points at himself. "I'm Elites new ace striker."

"Sorry, mate." Xander grins, showcasing his charming dimples. "That position is already taken by me."

"Screw both of you." Ronan physically shoves them out of the way and takes my hand in his. "Do you know how worried I was, Ellie? I didn't throw a party for an entire week."

"Some commitment from the devil," Teal mutters from her seat next to Cole.

They're the only calm people in this place.

Teal's T-shirt for the day reads, *I'd agree with you, but we'd both be wrong.*

Ronan doesn't pay her attention and continues in his overly dramatic speech. "*Bah alors,* Ellie. You can't get hurt when we're going to get married."

"Do you want to meet your maker, Astor?" Aiden's sombre tone shoots towards us like sharp knives.

I suppress a smile with the back of my hand.

Ronan cocks his head as if deep in thoughts. "No?"

He leans over and takes both mine and Kim's hands in his. "Seriously, though. I've been praying you survive and King doesn't so we can have that threesome we agreed about."

"I heard that," Aiden says from above him.

"Remove your fucking hand." Xander's lighthearted mood vanishes as he glares at Ronan.

Kim blushes something fierce before she pulls her hand from Ronan's.

Aiden smiles at Ronan, but there's no humour whatsoever in it. "Isn't that your dominant hand, Astor? It would be a shame if it somehow didn't work tomorrow."

Woah. Aiden can be really scary if he chooses to.

"Sick fucker," Ronan whines, dropping my hand.

I catch Cole's lips moving in my peripheral vision. 'Pussy,' he mouths at Ronan.

"*Fais chier, connard.*" The latter flips him the finger.

Cole just smiles. He's like a cat toying with a mouse.

A hunter with a prey.

He sets the trap and sits back to watch his prey being caught.

I'm beginning to learn Cole only shows the tip of the iceberg to the world. There's a whole lot of secrecy and darkness underneath the surface.

I can only imagine what it feels like to be his enemy.

Shivers.

After a while of joking and jesting—and Aiden sulking on

the side—they stand to leave, promising to visit when I get discharged tomorrow.

"You don't have to come." Aiden shoves every one out of the door. He pauses at Xander. "You and I need to talk."

Xander's ocean eyes snap back to Kim who's still standing beside me.

She pales, her hands digging into her skirt before she pulls at the sleeves of her pullover. She's been doing that a lot since she came in.

Actually, she's been having this wild gaze for a few days now.

Kim smiles, but she sucks at faking them. The grimace falls way too soon as she leans in to kiss me.

"Are you okay?" I clutch her hand.

"When you're out," she gulps. "I'll tell you everything."

"Okay."

She hugs me again, sniffing in my neck. "I'm lucky to have you in my life, Ellie."

"So am I, Kim."

Xander doesn't leave. He stands by the side of the door, slightly blocking it. He doesn't attempt to give way and Kim has to stop.

"Can you move?" she snaps without looking at him.

"No." He stares at the top of her green hair, crossing his arms over his chest.

"Just move out of the way, Xan—"

"Don't say my fucking name." He cuts her off.

Kim's face reddens as she slams her shoulder into his shoulder and brushes past him.

He nods at Aiden and then follows her.

Aiden continues to watch down the hall with that calculative look before he shuts the door and joins me.

The mattress shifts as he sits beside me and wraps his arm around my shoulders.

"What the hell was that all about?" I ask him. "Why did you tell Xander you needed to talk?"

"It's for Reed's sake."

"K-Kim? Is she in danger?"

"Not yet."

"Not yet?"

"I know how much she means to you." He sighs. "I'll make sure she's safe."

"What the hell is that supposed to mean?"

"Hear her side of the story first." He strokes my hair back. "And then we'll talk, okay?"

I nod slowly. As much as I want Aiden to tell me everything, Kim is my best friend. I need to hear what the hell is wrong from her.

Aiden retrieves the plate of the cut apples and places it in front of me. He's back to sulking, but he still feeds me the slices.

I try to tell him that I can use my hands, but he's not listening.

I take a bite and munch on it slowly. I study his profile as I eat. The strong jawline, the metal eyes and the dark strands I'm itching to ruffle up.

He's mine.

All mine.

The thought fills me with a strange type of empowerment.

This boy who told me he'd destroy me is now my number one protector and carer. He would do anything to make me happy.

Turns out his plan with Agnus was about the Rhodes deal. Aiden and Dad's right hand somehow convinced Tristan Rhodes he could get better results if he hired both King Enterprises and Steel Corporation in their respective field—King for imports and exports, Steel for copper and their mass productions.

Jonathan and Dad, ex-friends and rivals, are now partners.

This deal brought a certain type of peace to their strained relationship. I don't have to worry about Jonathan anymore either.

Levi told me about the threat Aiden made against Jonathan. If he comes near me or interferes in our relationship again, Aiden will leave him without an heir.

I never wanted Aiden to go against his father, but the fact that he's doing it for me makes me feel all fuzzy inside.

"Are you still mad about earlier?" I ask after the third bite.

"Hmm. So you knew I was mad."

Oops.

He removes the hospital table and lowers himself atop of me. Before I can blink, Aiden grabs both my wrists and pins them onto the pillow over my head. "Was it fun, sweetheart?"

"Maybe." I bite my lower lip, my heart hammering so loud, I'm sure he can hear it.

This side of Aiden is my addiction and my damnation.

I love his intensity and his madness.

I'm in love with his dark mind and twisted soul.

"Looks like I need to remind you who you belong to. Isn't that right?"

I remain motionless, excitement and thrill filling me to the core.

His free hand caresses my bottom lip. "Answer me."

"Yes."

And then his lips claim mine.

EPILOGUE

Aiden

Three months later

Negative energy hums under the surface. It mounts and soars with every second. The loud music and drunk people at Astor's place aren't helping.

Knight passes me a joint, but I shake my head.

Fuck this shit.

I'm pissed off.

And I know exactly why I'm pissed off.

Tonight was a semi-final game and Elsa came to watch and stayed through the entire thing. Yes, she finally came to one of my games. This time, it was for me and not for some other fucker.

To top it off, she wore my T-shirt. Number eleven, King. I had to stop myself from flying off to the stairs, remove that shirt and fuck her on the spot.

All the annoying people present put a halt to my fantasy.

Instead, I gave it my all during the game. I might have scored two goals to see that spark in her blue eyes.

Unlike common belief, I'm a giver. I just take more than I give.

Now, back to tonight's actual problem. Elsa and I were supposed to go to the Meet Up where I could worship her body all night.

I had plans that started with her moaning and end with her screaming my name.

See? A giver.

Last minute, Elsa decided she wants to come to Astor's fucking party. I told him to cancel it, but the twat disappeared somewhere to drink and fuck—probably at the same time.

I'm stuck here with a grumpy Knight who's been smoking more weed than a hippie and groaning like a divorced old man thinking about pensions.

Nash vanished. He's been disappearing without notice a lot lately.

Elsa is nowhere to be seen.

I pull my phone and read our last conversation.

Elsa: Wait for me at Ronan's party.

Aiden: No.

Elsa: Come on. Do it for me?

Aiden: Still a no.

Elsa: Please?

Aiden: I'm fucking you all the way to Sunday at the Meet up. You don't get to change your mind.

Elsa: I didn't change my mind. You get to fuck me all the way to Sunday and more if you wait at Ronan's house.

That's the text that convinced me.

I shouldn't blame Nash for thinking with his dick when I do the same sometimes.

Okay, most of the time.

Elsa sent that text more than an hour ago, but she's still not here.

Van Doren is in the middle of the floor, dancing and flirting with all the girls he can see.

His goth sister is tucked in the corner, almost blending with a plant. If the Marquis de Sade and Snow White had a spawn, it'd be her.

Usually, Elsa would be with them. If she's not, only one other person remains.

I nudge Knight with my elbow. "Where's Reed?"

"Fuck if I care."

"I didn't ask if you cared, I asked where she is." I hold up a hand. "And don't even pretend that you don't know where she is at all times."

He gives me one look over. "Even if I knew I wouldn't tell you. How about that, King?"

The little bitch.

I'm about to strangle the answer out of him when my phone vibrates.

Elsa: Remember our room in Ronan's place?

I don't even have to think about which room she's referring to. There's only one room in Astor's mansion that's completely ours.

"Hey, Knight?"

"What?" He grumbles from his seat next to me. He's been sitting there like a zombie for the past hour.

"Do you know what Reed said about you the other day?"

His eyes spark for the first time tonight. Sorry fuck.

He masks his reaction all too soon, though. "I don't care."

"Are you sure? It was kind of taboo."

His Adam's apple bobs with a swallow. When he speaks, his voice is quiet. "What did she say?"

"Even if I knew, I wouldn't tell you. How about that, Knight?"

I grin, walking away. I can feel him flipping me off even without having to turn around.

Taking the steps two at a time, I find myself on the second floor. The music from downstairs eventually fades.

My muscles tighten at the promise of finding Elsa. I haven't touched her since yesterday and something feels off.

I take back my thoughts about the possibility of getting enough of Elsa. It won't happen. Not in this lifetime.

My fucker friends tell me I'm too possessive. I ignore their comments in front of Elsa, but I mess with their lives any chance I get behind her back.

Since Elsa's discharge from the hospital, she's become a new person.

For one, she's more open about her affection for me. She's more demanding when it comes to what she thinks is her right, but most of all, she's all in as much as I am.

I can now feel it when she opens her eyes and smiles instead of frowning. When she hugs me instead of pulling away.

We still live separately, but I plan to change that once we're at the university.

The fright she gave me at the hospital will never happen again. Dr Albert, her heart physician, has been watching her condition intently. The meds are enough to regulate her palpitations for now. She's stable and healthy, but he told us to keep a close watch on her in case she hides the worsening of her condition again.

Forget about her aunt, uncle, and father. I've become much worse than them when it comes to monitoring her. I can tell Elsa doesn't like it sometimes, but I made it clear that there will be no more fucking around with her health.

There's no way in fuck I'll let her be in danger like that time in the basement.

As soon as I arrive at the door, I push it open. The bedside lamp is the only light that's on.

This is where I first had Elsa all for myself and the first time she wrapped those lips around my cock.

My back leans against the door as I lock it. "Sweetheart?"

"In here," she calls from the bathroom. "One second."

"Take all the seconds," I call back as I remove my jacket, my shirt and then my trousers and boxer briefs.

If she thinks we're here to party, she has another thing coming.

I'm facing away from the bathroom, placing my clothes on the chair when tiny arms surround me from behind. Now I know why she can be so quiet when she moves. She gained that habit ten years ago when she snuck around to come meet me.

"Wow," she breathes against my back. "You're ready."

"I'm always ready, sweetheart."

Her lips find my back in a chaste kiss as she murmurs, "I'm also ready."

Her torso that's glued to my back is fully clothed so she can't be naked.

We can fix that.

I turn around and freeze.

Elsa stands in front of me with her hair falling on either side of her breasts. She's wearing my Elites' shirt with number eleven and my last name on it.

She's obviously not wearing anything underneath judging by the visible peaks of her nipples. The thing barely covers her pussy. Her long, athletic legs are completely bare as she fidgets.

"What do you think?" she asks carefully. "Do you like it?"

"Like it?" I growl, lunging at her like a fucking caveman.

She squeals as I pick her up and throw her on the bed. Her arms loop around my neck and her legs wrap around my waist.

My lips find hers in a savage kiss, long and desperate. I've been starving all day for her taste. "You know how much you made me wait, sweetheart?"

"Was it worth it?" she pants against my mouth, her chest rising and falling in a quick rhythm.

"Fuck right, it was, but you're going to make it up to me." I run my tongue over the shell of her ear. "I was promised to be able to fuck you all the way to Sunday."

She laughs, lust shining bright in her eyes. "And if I say no?"

"I'll fuck you all the way to Monday."

Challenge rises in her blue gaze. It's a game of ours, something we do when Elsa wants me to go rough and merciless on her.

"And if I say no again?" Her voice is barely a murmur.

"We can go on until Tuesday."

She reaches between us and runs her finger over my cock. It

was semi-hard since she hugged me. At her touch, my dick snaps to life in an instant.

The fucking traitor is on an Elsa-Viagra pill. She's the only one who's able to revive him to life.

"Fuck, sweetheart. If you don't move your hand…"

"What?" she challenges.

"I'll tie you up," I whisper darkly into her ears and feel her sharp intake of air.

We don't do this often, but whenever we do, Elsa lets go completely. My little Frozen gets off on having her will taken away by me during sex. She's slowly admitting that fact to herself.

Baby steps.

She releases my cock and reaches to take off the T-shirt.

I clutch her hand, stopping her in her tracks. "I'm going to fuck you with my name branded on you, then you'll ride me wearing it. Then I'll take it off, tie your hands with it and fuck your little arse."

A red hue covers her cheeks. I revel in her reaction to my words as she nibbles on her bottom lip. "All the way to Sunday?"

"All the way to fucking Sunday, sweetheart."

My lips find hers as I ram inside her in one brutal go. My abs tighten with the ruthless force of my thrust. She arches off the bed. Her arms and legs grip around me like a vice.

In moments like these, when Elsa and I are one, the entire world vanishes.

The need to possess her beats under my skin and claws in my bones. It's more than an obsession or even an addiction. It's light in the darkness burning me from the inside out.

The more she holds on to me like I'm her anchor, the harder I fall into her warmth.

Being with Elsa is exactly like it was ten years ago. She always brought peace to my chaotic head.

The only difference is that I became more perverse about her company.

Kissing and hugging aren't enough anymore. Now, she's mine, body, heart and soul.

First, she engraved herself under my skin, then in my brain and then into my heart. She made a cosy place for herself in there. Now, that damn thing only beats for her.

After I come deep inside her walls and bring her to orgasm two times in a row, Elsa lies limp, appearing all spent.

I'll probably need to draw her a bath.

"Did I tell you how crazy your stamina is?" She rolls onto her side and props her elbow, facing me.

I tug on the T-shirt that's still covering her tits. "We still didn't do the round with this off."

"I give up." She laughs. "I completely give up."

"Good. Because I wasn't kidding. I keep my promises, sweetheart."

A twinkle shines in her bright eyes as she nibbles on her bottom lip. She then releases it fast, thinking I won't be able to read that gesture.

It's useless. I already know she has something in that busy head of hers.

"What is it?"

She says nothing.

My lips tug in a smirk. "Tell me or I'll add another round of thorough fucking."

"You said you keep all your promises," she starts.

"I do."

"How about promises from ten years ago?"

So it's about that. I smile on the inside, but I show her nothing. "I don't know. You still didn't decide on your university."

We've been talking about this for the past few months. I was more than willing to ditch Oxford and go to Cambridge—even if it's not the best for business management and it'd piss Jonathan off.

None of that mattered. I already decided Elsa and I will live together at university. I won't do the whole long-distance bullshit.

"I'm ditching Oxford," I tell her matter of factly. I don't care what anyone has to say about it.

"Bummer." She pouts. "I was thinking of applying there."

"You were?"

"Yes. Dad and I talked and I decided to go back to my initial dream."

"Your initial dream?"

"Yeah. I showed you the drawings when I was young."

"Building houses."

She nods frantically. "I'll go to the School of Architecture at Oxford."

"And we'll live together." I know I'm burning steps, but I have to hit the iron while it's hot.

Truth is, I can never get enough of Elsa. It kills me to send her back home every other night.

I want her with me all the fucking time. I want to sleep surrounded by her warmth every night and wake up to her face every morning.

I expect her to fight and tell me she needs to think about it.

My mind is already filled with a thousand ways to convince her. I can sabotage her dorm application. I can trick her into thinking she's rented a house with a roommate and then surprise her by showing up. I can—

Elsa reaches under the bed and brings out a bucket of chocolates. She kneels by my side, cradling the thing as her face turns bright red.

A bucket of chocolate? What the fuck?

Wait.

The name of the brand stares back at me.

Maltesers.

"When I grow up, I'm gonna buy you a bucket of Maltesers."

"Why?"

"Because Dad says you have to buy gifts for the one you marry."

"Marry?" I whisper.

"Yup!" She grins. "When I grow up, I'm going to marry you."

"I'm keeping my promise, too," she murmurs.

"You're not the one proposing, I am." I groan, pulling her and the stupid bucket into me. "I'm going to fucking marry you, Elsa. You'll be my wife. My family. My fucking home."

She nods several times, tears shining in her eyes. "You'll be my home, too, Aiden. Always."

Always.

I crash my mouth to hers.

Elsa is mine.

Fucking mine.

Just like I'm hers.

Always.

Next up, I'm going to put a fucking baby in her.

EPILOGUE

Elsa

Three years later

"As I was saying, you can't argue with me using some theory. Be an actual nerd and prove it in real time."

Aiden stares at our classmates with his signature poker face. I swear he's become even more tenacious about hiding his emotions.

I'm lucky I met him at eighteen because twenty-one-year-old Aiden would've driven me bonkers.

Scratch that. He does, but I know him well enough to counter him at every turn now. I don't always win, but the challenge is worth it.

Our colleagues stare at him with questions and no answers.

Only Aiden would call university students nerds to their faces. When I told him not to do that, he said he's a firm believer in calling things by their names.

"Anyone?" he challenges. "Yeah, I didn't think so."

He's lucky Cole isn't here. It would've morphed into a full-blown war if he was, and we'd be all sitting here watching them argue all night.

No one ever wins, but Aiden keeps insisting he takes it easy on him.

"Actually, there's one." A sinister voice comes from my right. His American accent differentiates him immediately.

I groan even before the twat joins the circle. I thought we were lucky tonight since Cole had things to take care of.

Turns out, no.

"What are you even doing here?" I ask. "You don't belong to this club."

"I do now." Deep green eyes fill with mischief as he waves his access card. "I had to be where all the cool kids go. Isn't that right, Pres?"

Our debate club president, Oliver, nods at the American's charming grin.

I roll my eyes. The only reason he joined is to challenge Aiden and Cole. I swear they attract lunatics like this American as if they were magnets.

Even Aiden didn't join the club out of goodwill. I joined first and he just slid in because 'he was interested'.

Interested, my arse. More like he wants to be here to shoo the flies away as he calls them.

Aiden's possessiveness knows no limits. He doesn't like how close I am to the other club members, so he barged in to make their lives hell. He can be so frustratingly argumentative when he chooses to.

"Good of you to join us, Ash." Aiden grins as sadism sparks in his eyes. "Now look away from my wife before I create a diplomatic problem between England and the US."

The all-American golden boy bursts into laughter, raising his hands. "All right, all right. You have it bad, dude."

Aiden wraps his hand around mine, interlacing our fingers as if to prove a point.

Our rings are above each other. Something Aiden likes to do a lot.

We've been married for two years, and he's been publicising it everywhere. Whenever someone stares in my direction, he nearly blinds them with the huge diamond ring he got for me.

It's not something I would wear, but I accepted it nonetheless. This ring was Alicia's, and I understand its emotional value for Aiden.

I soon found out he's also using it to mark his territory at every opportunity.

The press is the only medium he didn't use for publicity, but he didn't need to.

Our wedding, although exclusive to family and friends, made the headlines.

The King and Steel marriage was written about over and over in business columns and newspapers.

It's the start of a new era for both companies. While Dad and Jonathan aren't the best of friends, they learned to work together.

I still can't trust Agnus completely. He really is a psychopath and I'm always wary of him. However, Dad trusts him even though he might know exactly his nature.

Agnus plays a huge part in Dad and Jonathan's partnership. He's become a pillar of strength for our families and I can't hate him for that.

Even Aunt and Uncle's company, Quinn Engineering has been thriving since the partnership between King Enterprises and Steel Corporation.

Aunt was a little sad when I chose Oxford over Cambridge, but she quickly got over it.

"Do you have anything to add to the discussion, Ash?" Aiden asks his American friend.

All the team members focus on the latter.

Some girls blush. Others stare up at him with dreamy eyes.

If only they knew what lurks under the beautiful façade.

He's just like Aiden. If not a little more unhinged. I still have no idea why he left his prestigious college back in the States to join us here.

"Yes, actually." He flops into a chair, his arms hanging off the edge. "See, Aiden. I don't have to prove it to you because we're not under legal obligation. I can choose to prove it, but it's only voluntary."

"When does voluntary end and the obligation start?" Aiden shoots back.

They go on and on. The audience are watching the two titans clash with gaped mouths. Even the president doesn't dare to say anything.

Me on the other hand? I'm done watching two sociopaths trying to outsmart one another.

As Asher goes on and on about legal texts and whatnot, I squeeze Aiden's hand and whisper, "I'm tired. Let's go home."

He doesn't even stop to consider it.

Still clutching my hand, he stands, taking me up with him and cuts off Asher. "My wife needs to rest."

"Loser," Asher mutters.

Aiden smirks. "I'm taking a rain check."

"I'll be here," Asher calls to our backs as we head to the door. "Now, where was I?"

He launches into a long, one-sided argument.

"Why are you even friends with him?" I ask as soon as we're alone.

"Because he's fun, sweetheart. We need fun people who aren't politically correct."

"You mean sociopaths."

"Every society needs old-fashioned villains." He grins down at me, then his brows crease. "Why are you tired?"

"I'm—"

Before I can say anything, he slams his palm on the middle of my chest.

"Aiden!" I watch our surroundings. I know he's just checking my heartbeat—like he does every day. Actually, he sometimes sleeps with his head on my heart to make sure it's working properly.

"I told you to check my wrist pulse when we're in public," I whisper. "People are watching."

"Fuck people. I'll check my wife's pulse any way I like." He removes his hand and places two fingers on my neck. "Hmm. Your pulse is fine."

"It is," I say as we step into the cold air.

"Then what is it? Do you feel chest tightness?"

"No."

"Palpitations?"

I shake my head.

Aiden is strict as fuck when it comes to my health. He's more religious about my appointments than I am. He's continuously studying about heart conditions like doctors with degrees.

He's even considering taking a second course in medicine.

No kidding, he really is.

He steps in front of me, buttons my coat to my chin, removes his scarf and ties it close around my neck.

It smells of him, clean and masculine. I take a deep inhale, breathing him into my lungs.

Aiden takes my cold hand in his and blows warm air into them before he places them in my pockets.

I watch him with a smile on my face. This side of Aiden always gets me in a knot. He's so caring and attentive, I actually have nightmares about a life without him.

He's become such a constant I can't breathe without anymore.

Forget love and adoration, Aiden is fucking air to me. He's everything I want in life and more. For that reason alone, I move onto my tiptoes and plant a kiss on his lips.

He grins with boyish charm.

Aiden likes it when I surprise him with kisses or when I demand pleasure. He says it turns him on more than anything else.

"Come on, it's cold." He pulls on my cheek. "I need to get my wife home."

Right. Home.

Our place is about a fifteen minutes' drive from campus.

We spend it talking about classes while Aiden has his hand

up my thigh. I'm lucky to be wearing jeans, if I was in a skirt, he'd be bringing me to orgasm by now.

Aiden is still Aiden. Boundless and shameless.

He drives me crazy. I swear I fall for him a little more every day. I fall in love with how he prepares breakfast for me every morning. How he takes me on a run and watches my heart rate through it. How he carries me to bed from my desk every night when I fall asleep on it. How he fucks me as if he can't get enough of me.

I love his attentiveness and his protectiveness. Hell, I even love his possessiveness sometimes.

I love all of him.

We arrive at our place.

It's a two-storey house with a small garden I take care of. Aiden bought the land next to us for our one-year anniversary. He said it's a gift so I can build my first house.

Our actual house.

I've been going crazy since then, coming up with a thousand and one ideas. I'm even contemplating combining the two lands and having a blast with it.

For now, we live in a cosy house with an antique feel to it.

As soon as we're inside, I stop to remove my coat. Aiden yanks off his jacket and jogs to the kitchen—for my meds, no doubt.

I study our house with wooden flooring and dark decor.

A tinge of arousal hits me at the memory of Aiden taking me in every corner of this house. On the sofa, against the counter, and even on the floor near the entrance.

This place is filled with so many heartwarming memories.

After hanging the coat and scarf onto the hook on the wall, I tiptoe towards the kitchen. Aiden stands at the counter fussing with pills. He still reads the label every time. There's no risk of error with him.

I wrap my arms around him from behind and rub my cheek against his back.

Aiden might not be a football player anymore—except for the occasional games now and then—but his physique is still hard and toned.

We go on runs together and he works out when he has insomnia, although it's become rare since our marriage.

"What do you want most in the world, Aiden?"

"You." He doesn't even miss a beat.

I smile. "What else?"

"You healthy and happy and fucking mine."

God. This man will be the death of me.

"What else?"

"That's all."

"That's all?"

"Yes." He spins around and hands me the pills with a glass of water.

I swallow the meds as he watches me intently. I watch him, too. His tousled, inky hair, the mole on the corner of his metal eyes, and the hint of his arrow tattoos as the sleeve of his shirt bunches up.

He clutches my elbow. "Let's get you some rest."

I squirm free. "I'm not tired."

He raises an eyebrow and tilts his head. "If you're not tired, I'll fuck you in the shower like yesterday. I like it when you are horny, climbing up my body and clawing at my back."

"There's a reason for that."

"Whatever it is, I like the reason. Let's repeat it today." He grins and goes back to fiddling with the pills.

I take a deep breath. Okay, here goes.

"Aiden?"

"Hmm, sweetheart?"

"I'm pregnant. Six weeks, to be exact."

He freezes, the bottle of pills half-suspended in his hands.

Aiden wanted a kid three years ago, but he completely backed off when Dr Albert said it could be a danger to my life at that stage.

However, three months ago, Dr Albert told me it's safe to have a child. Since then, I've been without birth control. I wanted to give him a surprise on our second anniversary two months ago. However, I didn't fall pregnant.

I nearly cried every time my period came on time for the past three months.

Yesterday, my period was two weeks late. I took a test and boom, pregnant. I was so happy, I wanted to tell Aiden right away, but I kept it to myself until I had tests done with both Dr Albert and an OBGYN.

Aiden spins around. My mouth falls open. I never expected to see that expression on Aiden's face.

Fear.

Complete terror.

He grabs my arm. "Let's go to Dr Albert. He'll tell us how to deal with this—"

"No." I wiggle away from him. "I'm having this child."

"And I'm not having a child that will risk your life." Aiden's voice is authoritative and final. "I'd rather be childless than without you."

My eyes fill with tears at his statement because I know it's true. Aiden would be happy with just me by his side. I feel it in my soul.

But I want to give him more. I want to give him everything. I want to be the mother of his children.

"I'm not in danger." I cradle his cheek with my palm. "I talked to Dr Albert and the OBGYN and we had tests done. The baby and I are healthy."

He narrows his eyes. "Are you just saying that so I'd change my mind?"

"I know you'd barge into Dr Albert's house to make sure my words are correct, so no, I'm not bluffing. I have the test results and everything in my bag."

He jogs to it and spends minutes reading the papers over

and over again. I stand there, watching him, and waiting for his reaction.

He switched to stare at the ultrasound of a small life. A life he and I created.

"So?" I ask carefully. "What do you think?"

"You're pregnant." He stares between me and the ultrasound as if to make sure.

"Yes, Aiden." I cradle my stomach. "I'm carrying your baby."

"You're carrying my baby," he repeats, slowly approaching me.

When he's within touching distance, I take his hand and place it on my stomach.

It's still flat, but I can feel the life humming inside me. I can already feel the connection.

He stares at his hand and slowly strokes my stomach.

"We created a life, Aiden," I murmur. "Are you happy?"

He rips his gaze from my stomach to meet my eyes. "Are you?"

"I'm over the moon. This is the best gift you could've given me." I press my lips to his. "I love you."

He wraps his arms around me and I squeal as he lifts me off the ground and hugs me. My arms wind around him as he kisses my mouth, my cheeks, my nose, and my forehead.

"You're the best gift I've ever been given, my queen."

"And you're mine, my king."

THE END.

WHAT'S NEXT?

Thank you so much for reading *Twisted Kingdom*! If you liked it, please leave a review.

Your support means the world to me.

If you're thirsty for more discussions with other readers of the series, you can join the Facebook group, *Rina Kent's Spoilers Room*.

Next up in the series is Xander and Kimberly's book, *Black Knight*.

Love is impossible. Hate is an open game.

Kimberly

He was once my best friend, now he's my worst enemy.
Xander Knight is heartbreakingly beautiful.
Ridiculously popular.
Brutally cruel.
He's a knight but won't do any saving.

Xander

We started as a dream, now we're a nightmare.
Kimberly Reed is pathetically fake.
Terribly innocent.
Secretly black.
She can hide but never from me.

ALSO BY RINA KENT

For more books by the author and a reading order, please visit:
www.rinakent.com/books

ABOUT THE AUTHOR

Rina Kent is a *USA Today*, international, and #1 Amazon bestselling author of everything enemies to lovers romance.

She's known to write unapologetic anti-heroes and villains because she often fell in love with men no one roots for. Her books are sprinkled with a touch of darkness, a pinch of angst, and an unhealthy dose of intensity.

She spends her private days in London laughing like an evil mastermind about adding mayhem to her expanding universe. When she's not writing, Rina travels, hikes, and spoils cats in a pure Cat Lady fashion.

Find Rina Below:

Website: www.rinakent.com

Newsletter: www.subscribepage.com/rinakent

BookBub: www.bookbub.com/profile/rina-kent

Amazon: www.amazon.com/Rina-Kent/e/B07MM54G22

Goodreads: www.goodreads.com/author/show/18697906.
Rina_Kent

Instagram: www.instagram.com/author_rina

Facebook: www.facebook.com/rinaakent

Reader Group: www.facebook.com/groups/rinakent.club

Pinterest: www.pinterest.co.uk/AuthorRina/boards

Tiktok: www.tiktok.com/@rina.kent

Twitter: twitter.com/AuthorRina